D0242146

*For Leonardo & Isabella:*
*May you always find the silver lining.*
*xxx*

## One

# SHETLAND

STELLA hung over the wooden rail and watched the inky waves, far below.

*I know you're down there . . .*

As if in answer, a sudden swell made the ferry tip and her stomach rolled. She'd never liked being out on the open water, but the nightmare had made it worse. She couldn't remember all of it. Deep, dark water. The feeling of drowning. In the daytime, the details always faded, like mist in sunlight.

Mum always blamed it on Gran – all her tales of sea witches

and selkies, blue men and sea monsters. Stella didn't really believe the stories any more, but deep water still made her uneasy. She couldn't shake the feeling there was something down there, watching.

"We're close now," said Dad, his eyes twinkling. "The edge of the world!"

It did feel like it. They'd been travelling for ages. Always north. Until the air was clear as crystal and the only sound was seabirds.

Dad nudged her. "You excited to see Shetland again?"

"Can't wait," she said.

Ever since they'd moved away, Stella had been longing to come back, but now it was really happening, it felt alarmingly real.

"It'd be better if you were staying too."

Dad put an arm round her shoulder. "We've talked about this."

"Just for like, a few days?"

"You know we can't," said Dad. "That's the whole point of you coming here. Mum and I have got to work."

*Work. Always work.*

Other people's families went on holiday together. That was the point of holidays.

"It's important, what we're doing," said Dad.

*More important than me.* Stella narrowed her eyes at Dad, but he just smiled at her.

"I could come with you?" she said. "I could help."

"Don't be daft," said Dad. "You'd be bored out of your mind.

Besides, I don't think they allow children on research vessels."

Stella pulled a face to show what she thought of that.

"Hey, you're the one who's been pestering us to come back here!" said Dad.

It was true, but Stella had always imagined *all* of them coming back, as a family. Not just her, on her own. She *was* excited to see Grandpa again. The bit she wasn't looking forward to was Mum and Dad leaving. Six weeks was a long time.

Dad shook her gently by the shoulder. "Happy thoughts, remember?" he said. "I know you're nervous, but you're going to have a great time."

Stella curled her toes inside her shoes. Maybe she would. Maybe it would be amazing.

"Come on," said Dad. "Name one thing you're looking forward to."

Stella thought about it for a moment. "Hot chocolate," she said. *In a big mug. With cream instead of milk. And loads of shortbread to go with it.*

"More than I'd be allowed at home," she added, daring Dad to disagree.

"Sounds like a plan," he said. "With cream? Shortbread to dip?"

Stella nodded. He remembered.

"So, hot chocolate. What else?"

"Seeing puffins again," she said. "Real live puffins."

"*Tammie norries*," Dad reminded her. "Get Grandpa to take

3

you to the lighthouse. They're nesting, this time of year. You'll be able to get right up close."

It was hard to stay cross with Dad, even when he deserved it. Somehow, he always knew what to say.

*Puffins. Right up close!*

"I'm looking forward to staying with Grandpa, too," she said.

It would be strange seeing him without Gran. They were always a pair. Salt and pepper. Bread and butter. Gran and Grandpa.

Now it was only Grandpa, but it would still be brilliant to see him. It had been such a long time! Six whole years. The last time she saw him, she was only five.

"Do you think he'll recognise me?" she said.

Dad smiled. "He'll recognise you alright. But I daresay he'll be amazed. His favourite little girl, all grown-up and independent," he said.

Stella's heart glowed with pride. She stood up straighter, turned her face into the wind and let her knees bounce, riding the movement of the boat, like a proper Shetland sailor.

The deck bucked over a wave and she grabbed for the rail again. How did Dad make it look so easy?

"There it is," he said and pointed at the horizon.

Stella squinted at the distant dot and her stomach flipped like a mackerel. Soon she'd have to say goodbye.

The Shetland mainland looked like a little limpet. A small grey hump hunched low in the sea. As the boat drew gradually closer, the cliffs loomed taller. Seagulls whirled and swooped down the sheer rock face like stunt pilots.

On the skerries, close to the shore, dozens of seals were sunning themselves like fat black sausages. Stella pointed at them in excitement. "Sleeping selkies!"

"I'd forgotten you used to call them that," said Mum, joining them at the rail.

"They've made a welcoming party for you," said Dad. "Remember the selkie story?"

"Of course I do," replied Stella. "I've got the book with me."

"*Shetland Myths and Magic*? No wonder this rucksack's so heavy!" said Mum, hefting it in her hand. "How on earth did you fit it in?"

"I took some stuff out . . ." said Stella.

"What?!" said Mum. "What stuff?"

Stella could practically see the packing lists scrolling through Mum's mind.

"Nothing important," she said. "Just spare socks."

"There wasn't spare anything!" said Mum. "And I already packed a stack of books for you. That one's falling apart!"

Stella felt a sudden twinge of embarrassment. *Shetland Myths and Magic* was very tatty now. And a bit young for her. But it was still her favourite.

"Gran always used to read it to me," she said. "Coming back here, I just felt like . . ."

"It was a good idea," interrupted Dad, firmly. "Grandpa will be pleased."

Mum shook her head and looked doubtfully at Stella's two bags – probably wondering what else she'd taken out.

Dad put a reassuring arm round Mum's shoulder.

"It's not a problem," he murmured into Mum's hair. "Socks can be washed. She's going to be just fine."

Stella gave him a grateful smile.

"Come on, tell us what else you're looking forward to," said Dad.

"The northern lights?" she said.

Dad shook his head. "Not this time of year. Right now, it's the *Simmer Dim* – summer twilight, so it won't get properly dark."

*Never dark?* thought Stella. *I'll be able to stay up all night!*

"That doesn't mean you get to stay up all night, mind," said Mum.

Mum did that sometimes – knew exactly what she was thinking. Usually when Stella was trying to get away with something.

"It's the holidays," said Dad. "A few late nights won't hurt."

"I was thinking more of your father," said Mum. "I should think he'll want his sleep, even if Stella doesn't."

"You'll be fine with Grandpa, won't you?" said Dad.

It wasn't a real question. It was just to make Mum feel better. She almost told him that, but a glance at Mum's face changed her mind.

"I'll be responsible," she said. "And super helpful. And I'll go to bed at bedtime. And I'll wash my own socks if I haven't got enough. You don't have to worry. I'll be completely fine."

*I will,* she thought. *I'll be fine.* Her stomach was doing little somersaults. *Just think of it as an adventure,* she told herself.

Stella breathed in as they slipped through the narrow opening in the harbour walls, as though she could make the boat thinner by sucking her tummy in. The harbour was packed with fishing boats, their lines clinking and clanking.

There was a great whirr and growl of thrusters as the ferry lined up neatly alongside the wall. Two crewmen leapt ashore and looped ropes around the bollards that sprouted on the dockside like massive mushrooms.

Stella peered over the side. Ropes of dark-brown seaweed tangled beneath the surface. She counted five jellyfish.

*I do NOT want to fall in there.*

A scrap of the nightmare surfaced in her mind: a feeling of being trapped, tangled in seaweed.

Dad picked up her suitcase in one hand and walked down the gangplank, as calmly as if he were taking an afternoon stroll, then headed off along the dock.

Stella glanced back at Mum. Dad had made it look easy, but now it was her turn.

She took a deep breath for courage. Also, in case she fell in.

*Don't think that! It's not going to happen.*

The gangplank bounced as she walked along it. Three short

steps – with her arms out wide, like a tightrope walker – then she jumped off, onto the concrete, and let the breath out again.

It felt good to have solid ground under her feet.

## Two

# A STRANGE CATCH

MUM put Stella's rucksack down and stood there, looking up and down the dock. There was no sign of Grandpa, and Dad had gone looking for him.

"Honestly, of all the days for him to be late," she said.

"Maybe he got held up in traffic?" said Stella.

Mum gave a short laugh. "Traffic? The only thing likely to slow you down here is rabbits."

"Oh." Stella looked up the road. Mum was right. She could only see one car. A big, boxy car, caked in mud, parked in the long grass.

It looked as though it had grown there.

"Anyway, Grandpa's picking you up in *Curlew*," said Mum. "His boat," she added, in response to Stella's puzzled look.

"Another boat!" groaned Stella. She wrapped her arms around herself and bounced on her toes.

Maybe Grandpa had forgotten. Maybe he wouldn't come at all? Then Mum and Dad would *have* to take her with them.

"Over here!" called Dad, from the other end of the dock.

She turned to see Dad approaching, Grandpa by his side.

It was strange seeing them together without Gran. Gran always walked in the middle.

*Between my two fine men-folk.*

Stella pushed the thought away and focused on Grandpa. He was shorter than she remembered. Had he shrunk?

*No, I've grown!*

Stella always used to greet him by running at top speed. Grandpa would catch her and throw her up in the air. He didn't look strong enough now. She might knock him over.

"Good crossing?" said Mum, as they approached.

Grandpa nodded. "There was a fair breeze," he said. His voice creaked and crackled, like he hadn't used it for a while. He cleared his throat before continuing. "You brought the sun with you. We've not had any bad weather for a week or more." He glanced out to sea and sniffed. Dad always did that too. *Smelling the weather*, he called it.

Mum stepped forward and gave Grandpa a brief hug. "Thank

you so much for having her. I know it's short notice – we're really grateful."

The butterflies in Stella's stomach suddenly felt as big as seagulls.

"It's fine," said Grandpa, patting Mum's shoulder and turning towards Stella. "Be nice to have some company, for a change."

Mum glanced at Stella and raised her eyebrows very slightly, but a horrible shyness had snuck up and glued Stella's mouth shut.

Dad gave her an encouraging nod.

*Do something!* she thought.

She found herself sticking out her hand.

*No! Stupid brain!*

Shaking hands was extra polite – for meeting strangers, not family. *Now he's going to think I'm weird.*

Grandpa looked at her hand in confusion for a moment, then shook it solemnly.

"It's official then," said Dad. "You've arrived." There was a hint of amusement in his voice.

Stella flashed her eyes at him. It wasn't funny. This was the first time she'd seen Grandpa for ages and now he was going to think she was weird.

"Off we go then," said Grandpa. "*Curlew*'s down the end."

Stella hoiked her rucksack onto her back. It was heavier than she expected. Maybe Mum had a point about the books.

"You alright with that?" said Mum, looking doubtful.

Stella hitched the straps so they didn't cut so hard into her shoulders.

"Fine," she said, and smiled to prove it.

If she was going to spend the whole summer being grown-up and independent, she might as well start now. It might make up for that awkward handshake . . .

Grandpa gave a nod of approval, then clapped a hand on Dad's shoulder. They walked on ahead.

As Stella followed along behind, Mum took the opportunity to give her a hundred and one last-minute instructions.

"The trick is to be prepared," said Mum. "Think ahead. The weather can change in an instant. And don't go swimming. There are strong currents."

"Mum, I know!" said Stella. "You've told me already."

It was already really hard to be excited, not terrified. Mum wasn't helping.

Instead, Stella focused on the boats. They were really pretty, with tall, elegant masts and brightly painted wooden hulls. She wondered which one was Grandpa's.

Dad hopped down into a boat that looked like a floating bathtub, with a small shed in the middle of it. It looked very small and silly between the tall sailing boats on either side. Why couldn't one of those have been *Curlew*?

Stella pictured it being tossed about by the waves and her stomach clenched.

Dad stowed her suitcase in a deep locker under one of the benches, then reached up for her rucksack. Stella shrugged it off and handed it to him.

There was a low burble as Grandpa started the engine. Mum squeezed Stella in a tight hug. "Stay safe," she said. "I love you."

"Love you too," Stella mumbled into her shoulder.

"We all set?" asked Dad.

Stella took his outstretched hand and stepped down into the cockpit. She sat down where Grandpa pointed, on the seat at the back. The wooden slats were knobbly and uncomfortable, and the cockpit smelled of engine oil and fish. She swallowed hard.

Dad leant forward and kissed the top of her head. "Bye then, poppet," he said. Then, in one swift movement, he was up and out of the boat, untying the ropes and throwing them to Grandpa.

It was too fast. She wasn't ready.

Stella stood up.

A gap of oily water was already opening between the boat and the harbour wall.

"Sit down, lass," said Grandpa. "You'll fall in."

She sat down quickly and twisted round to face Mum and Dad. They were both waving. She waved back, hard enough to make the boat wobble.

Grandpa revved the engine and turned them towards the open sea.

"Love you!" called Mum.

"Have fun," called Dad.

Stella didn't shout back. Right at this moment, she didn't feel grown-up or independent. Her throat was clogged with tears.

Mum and Dad blew kisses. Stella snatched them out of the air and held them tight to her chest. Normally it was her and Mum blowing kisses to Dad. This time, it was them staying behind, her leaving.

*I'm on my own,* she thought, with a shiver of daring. *Well, nearly.*

She cast a furtive glance at Grandpa.

His faded blue cap was pulled low against the sun and his gaze was fixed on the sea ahead.

He hadn't said much yet. Then again, neither had she.

\* \* \*

The crossing wasn't as bad as she'd feared. The sturdy little boat thudded across the water, and for some reason it didn't make her stomach lurch like the roll of the ferry. Stella began to almost enjoy it. The roar of the engine meant she didn't have to think of anything to say to Grandpa, and that was good.

*Me and Grandpa. On an adventure.*

As they approached the shore on the far side, Grandpa slowed the engine. They definitely weren't there yet – there was no sign of a house, or a jetty.

Ahead of the boat, a tall column of rock speared the sky – that seemed to be where they were heading.

Sure enough, when they were a few metres away, Grandpa killed the engine. Stella's ears rang with the sudden silence, until the sea sounds crept in – the whisper of the wind, the salty whoosh of the waves curling around the base of the rocks.

Grandpa peered up at the towering sea stack and shaded his eyes with his hand.

"What are you looking for?" said Stella.

Grandpa heaved a sigh. "I'd thought to show you the cormorants. Your Dad said you like birds?"

Stella nodded and looked up. There weren't any birds, just a bare rock.

"This place is usually packed with them. I don't understand it," said Grandpa, with a brief scowl. He shook his head in disappointment. "Perhaps the storm petrels . . . We could maybe go out one evening and watch them coming home to roost?"

Stella nodded. "I'd love that. It doesn't matter about the cormorants. I'm sure I'll see lots of other cool stuff while I'm here."

"Ha!" Grandpa's eyes brightened and he stood up and moved to the bow. Stella gripped the seat as the boat wobbled alarmingly. He dragged a large cool box back to the cockpit.

"Here's something you won't have seen before," said Grandpa, a note of triumph in his voice. "Did some fishing on the way here. Take a look at this monster." He lifted the lid.

Stella leant closer to look, but recoiled from the stink. It smelled like fish, but it didn't look like one. It was mostly mouth –

a wide toad-like mouth, bristling with pointy teeth. Its eyes were two small pools of milky jelly and they were too far apart.

"What," she asked, "is that?"

"Supper," replied Grandpa.

Stella looked at its warty skin and swallowed. She hoped Grandpa was joking. There was no way she was eating something that looked like that.

"It doesn't look like a normal fish," she said.

"No. It's a rarity alright," said Grandpa proudly. "I've never caught one on a line before. They're not found near the surface, as a rule."

"But what is it?" said Stella.

"A *masgoom*," said Grandpa. "An anglerfish. Lives way down deep. Probably never seen the light of day, until now."

He lifted the fish out of the box with one hand. Its brown skin wrinkled into slimy folds between his thick fingers. A long wormy piece of skin dangled from between its eyes. Grandpa lifted it and waggled it about.

"This is its lure, see? Glows in the dark. Looks like a tasty little morsel, but then . . . *Omp!*" He snapped the wide mouth closed.

Stella jerked back and pulled a disgusted face.

Grandpa mirrored her look of revulsion, then smiled. "It's not a pretty sight, I'll grant you. Makes good eating, though."

He put the fish back in the box, closed the lid, and wiped his hands on his trousers.

*I wish it had stayed where it belonged*, thought Stella. *Down in the dark.*

"Why would it come up?" she asked.

"Don't know," said Grandpa. "Odd, really. Still, lucky for us!"

"Maybe something big was chasing it?" said Stella, with wide eyes.

"Could be." Grandpa nodded.

Stella's mind raced through the possibilities. *A giant squid. A huge shark. A killer whale. Something big and scary enough to make it swim all the way to the surface ...*

"Wait, I have seen one!" she blurted and yanked her rucksack towards her. She undid the buckle and pulled the book out of the top.

"*Shetland Myths and Magic*," said Grandpa, softly. "You kept it."

Stella flicked through the book, intent on finding the right page. "Here. Look. It's here," she said.

Grandpa patted the seat and she slid round next to him so he could see.

"I always loved the pictures in this book," he said, with a nod of approval. "Must have been painted by a fisherman. They're all so true to life."

Stella had always thought the creatures in it were made-up monsters. The boat suddenly felt very small on the open water. She moved a bit closer to Grandpa.

Grandpa squinted at the book and smiled. "Here, see? Wolf

fish, cut throat eel, fangtooth, viperfish, squid." He pointed each one out. "They all live way down deep – midnight depth. It's usually only deep-sea trawlers that pick them up."

*Midnight depth.* A shiver crept up Stella's spine.

She turned the page and the sea witch stared up at her.

"That story used to give you nightmares when you were small," said Grandpa.

"Mm." She decided not to tell him that it still did.

"Your Mum was not best pleased, if I recall?"

Stella gave him a conspiratorial smile. "Gran still used to read it though," she said. "We'd just wait until Mum wasn't around."

Grandpa looked away for a moment, blinking.

*Was she not meant to talk about Gran?*

Worry crawled through Stella's chest. Dad hadn't said not to, but she wasn't sure what was right. It would be hard not to mention Gran at all, especially here. She chewed her lip and looked down at the book.

The edges of the page were a dark tangle of spines and scales, suckers and tentacles. A whirlpool of monsters, fleeing the sea witch as she rose from the depths.

"Why do you really think the *masgoom* was up at the surface?" she said, changing the subject.

"Well, it wasn't escaping a sea witch, if that's what you're thinking," said Grandpa.

Stella shook her head.

"Probably a shift in the currents," said Grandpa. "Or it might have been stirred up by a storm."

Stella looked over the side. They weren't far from shore, but the water was darkest blue, almost black. She tried to imagine how far it was to the bottom, but the thought made her head spin.

"Can we go now?" she said.

# Three

# GRAN'S MUG

THREE *whole days, and no fun,* thought Stella. *How am I going to last the whole summer?*

"Grandpa?"

Grandpa had disappeared into his room after lunch. He didn't like it when she 'bombarded him with questions'. Which was tricky, because now Stella had got used to being here, she had lots of questions, like:

"Where do you go shopping?" *The mainland.*

"Have you got any friends?" *Not these days.*

"Where can I wash my socks?" *In the sink.*

"How do you talk to people without a phone?" *I don't.*

And, more importantly, "How will we know when Mum and Dad are coming back to get me?"

"They'll write and let us know," Grandpa had answered. After that, he'd gone into his room and hadn't come out.

That was about half an hour ago.

Spending time with Grandpa was not going well. No matter what he'd said to Mum, Grandpa did *not* enjoy having company. Not Stella's, anyway.

The more she talked, the grumpier he got.

She'd tried being quiet, but she couldn't keep it up – not for as long as Grandpa. After a while, she just had to talk, otherwise it felt like she might burst.

Grandpa's grumpy silences cast a massive black cloud over everything.

Things had started to go wrong as soon as they got home. Grandpa hadn't been joking about having the fish for supper.

She'd tried to eat it. She really had. But every time she brought a forkful to her mouth, she remembered its warty skin and pale jelly eyes, and her throat closed up. She couldn't do it.

Grandpa was not pleased. He'd said quite a lot of things about "city living" and "children who think fish comes out of a cardboard box, in orange rectangles".

It was slightly true, but also really mean.

He'd made her mashed potato in the end, but Stella felt she'd failed some important test.

That was what caused *The Tools Incident.*

The next day, she'd decided maybe she could make it up to him by being helpful – tidying up a bit – but Grandpa took it completely the wrong way. After that, he'd said she wasn't allowed to touch his tools at all, she was never to go in his shed again, and that from now on she had to stay where he could see her.

Which mostly meant: *in the house.*

Grandpa's tools were still all over the kitchen table, like an incoming tide. She used the edge of her book to push them a bit further away. That didn't count as touching them.

She looked down at her bird book and heaved a sigh. What was the point of even bringing it, if she was going to be stuck inside the whole time?

She flipped to the puffins page. The only birds she'd spotted so far were herring gulls, swooping past the window. You could see them anywhere – even back in Southampton – nicking chips and pecking rubbish. There was nothing special about herring gulls.

"Grandpa!" she said, a bit louder this time. Not quite a shout, but loud enough that he couldn't pretend he hadn't heard.

She heard a creak of old bed springs as he got up, then his door opened and he came out. "What is it?"

"Can we go to the lighthouse today?" She gave him her sweetest smile.

"No. Not today. Maybe tomorrow. Or the day after."

"What about if I go there by myself? You could tell me where it is?"

"Not on your own. You don't want to get swallowed up by a peat bog, do you?"

Stella shook her head. Of course she didn't.

But was it really that dangerous out there? Dad had made the island sound amazing. Grandpa's version of the island was very different: peat bogs that wanted to swallow you whole, cliffs just waiting to crumble under your feet. The first day, it had scared her, but now she was starting to wonder if they were all just excuses not to let her go out.

"What about down to the beach? It's really close. I remember the way."

"Can't walk on the beach now. It's nesting season. Storm petrels. Remember them?"

Stella heaved a deep sigh and nodded, she did. They laid their eggs under the rocks. It meant the beach was a no-go zone until all the chicks had hatched. "I didn't mean *on* the beach, just *near* the beach. Maybe tonight, we could watch them come home to roost—"

But grandpa was already shaking his head. "I've got to round up the sheep this afternoon, check them for flystrike, so I'll be fair shattered this evening. It'll be an early night for me."

"Okay, but *I* could go down there and—"

"At night! By yourself? Not a chance." Grandpa turned to go back into his room.

"Wait, Grandpa . . ." said Stella

He paused in the doorway. "What?"

"I've got nothing to do," said Stella.

*I'm bored!* is what she would have said at home, but she was pretty sure that would annoy him. It was very easy to annoy Grandpa.

"Hmm." A frown flicked across his face, then his eyes lit up. He went off down the corridor and reappeared with a battered wooden crate.

"Don't know why I didn't think of this before," he said. He plonked it down on the table. "These used to keep you busy for hours."

Stella looked at the crate with a sinking feeling.

"I'm sure you'll find something in there to entertain you?" said Grandpa.

Stella rooted through the contents, but there were no surprises: faded wooden building blocks, a chunky fishing boat with a tattered cotton sail, a sparse collection of farm animals and a roll of green felt to stand them on.

Baby toys.

"Grandpa, I don't really play with stuff like this any more," she said. "I'm eleven."

Grandpa looked crestfallen for a moment, then his mouth

tightened. "Suit yourself," he said. He picked up the crate and stomped off down the corridor.

"Sorry," she called after him.

Frustration coiled in her chest. This wasn't what this holiday was meant to be like. It was meant to be fun! Grown-up fun – with adventures and exploring – not boringness and baby toys!

She'd been imagining coming back here for ages – ever since they'd left. But it was nothing like she remembered.

Stella looked around the room, trying to picture how it used to be. Above the fireplace, there was a pale rectangle on the wall, like the ghost of a window.

Gran's painting of the seal, she realised. That's what used to be there. The gap made the wall look bare and sad.

*Why would he take it down?* she wondered.

She hadn't noticed before, because of all Grandpa's mess, but all Gran's stuff was gone. Not just the painting, everything: the knitted chicken, the tufty rug, the driftwood seal that lived on the windowsill.

Where were Gran's things?

She stood up and opened the middle drawer of the dresser. It was where Gran used to keep their beach treasures – mermaids' purses and more periwinkles than you could count.

It was empty.

She slid it closed.

Grandpa reappeared carrying a sack of chicken feed. He held it up. "If you're too old to play, why don't you make yourself useful?"

Stella shrank back and shook her head. If she hadn't run inside at top speed yesterday, the rooster would have pecked her to death. No way she was doing that again.

He gave a slight shrug, as though she was missing out.

"Grandpa, where's Gran's stuff?" said Stella.

Grandpa froze for a moment, then turned away towards the door.

"The seal painting is gone," she pointed out. "And the knitted chicken. Even the rug!"

As Grandpa bent to pull his wellies on, she was gripped by a horrible suspicion.

"You haven't thrown it all away, have you?" she said.

"No!" Grandpa burst out. He looked horrified.

Stella sat very still.

"Of course I haven't thrown them away," he muttered, snatching up the bag of chicken feed. "What do you take me for?"

The door banged shut behind him.

*I only asked!*

Stella took a deep breath and let it out again.

She looked around the room again. The only familiar thing of Gran's left was her armchair, standing opposite Grandpa's, in front of the fireplace. Stella used to snuggle there on Gran's lap, to listen to *Shetland Myths and Magic*.

When Gran read, all the 'r's had a warm purr and 'i' made that *ee* sound that you can only say properly if you're smiling. Gran made the stories real – the way she told it, every storm was a sea witch approaching, every seal a selkie in disguise. The whole island was magical.

The memory swallowed Stella's heart like quicksand.

Nothing was the same without Gran here. Especially not Grandpa.

He used to be a proper Grandpa – whistling, making up stories, telling jokes. Back then, he knew how to smile. He hadn't smiled once since they'd got back to the house. Not once.

*He's not Grandpa, without Gran,* she realised.

Stella pursed her lips and shook her head. She had to do something. Remind him how to be happy, like he used to be. Then everything would be better.

*Make yourself useful,* he'd said. Well, she could do that.

She was always helping Mum at home. In fact, she was brilliant at making herself useful – just not if it involved evil roosters, that's all.

*I'll bake something,* she thought. *He'll like that.*

Stella nodded to herself. She'd made biscuits on her own before – even the oven bit.

She looked up at the dresser and a smile spread across her face. Gran's cookbook was still in the same place, tucked away in the corner of the top shelf. In front of it was Gran's favourite mug – the one with puffins on it.

*So he didn't get rid of everything!*

It was perfect. She'd make shortbread. Grandpa always used to love shortbread. Maybe they could even have hot chocolate with it.

Stella couldn't reach the top shelf, so she pulled a chair over to stand on.

The row of plates on the middle shelf looked apologetic, peeking out from behind piles of letters, rowlocks for the boat, and boxes and bottles of medicine.

The top shelf was crowded with Grandpa's little driftwood carvings – angels, mostly. They were grey with dust. She wrinkled her nose. She was pretty sure the little black dots between them were mouse droppings. The house hadn't been cleaned for ages.

*Gran probably used to do it,* she thought. *Maybe Grandpa doesn't know how.*

She stretched on tiptoes and reached to move the mug out of the way.

"Don't touch that!" barked Grandpa, from behind her.

She jumped in fright and her fingers grazed the handle.

"No!" Grandpa shouted, and lunged to catch it.

Too late. Stella's stomach fell with it, all the way down to the flagstone floor.

*Smash.*

A terrible, sharp-edged crash. Shattering all her good plans into jagged white triangles.

"Your Gran's . . ." started Grandpa. "What did you think you were DOING?"

Stella climbed down off the chair. Shards of broken china crunched underfoot.

"I was . . . I was trying to help!" she stammered. *Trying to make you happy,* she thought, but the words got stuck in her throat.

"Some help!" yelled Grandpa. "Are you wilfully destructive, or just plain clumsy?"

She stared at his thunderous face and a dark feeling washed over her, sucking away any kind thoughts.

"Well? Which is it?" he bellowed. His cheeks had gone scarlet and his eyes bored into hers. She didn't even recognise him any more.

The grandpa she loved was gone.

She turned and ran.

Out the front door. Down the path. Banging the gate open on its rusty hinges. Away from the roar that chased her up the path: "Stella? Get back here! Stella!"

The horizon blurred with tears and she sniffed. *He probably wishes I'd never come.*

There was nothing ahead but bristly grass, grey rocks, and dark humps of heather. The wind came barging over the top of the cliff and shoved at her with icy fingers.

Gran's stories were wrong. Nothing here was magical.

She'd never felt so alone.

But she wasn't going back to Grandpa's. Not yet, anyway.

'Clumsy, or wilfully destructive?'

*It wasn't my fault! If he hadn't shouted . . .*

Stella ran. No idea where she was going, just anywhere but here.

*Gran's favourite mug! Why that one?*

Her foot caught and she tripped, landing in a tumble of elbows and knees. "Ow!"

She stood up, brushed off her trousers and looked back.

A bag. A green cloth bag, with a long loop of shoulder strap – that's what she'd tripped on. Who would leave a bag in the middle of nowhere, just waiting to trip someone up?

"In a hurry, were you?" said a cheerful voice.

Stella froze. There weren't meant to be other people here. Grandpa's was the only house on this side of the island.

The old woman stood ahead of her, a little way off the path. How had she got there?

Stella stared, her heart beating fast. The woman didn't look like an islander – no thick coat or sturdy trousers, not ready for the outdoors at all. Her cardigan was thin and floaty, and her long skirt draped through the grass.

It was like she'd just appeared – popped out of the hillside like a trow. Gran's stories crowded into Stella's head, whispering warnings: *Taken to a trowie mound and never seen again . . .*

*Don't be silly,* she thought. *You're too grown-up to believe stuff like that.*

But it was hard to feel certain, on an empty hillside, with no one else around. For a split second, she wished Grandpa was there, but shrugged the thought away.

"You didn't need to be running," said the old woman. "You're early."

The hair on the back of Stella's neck prickled.

"Early for what?" she said.

"To meet me, of course," said the old woman, with a smile.

Stella shook her head. "But I wasn't—"

"I'm Tamar," interrupted the old woman, sticking out her hand.

Stella stood up a bit straighter and tried to pull one of her socks up with the side of her shoe.

"I'm Stella," she said, and shook Tamar's hand.

She didn't know what else to do. It would have been rude otherwise.

Who was Tamar meant to be meeting? Not her, that was for sure. And it wasn't exactly the sort of place where you came to meet people. Apart from her, Grandpa, and now Tamar, there was nobody else here.

The wind threaded its way through Stella's jumper and she shivered.

*Always wear your coat,* said Mum in her head, too late to be helpful.

Tamar held up one hand, as though hailing a bus. Her purple cardigan billowed around her. She pinched her finger and thumb together, and the wind stopped.

Stella stared at her.

Had she imagined it?

*No.*

Tamar had just reached up and stopped the wind.

*A witch,* whispered a corner of her mind.

She knew the story by heart. She could hear Gran reading it: *See how sea witches turn fair weather foul, suck ships down their whirlpools and make the winds howl.*

*It's just a story,* she told herself, but a niggle of fear crawled into her chest.

"So, have you come far?" said Tamar.

Stella shook her head.

"Do you live near here, then?"

The questions were so ordinary.

"Kind of . . . Well, no. Not really." Stella knew that didn't quite make sense, but it was complicated.

"Kind of, no, not really?" said Tamar, looking puzzled.

"I did live here, before," said Stella, "But we moved away. So I'm just, er, visiting."

Tamar's face lit up in a smile. "Welcome home, then!"

A small flower opened in Stella's heart.

*Welcome home . . .*

She took a deep breath and felt something heavy lift from her chest.

"Thank you," she said.

Was it magic, or had Tamar just said the right thing at the right moment? Suddenly the whole island felt a little brighter, greener, more familiar.

Like home.

*Why couldn't Grandpa have said that?*

But the thought melted away into the warm feeling of having arrived.

Tamar stepped past her and picked up the bag. "Right, that's introductions done. Now, you'll be needing this." She held out the bag.

Stella frowned in confusion. "What for?"

"I need you to fetch me a cloud," said Tamar.

And just like that, the weirdness was back. There was a long pause, filled only with the distant hiss of the waves against the cliffs.

"Um, I can't do that . . . Clouds are, well, clouds," said Stella.

"Of course you can," said Tamar. "Just because you haven't done it before doesn't mean you can't. Go and fetch me a cloud."

# Four

# THE CLOUD

TAMAR stood there, holding out the empty bag, as if fetching a cloud were a perfectly normal, everyday thing to ask someone to do.

"Any time now would be good," she said.

The wind lifted her tufty white hair. She definitely looked like some sort of witch. Either that or she was completely bonkers. Stella wasn't sure which was worse.

"How?" she asked, cautiously.

"Now you're asking useful questions," replied Tamar. "Climb

up the nearest hill. Clouds like hills, so that's where you'll tend to find them hanging around. You may need to walk up a number of hills, but when you've found one, you just call it in, grab a hold of it and stuff it into the bag."

"Like that one?" said Stella. She pointed to a small white cloud on top of the nearest ridge.

"Perfect. Well spotted!" said Tamar. She held out the green bag and nodded. "Off you go then."

Stella hesitated. "Just so you know, I don't think I can do it," she said.

"Well, why on earth not?" said Tamar

Stella looked at the cloud. It was perched at the top of the slope, like a fluffy pompom. *Because you can't catch clouds,* she thought, but she couldn't say that. "It's probably not something I'd be good at," she said.

"Balderdash!" said Tamar. "You don't know until you try. Have you ever tried to catch a cloud before?"

Stella shook her head.

"So, you might be absolutely brilliant at it?" said Tamar.

"It's not very likely—".

"It's a possibility though?" said Tamar.

Stella sighed. After a few days with Grandpa, she was getting good at knowing when she'd lost an argument. "I'll have a go," she said.

"That's the spirit!" said Tamar.

Stella took the bag from her and stepped off the path. The slope was steep, rugged, and not at all easy to climb. The purple clumps of thistle looked really pretty, until she put her hand on one, and its sharp thorns stuck in her palm.

By the time she got to the top of the hill, Stella was out of breath and her shoes were wet from squelching over the boggy peat. She'd reached the cloud though.

It was more of a fog, really, once you got up close to it. She wondered what she was supposed to do. The air was clammy and cold, and she couldn't see further than a metre or two in front of her.

Feeling a bit silly, she held out the bag and flapped it about a bit, trying to scoop up some cloud. She looked inside, but the bag was still, very definitely, empty.

Stella tried holding the bag open and calling to the cloud in a sweet voice. "Here cloudy, cloudy, cloudy . . ." The neighbours at home always got their cat in at night by calling to it like that. It didn't seem to work on clouds though.

She dropped her arms, letting out a small puff of frustration. Whoever heard of sending someone out to get a cloud? It was ridiculous.

*But Tamar seemed so sure!* she thought. *And wouldn't it be amazing?*

Stella closed her eyes and imagined that the whole cloud on top of the hill was thick and soft, like cotton wool. Keeping her eyes tightly closed, she put out her hand and mimed taking hold of it. She wasn't sure, but thought maybe she could feel it, light as a dandelion fairy clock between her fingers. She stuffed the imaginary cloud into the bag and closed the top.

When she opened her eyes and looked at the bag, it didn't look empty any more. In fact, it looked quite fat – like a bag with a cloud inside it might look. Stella shook it gently.

It was definitely full of something.

She suddenly realised a cloud would probably find it pretty easy to get out of a bag.

She had to get it back to Tamar. Now! Before it escaped.

She rolled the top of the bag tightly closed and set off at a jog, dodging the thistles and jumping between tufty clumps of grass. It was much easier going down. When she got back to the path, Tamar tilted her head.

"So?" she said.

Stella grinned and tried to catch her breath. "I've got it!" she announced.

Tamar raised her white fluffy eyebrows

"Well, I think I've got it . . ." said Stella.

The bag had deflated a bit on the way down. Maybe it had got out?

"Let's see now, shall we?" said Tamar, taking it from her. Gently, she opened the top and peered in.

*CRACK, FLASH, BOOM!*

A spike of lightning shot out and zapped Tamar right on the nose. Stella leapt backwards and threw her hands over her face.

*I've killed an old woman!* she thought. *A magic old woman. The only magic person I've ever met, and I've killed her!*

Was Tamar fried to a crisp? Stella didn't want to look. She wasn't sure what would happen to someone hit by lightning, but she was sure it would be horrible. Maybe they'd catch on fire. Maybe bits of them would melt. Whatever it was, it was going to be disgusting.

She sucked in a breath of cold air, full of the electric smell of storm and kept her hands clamped tight over her eyes.

Tamar cleared her throat.

Stella peeked through her fingers. Tamar's hair was standing on end. Her face was black and sooty and thin plumes of smoke were coming out of her nostrils. Her eyes were scrunched shut and she was holding the bag tightly closed, at arm's length.

*Definitely magic,* thought Stella. *If she was normal, that would have killed her.*

Tamar drew in a deep breath that sucked all the smoke back up her nose. Then she let it out again, in a long slow sigh, and opened her eyes.

"When you were coming back here," she said slowly, "you didn't happen to . . . shake the bag, did you?"

"You didn't say anything about not shaking it!" burst out Stella.

Tamar stiffened and her eyes glittered. Stella suddenly remembered she might be a witch.

"I mean, sorry," she said, quickly. "Are you okay?"

The glitter softened to a twinkle. "Woke me up a bit," said Tamar, with a wry smile.

She plumped herself down on a nearby boulder and patted her hair flat with her free hand until it wasn't standing straight up any more. Every time she moved, the bag let out a low throaty rumble, which Tamar pointedly ignored.

"That's not what's meant to happen, is it?" said Stella.

"No," said Tamar. "This complicates things."

Five

# LETTING THE CLOUD OUT OF THE BAG

"DID I do it wrong?" asked Stella.

Tamar shook her head. "It's my fault. I shouldn't have sent you when you were in a temper."

Stella frowned. *How did Tamar know about that?* And what did it have to do with anything, anyway? She'd been happy up on the hill – she hadn't thought about Grandpa once, until now.

"I'd suggest you walk away," said Tamar.

Stella's heart sank.

*I don't want to go,* she thought. *This is actual magic! And I can't go home. Grandpa will still be mad at me.*

"I'm sorry I shook it," she said. "I didn't know I wasn't meant to."

"Of course you didn't. You couldn't be expected to," said Tamar. "You don't need to go far, just stand back a bit. I'm going to let the cloud out of the bag."

"What?" said Stella. "You can't!"

"The longer we leave him in there, the crosser he's going to get," said Tamar. "I don't want my bag to get scorched."

"Your bag!" said Stella. "What about me? If I get hit with lightning, I'll get more than scorched. I'll probably die!"

Tamar wrinkled her nose and shook her head dismissively. "You'll be fine," she said. "If you caught the wrong cloud, he'll just fly away. If he's the right one, he's not going to kill you. I wouldn't have asked you to catch him if there was any danger of that."

Stella backed away, her eyes fixed on the bag.

"Maybe a bit further," said Tamar. "Just to be on the safe side."

Stella scampered across to the nearest outcrop of rock and crouched down. If the cloud looked like firing lightning, she'd throw herself to the ground. Hopefully the rocks would shield her. She wasn't sure it would work, but it was the best she could come up with on the spot.

Tamar gripped the bottom of the bag with one hand, unrolled the top, and flapped it hard. The cloud poured out like a long

41

grey streamer, and gradually faded into a fine haze.

*It's gone,* thought Stella, with a twinge of regret.

She stood up and began to walk back to Tamar. After only a few steps, her scalp began to prickle – like she was being watched.

Stella looked behind her, but there was nobody there, only a flutter of sparrows in the bushes. Then she looked up.

The cloud was floating above her head.

She tensed for a moment, but there wasn't any sign of lightning. Not even a spark. The cloud was back to being a white powder-puff.

Stella smiled. *I did catch the right cloud!*

She pointed. "Go on," she said. "That way. Tamar's over there."

The cloud didn't move.

She suddenly felt a bit foolish. It couldn't hear her – it was a cloud. It was just floating where it had ended up, when it came out of the bag.

Wasn't it?

She stretched up to try and touch it, but found it was just out of reach. She flapped her hands to waft it in the right direction, but it stayed put – a white circle against the grey sky.

Stella set off towards Tamar. As soon as she moved, the surface of the cloud heaved, like someone rolling over under a duvet, and it began to follow her.

She walked a bit faster, but the cloud caught up, its shadow raising goosebumps on her arms.

Stella frowned up at it. *Surely, if anyone, it's meant to follow Tamar?* she thought.

Perhaps Tamar's magic had gone wrong, somehow?

"Tamar?" she said. "Look." She pointed at the cloud above her head. Tamar beckoned.

When Stella reached her, she saw that Tamar's face was creased with amusement.

"Your cloud is following me," said Stella.

"He's not my cloud. He's your cloud now," said Tamar, trying not to laugh.

"No, he's not. I caught him for you!" she said.

"You caught him so that I could find out whether you could," said Tamar. "But you caught him, so now he's yours."

A fresh breeze came in from the sea and the cloud swayed in the air. It looked very peculiar, floating there all on its own. Stella tried to imagine what Grandpa would say if she came back with her own personal cloud. She couldn't.

What about when Mum and Dad came back? What about when she went back to school? Would it follow? She imagined standing in the playground with the cloud hovering over her head. What would the teachers say? What would *everyone* say?

Stella couldn't think of a nice way to explain all this to Tamar. "Um, I don't think I really want a cloud," she said awkwardly.

"Bit late for that now," said Tamar. "Anyway, you should be pleased. Clouds are hard to catch. They only let themselves be caught by people they really like. This cloud has obviously taken a real shine to you, so he's yours now."

"What do you mean, mine?" said Stella. "Like a pet?"

She looked up at the cloud again. It was gradually shading from white to grey, to very dark grey.

A raindrop landed right in her eye.

She had just a split second to feel relieved it hadn't fired lightning, before the downpour started.

It was like standing under the shower with her clothes on. Stella scrunched her eyes closed. "Stop it!" she squawked. "Stop!"

Tamar folded her arms and smiled broadly, as though she was watching a very entertaining show.

"Why is it raining on me? Make it stop!" spluttered Stella.

"I think you offended him," said Tamar.

"Offended? How?" said Stella, wiping water out of her eyes. She tried holding her hands between her and the cloud. It didn't help. The rain gushed through her fingers, plastering her hair flat to her head.

"Hmm. Well, first of all, you said you didn't want him, but most likely it was when you called him a pet," said Tamar.

"I'm sorry I called you a pet!" yelled Stella, in a very un-sorry voice. "I don't know what you are. I've never met any clouds before." She was starting to wish she hadn't met this one.

The rain stopped, like a tap being turned off.

"So, he's not a pet," said Stella, wiping her face on her arm. "What is he then? You're the one who said he's mine."

"He's more like a teammate. A partner. A friend, if you like," said Tamar.

Stella snorted and glared up at the cloud. "I suppose I should be glad he's not firing lightning at me?" she said.

At the word lightning, the underside of the cloud turned a muddy shade of orange and began to crackle with sparks.

"No! Help! I'm sorry!" squeaked Stella. She threw her arms over the top of her head.

The cloud gave a small rumble and faded to white again.

"That," said Tamar, "was a cloud making a joke! It seems you have picked a particularly feisty one. Seems fitting really, given your temperament."

Stella stared at her.

"Come on," said Tamar. "You'd better come with me." She turned and began to walk away, the tail ends of her long cardigan flapping behind her.

Stella hesitated. Being able to control the weather, that was a sea witch power . . .

In Gran's story, the sea witch made a storm that drove the boats onto the rocks – she tried to drown all the sailors. Stella remembered begging Dad not to go out on the boat in case the sea witch got him – that was what made Mum really annoyed with Gran.

*I don't believe in sea witches any more*, Stella reminded herself.

Then again, this morning, she wouldn't have believed you could catch clouds.

"I'll tell you everything you need to know about having a cloud," Tamar called over her shoulder.

A tug of guilt made Stella hesitate. She ought to go back home first. Let Grandpa know where she was going. Say sorry about Gran's mug.

But how could she, with a cloud following her?

*Besides, it's probably better to give him time to calm down.*

She cast a worried look up at the cloud, then turned to follow Tamar.

The cloud trailed after her, like a balloon on a string.

## Six

# SPINNING A YARN

A S they rounded the hill, Tamar turned down the slope
towards an ancient croft house. It nestled low into a fold
of the hillside and looked out over the bay. The stone walls had
moss growing in all the cracks, making it all but invisible against
the scrub of heather behind. The thatched roof was covered with
a loose net of ropes, with rocks strung on the end, presumably to
keep the roof on when the gales came in from the sea. Somehow
the small windows didn't make this house look mean and angry,
like Grandpa's house. It just looked cosy.

Tamar wasn't tall, but even so, the doorway was so low that she had to duck her head to go inside. Stella followed her in and closed the door quickly behind her.

The warm smoky smell of peat wrapped itself around her. It reminded Stella of when she was little. She took a long slow breath and held it in, trying to hold on to the memory like a hug.

As her eyes adjusted to the gloom, Stella looked around. She'd half expected Tamar to live in some sort of witchy hovel filled with skulls and cauldrons. It wasn't like that at all.

A fire glowed in the grate, casting a warm light. Bundles of herbs hung from hooks on the low beams. The far wall was full of shelves, from floor to ceiling, crowded with colourful reels of yarn, glass bottles and jars. A pale grey curtain was drawn across the window.

"Dingy in here," grumbled Tamar. "Can't see a thing." She waved a hand at the window and the curtain dissolved.

"How did you do that?" said Stella, hoping that Tamar couldn't make her disappear just as easily.

"Curtain of fog. Fog doesn't like being waved at. If you wave at it, it dissolves. Don't ask me why. Still, saves having to draw the curtains."

A shaft of sunlight shone in, making dust motes sparkle in the air. Stella's face prickled with cold. It wasn't dust. It was snow! Really fine snow. Falling indoors! She wiped a hand across her cheek.

"Oops, sorry about that!" said Tamar. "Pesky stuff. I opened a dusting of it this morning. I must have forgotten to put it away. It'll pass in a minute."

The snow whirled away, as though a breeze had blown through the room. It streamed up into the far corner of the ceiling and spun in a glittering circle.

"I said, it'll pass in a minute!" said Tamar, raising her voice and banging the bottom of an empty jar on the kitchen table. "It had jolly well better pass, or I'll break out some Sahara sunshine – then we'll see how frisky it feels!"

The snow swirled towards her, formed a fine shimmering column, then fell into the open jam jar.

"That's more like it," said Tamar, screwing the lid on. "Fancy snowing on our guest! What's she going to think of us?"

"It's better than being rained on," said Stella.

"You can hardly blame me if you get rained on by your own cloud," said Tamar. "Here, this will have you dry in no time," she said, handing her a towel.

Stella rubbed the towel over her hair, but when she put it to her cheek, it squirmed in her hands and tried to wrap itself around her face. She snatched it away and held it between finger and thumb, until Tamar took it and hung it on a hook by the sink. Stella watched it suspiciously, but it just hung there, looking like a perfectly ordinary towel.

"Make yourself comfortable," said Tamar, waving a hand at one of the armchairs by the fire.

Stella went over to the armchair and looked at the blanket hanging over the back of it. A blanket was much bigger than a towel. She had a sudden horrible image of it leaping off the chair and wrapping itself round her, like some kind of monster cocoon. She poked it with one finger, but it didn't move, so she sat down on the front edge of the chair and perched there.

Tamar sat down opposite her. "So, you moved away, but you're back, yes?"

Stella nodded. "At least for the summer. I don't know where we'll be after that. We move with Dad's work."

"So, where did you call home before?"

*Nowhere,* thought Stella. They'd lived in three different places since leaving Shetland and none of them had felt like home. She wasn't sure how to explain that though.

She gave a small shrug. "We were in Southampton last."

"And who are you here with?"

"My grandpa," said Stella, with a twist of her lips.

"Not going so well?"

"No."

Amazingly, Tamar didn't put on a sympathetic face or pester her with questions. She just nodded. This was good, because Stella didn't want to talk about Grandpa right now.

"Now, where's that cloud of yours got to?" said Tamar.

Stella glanced towards the door and her heart skipped a beat. Something was moving in the shadows. She thought for a moment it might be a rat, but it wasn't. A mist was creeping under the door, pooling like cold smoke in the cracks between the flagstones. She pointed.

"Oh, don't tell me you shut him outside!" said Tamar, pushing herself up out of the chair. "Can't you at least make an effort to get along with him?"

"I didn't mean to," said Stella, which wasn't true. "I didn't realise that clouds could come inside houses," she said, which was closer to the truth. She had hoped clouds couldn't come inside houses and had shut the door quickly to make sure.

Tamar stomped over to the front door and threw it open. The cloud came tumbling in as though it had been leaning on the other side. It bounced through the legs of the kitchen chairs, shedding feathers of mist, and finally sprawled to a stop in front of Stella's knees.

Stella watched it carefully, to see if was going to turn thundery, but instead, it gathered itself up into a neat ball and floated there, pale and round, as though waiting for something.

"Poor thing," said Tamar. "Honestly! What a way to treat a new cloud." She closed the door and came over to the fire again. As she sat down opposite Stella, the cloud unfurled, splitting into pale wisps that curled between the chair legs and up over the edge of the little fireside table.

Stella shuffled back in her seat. She felt a bit uncomfortable sitting this close to it, when it was behaving like this. She was worried it might wind itself round her ankles or snake its way up her nose or something.

The tendrils of mist streamed up and twined together like a ghostly ball of wool, until they had blended into a whole cloud again, floating just above the surface of the low table.

Tamar stroked the top of the cloud and raised her eyebrows. "So, you'll be wanting to know what you can do with your cloud, now you've caught him?" she said.

Stella's lips twitched. The first thing she wanted to know was how to stop him following her.

Tamar tilted her head to one side, as though she'd heard a noise, then stood up.

"One of my clouds has just arrived," she said. "That's good timing."

"I didn't know you've got a cloud too," said Stella.

"I've got lots," said Tamar. "Only one that's full right now, though."

*Full? Full of what?*

Stella hoped it wasn't rain. Her clothes were still damp after the last downpour. She edged closer to the fire.

Tamar leant over the sink and cracked the window open. A whisper of mist crept inside and wound across the room in a sinuous grey line. It curved towards Stella and she put a hand over her mouth, so she didn't accidentally breathe it in. At the last moment, it turned away.

There was a sudden chill around her ankles. Stella glanced down to see her cloud doing a bad job of trying to hide under the little table.

The snaking ribbon of cloud made its way to an old wooden spinning wheel in the corner. As it looped neatly around the rim, the spinning wheel wobbled and tilted.

"Whoa, whoa! Wait!" said Tamar. She grabbed the frame of the spinning wheel and leant on it, pinning it to the floor. "Give me a hand," she said to Stella. "There's a jug of water on the table over there."

Stella jumped up and fetched the jug. "What do you want me to do with it?" she said.

"Pour it out," said Tamar.

Stella tipped a little splash of water onto the floor.

"All of it," said Tamar.

Stella poured until the spinning wheel stood in a big puddle of water and the jug was empty.

Tamar nodded. "Good." She stepped back and pointed a stern finger at the puddle. Frost curled across the surface of the water like lace until the pool froze into a circle of ice.

Stella laughed in surprise. "Cool!"

"Precisely," said Tamar.

Stella smiled. *Imagine being able to freeze stuff, just by pointing at it!*

She grinned at the thought of making instant ice lollies.

That would be popular at school. It might even make up for the cloud . . .

*No,* she realised. *It won't. That's not something people will ever get used to.*

Tamar nudged the spinning wheel. It was solidly frozen to the floor. "Good. That should hold it," she said. She took the jug from Stella, with a nod of thanks, and went over to the sink to refill it.

Stella crouched down and touched the circle of ice. It was so cold that her fingertips stuck to it. She snatched up her hand and stuffed it under her armpit.

Tamar turned around. "Oh, I forgot to say, don't step on the ice," she said. "It'll freeze you to the floor, and that wouldn't do, would it?"

*You might have told me that before,* thought Stella.

She inspected her fingers. They were bright red with cold. She wiggled them to make sure they still worked, then tucked them back under her armpit.

"Alright, we're ready now!" called Tamar.

The ribbon of cloud tightened into a straight line and the spinning wheel creaked. The wheel started to turn with a gentle humming noise, and a gossamer-fine yarn began to appear on the reel.

"Good cloud, this one," said Tamar. "Had him for years. Spins himself these days, which saves a bit of time."

Stella looked up at the shelves. She'd remembered right – in amongst the bottles and jars, there were reels of yarn. Loads of them, in almost every colour of the rainbow. A smile crept across her face.

"Did you make all these out of cloud?" she asked.

Tamar nodded. "Most of them," she said, and walked back to her armchair.

Stella watched in fascination as the spiral of yarn climbed up the reel. As it got thicker, it began to sparkle and shine, like moonlight on snow. She glanced down at the grey line of cloud. "Why is it coming out silver?" she asked.

"It's magic. Pure magic," said Tamar, as though that explained everything.

Stella shook her head, to let her know that it didn't.

"Magic is silver," said Tamar. "Or the kind that the clouds fetch is, anyway. Clouds are magic gatherers, you see. They collect up magic and bring it back to be spun."

"Oh . . ." said Stella. She looked at her cloud, poking out between the table legs in pale grey tufts. "Why aren't the clouds silver, then?"

"You've heard of every cloud having a silver lining?" asked Tamar.

"No."

Tamar raised her eyebrows in surprise. "Oh! Well, originally, of course, it was simply a literal description of clouds. Nowadays it means there's always something wonderful to find, if you bother looking for it."

Stella grinned. *Magic gatherers? Spinning clouds? This was wonderful.*

She stood up and went over to sit with Tamar.

"So what do you use the magic for, once you've spun it?" she said.

"Weaving, of course" said Tamar. "Have you never heard of weaving magic?"

"Yes, but I thought only witches . . ." Stella clamped her mouth shut on the sentence.

Tamar just looked at her and waited.

Stella bit her lip. Maybe it was better to know.

"Are you a witch?" she asked, with only a small tremble in her voice.

"No," said Tamar emphatically. "Witches weave spells. That's different."

"Oh," said Stella.

Tamar picked up a poker and prodded the glowing bricks of peat in the fireplace until a shy flame licked up the side. The firelight made her look even witchier than she had before, but Stella decided not to think about that.

Tamar knew magic. That was the important thing.

"We'll get your cloud spinning, in due course," said Tamar.

Stella looked down at her cloud. He was still hiding under the low table. He didn't look like he fancied being spun.

*Surely you want to know how to spin magic?* thought Stella. *I do, even if you don't.*

Stella prodded him with the tip of her toe, coaxing him out from under the table. He didn't look very happy. She surreptitiously wafted him until he was floating above the table again.

*There,* she thought. *That's better.*

"You were going to tell me about having a cloud?" she prompted.

Tamar blinked and looked at her. "So I was." She narrowed her eyes, as though sizing Stella up, then she adjusted the cushion behind her and settled back in her chair. "Thousands of years ago," she started, "when the world was young and all magic was the colour of moonlight—"

*This sounds like one of Gran's epics. The ones that take weeks.*

The cloud gave a little shudder and slid off the table.

Tamar leant forward and peered at it. "Boring you, am I?" she said.

Stella shifted in her seat. She did want to hear the story, but she didn't have days. Grandpa would go nuts if she didn't come back soon.

Mainly, she needed to know how to stop the cloud following her. Especially inside houses.

"Can we skip to the bit about clouds?" she said. "I'm sure he'd be interested in that bit."

Tamar sat up and heaved a sigh. "Fine," she said. "The short version is – you're a weather weaver."

"A what?" said Stella.

"A weather weaver," said Tamar. "People who fish are fishermen. People who farm are farmers. People who weave weather are weather weavers." She turned towards the spinning wheel. "Ah, all done."

The wheel had stopped and the grey ribbon of cloud had vanished.

Stella's cloud scooted out from under the table and across the floor. He nosed around the legs of the spinning wheel and extended a misty point up towards the reel of thread.

Tamar went over. "Stop that!" she said. She lifted the reel of magic from the wheel and gently batted the cloud away. "Don't be greedy. Go gather your own."

"He seems a lot happier now your cloud's gone," said Stella.

"Probably felt a bit daunted," agreed Tamar. "It's one of my bigger clouds."

Stella stood up and went to the window. She couldn't see any clouds. The whole sky was just a smooth sheet of grey.

"Where's your cloud gone?" she said.

"You're looking at him," said Tamar. "He's grown large over the years."

Stella stared out of the window. The thought of a cloud as large as the sky stretched the inside of her head. It was too big. She looked back at her little cloud.

*No wonder you hid!*

He was definitely feeling better now the other cloud had gone.

He'd floated back to his spot above the fireside table and was looking distinctly fluffier.

"—thirsty towels, cloaks of invisibility, flying carpets," Tamar was saying.

"Wait, what?" said Stella.

"Things you can weave out of magic thread," said Tamar. "Have you been listening at all?"

Stella shuffled from one foot to the other. "I might have missed a bit," she said.

Tamar sighed. "I'm probably getting ahead of myself," she said. "You won't be able to get on to spinning and weaving until you and your cloud have mastered every weather. The full rainbow, as it were."

*Rainbows? Cloaks of invisibility? Flying carpets!*

Stella looked at her cloud with new interest. Maybe she could get used to it, after all.

The surface of the cloud suddenly glowed white, as though the sun had come out.

## Seven

# A FINE COLLECTION OF WEATHER

"SO, shall we get started with some weather?" said Tamar.

After lightning and rain, Stella wasn't keen to see any more weather, but Tamar's eyes were sparkling with excitement, so she nodded.

Tamar waved her hand at the wall of shelves with a flourish. "My personal collection of unusual weathers," she said with a proud smile.

Stella went over to look. The top two shelves were full of yarn, but the ones further down were crammed with bottles and jars. It reminded her of Mum's larder. The nearest jar seemed to be filled with small hard-boiled eggs. She squinted at Tamar's swirly handwriting on the label. "Puffin's Egg!" she read aloud and turned to Tamar in horror. "You can't take eggs from—"

Tamar shook her head. "Keep reading," she said.

Stella turned the jar round, until she could see the rest of the label. "Puffin's Egg Hailstones?" she said.

"Well, honestly! I wouldn't take eggs from puffins," said Tamar indignantly. "That would just be cruel. Poor things only lay one egg a year."

"I've never seen hailstones as big as this," said Stella. She'd been in a hailstorm last winter. She remembered the thrill of seeing the tiny balls of ice ping up as they hit the ground. These hailstones didn't look like they'd bounce. They looked like they'd hurt. "Why have you got them in a jar?" she asked.

"You never know. They might come in handy," said Tamar. She patted the top of Stella's cloud, making it bob up and down, then stood up and walked over to a glass cabinet in the corner.

Stella shook her head at Tamar's back. *When would giant hailstones ever come in handy?*

The next jar was tall and shaped like a glass bell. It was full of white lumps that looked a bit like sugar mice. Tamar's spidery handwriting was full of loops and wiggles that made it hard to read. "Snow Bones," she deciphered.

*What sort of creature had bones made of snow?*

The brown bottle next to it seemed to be empty. Stella ran her finger under the swooping curls of the letters. The bottle hummed, making her fingertip itch as she ran it over the label.

*Heart of Hurricane. DO NOT OPEN!*

Tamar plonked a large Kilner jar down on the side table with a bang, and Stella jumped. The brown bottle wobbled on the shelf and she put both hands up to steady it, her heart racing. The glass vibrated under her fingers, as though whatever was inside was trying to get out.

"I wouldn't be opening that one, if I were you," said Tamar.

Stella lifted her hands away carefully and looked at Tamar with wide eyes. "What would it do?" she asked.

"It might blow us both to kingdom come," said Tamar.

"Why would you keep it in your house then?" said Stella.

"In case of emergencies," said Tamar. She threw more peat into the fire. It landed with a thud, throwing up a shower of sparks that reflected like fireworks on the glass.

Tamar popped open the lid of the Kilner jar. "I think you'll like these," she said.

Stella went over and crouched down. At first glance, she'd thought it was full of bubbles, but when she looked closer, she realised they were fine, multi-coloured rings. They glowed like stained glass. "Wow! They're beautiful," she said. "What are they?"

Tamar raised her eyebrows and gave a conspiratorial smile.

"Rainbow? Bits of rainbow?" asked Stella, holding her hand over them. The light painted stripes on her skin.

"Mm-hmm," said Tamar, nodding.

"How did you make them into rings?" said Stella.

"What shape is a rainbow?" said Tamar.

"Sort of a curve," said Stella.

"Wrong!" sang Tamar, looking very pleased with herself.

"Go on? What shape are they then?" said Stella.

"They're round. Circular. Hoops. And how big are they?" Tamar asked, obviously enjoying herself.

"You're going to tell me they're tiny, like those little rings?" said Stella, her voice full of disbelief.

"There you are!" said Tamar. "You're catching on."

"But they're not!" said Stella. "I've seen rainbows as big as the sky."

"Ah, those would be wild rainbows," said Tamar, nodding sagely. "They can be enormous."

"So what are these then? Tame rainbows?" said Stella, wondering what a wild rainbow was like. She couldn't picture a snarling rainbow. Rainbows were too lovely to be fierce.

"Close," said Tamar. "These are home-grown rainbows."

Stella thought of the greenhouse at home and imagined what it would look like if, instead of tomatoes, it was full of rainbow plants.

"A rainbow is as big as the cloud that makes it," said Tamar. "If you catch a very small cloud, you can make little tiny rainbows like these. I should think your cloud would make rainbows about the size of a hula hoop."

Stella wondered whether hula hooping with a rainbow would be any different than doing it with an ordinary hula hoop. Maybe a bit more glowy. You could do it in the dark!

"Can we make one now?" she said, her eyes shining.

"Not yet," said Tamar. "You'll need to find your colours first. It's a process that requires patience."

Stella sighed. Patience was not her strong point. Mum was always telling her that. But if it meant making rainbows . . .

"I can be patient," she said.

"Good," said Tamar. "It is worth the effort. They're really very useful."

Stella frowned. *Useful?* "For what?"

"All sorts of things," said Tamar. "Mainly, I use them to split stories into truths."

"Do you mean truth?" said Stella.

"No. Truths," said Tamar. "Here." She lifted a fat little tube off the mantelpiece and handed it to Stella. "Try the yellow one."

Stella turned the tube round in her hands. It looked like a stubby telescope. It was smooth grey metal and at one end there was a small circular dial surrounded by tiny coloured dots. The arrow on the dial was pointing to yellow.

"Go on," said Tamar. "Look through it. That's called *gaa* glass, that is – a rainbow glass."

Stella held the eyepiece up to her eye and closed her other eye. She could see the kitchen table, all lit up gold, as though the sun was pouring in on it. It didn't look any closer, like it would through a telescope. "I don't think it's working," she said, and swung the tube round towards Tamar. "Oh!"

Tamar was transformed.

Her hair no longer stuck up in wiry white tufts. It flowed down over her shoulders in silky copper curls. Her face was smooth and unlined, and she was smiling the kind of smile that it was impossible not to join in with. A faint golden light shone out of her head – a shimmering halo. It was definitely Tamar, but she looked like an angel.

Was this who she really was?

Stella took the tube away from her eye and there was Tamar again. Her mad white hair stuck up in wiry tufts and the mischievous look was back in her eyes. "So? What did you see?" she said.

"Um, you looked quite different," said Stella.

"And that's a truth," said Tamar.

"The truth?" said Stella.

"No, just one of them," said Tamar, shaking her head. She took the tube from Stella and rolled it between her palms. "There's always more than one truth."

"There can't be," said Stella. "Otherwise it wouldn't be the truth."

"Life would be incredibly boring if there was only one truth," said Tamar. "The whole world would be tick or cross, yes or no, black or white. We wouldn't need rainbows to figure it out. There are many truths. Always."

"Can I see another truth then?" said Stella.

"No. I don't look as nice through the other colours," said Tamar, patting her thatch of white hair. "Allow an old woman a little vanity."

Stella pursed her lips. "So yellow shows you the prettiest truth," she said. "What do the other colours do?"

"Yellow is for joy and good intentions," corrected Tamar. "Each colour is a little window onto a different view of the world. They're all as true as each other. Red reveals violence, or fury—"

"What do you look like through the red one?" said Stella.

"Terrifying," said Tamar. She widened her eyes and waggled her fingers with a grin. "Blue is for loss, loneliness, grief. Green is belonging, groundedness. And so on. You get the picture."

"Not if you won't let me see them," said Stella.

Her cloud spun slowly. She wondered whether it was listening.

"Do you see things the same way you normally would, when you're flaming angry?" said Tamar.

"No, of course not," said Stella, shaking her head. Grandpa's shouting face popped into her head, the veins standing out on his forehead like worms. Did Tamar know what had happened this morning?

"So, there you are," said Tamar. "When you're seeing red, the world looks very different than it does when you're cheerful, or peaceful, or sad . . ."

The cloud turned over in a slow roll and started to drift up towards the ceiling.

"Rainbows are good for uncovering feelings and intentions," said Tamar. "Everyone's a proper mixture. Often they don't want you to see what's underneath. People hide all sorts of things, in the name of good manners. Sometimes because they're just downright deceptive. A *gaa* glass lets you see the hidden bits."

Tamar put the little tube back on the mantelpiece. "Now you'd best be getting home, I think. It's getting late."

Stella looked out of the window and her heart dropped into her stomach. A scarlet sunset striped the sky outside.

She'd been gone all afternoon! Grandpa was going be so mad. She ran to the door. "I should have been back ages ago!"

"Take the coast path," said Tamar. "It's the quickest route back from here. You'll be home in no time."

Stella put her hand on the latch and turned to look at her cloud. It was turning small circles in front of the fire. *He looks happy to stay here,* she thought with relief.

"Can I come back, tomorrow?" she said.

*If Grandpa ever lets me out of the house again . . .*

"Of course!" said Tamar. "I'll be here waiting."

With a swift nod, Stella slipped out of the door.

The sun was low on the horizon, casting a long path of gold across the tops of the waves. The sky flamed orange and red.

"I'm in so much trouble!" Stella muttered to herself. She ran down the slope to the path, startling a rabbit. It scampered away, its white tail flashing like a warning.

## Eight

# A PERFECT STORM

As she got close to Grandpa's house, Stella slowed. There was no point rushing in when she'd been out all day. Better to see what sort of mood Grandpa was in first.

The kitchen window was speckled with dust and grime, making it hard to see inside. She cleaned a little hole with the tip of her finger and put her eye up close.

Grandpa was sitting at the table, a pot of tea and a mug next to him. He had his coat and hat on.

*Maybe he's been out dealing with the sheep all this time,* she thought. *Maybe he hasn't realised I haven't been back?*

A cool breeze blew in from the sea, and somewhere in the distance, a sheep gave a groaning *baa*. Stella shivered. She couldn't stay out here all night.

The front door gave a loud creak as she pushed it open. Grandpa lifted his head and Stella's heart sank.

*Still angry.*

She pushed the door closed behind her, but decided not to take off her shoes, just in case.

The muscles in Grandpa's jaw twitched and the silence stretched as cold and deep as the ocean. All the way home, she'd been trying to work out how to say sorry – sorry for breaking Gran's mug, sorry for running away, sorry for everything – but the longer he glowered at her, the less sorry she felt.

*It's your fault Gran's mug got broken. It's your fault I ran away. It's your fault for shouting at me. All this is your fault.*

The accusations bubbled like lava inside her, but she didn't dare say them out loud.

"So. You're back," he growled.

Stella nodded and shifted from one foot to the other.

"I suppose you think it's FUNNY to run off and leave me imagining the worst?" He spat the words, between clenched teeth.

Her heart burned with the unfairness of it, but she shook her head. "No," she said.

"Were you trying to scare me? On purpose? Was that your plan?" he shouted. A white fleck of spit flew from his mouth.

"I didn't mean to be out that long," protested Stella. "It wasn't on purpose! I just . . . lost track of time."

Grandpa's face turned a strange shade of raspberry, and a vein started to pulse on the side of his forehead. "You lost track of time, you lost track of time," he said, in a horrid sing-song voice.

He was furious. She'd never seen him this angry.

"Where have you *been*?" roared Grandpa. He slammed his fist down on the table and the teacup jangled in its saucer. "I looked everywhere! I thought you were lost, or hurt, or dead! But it turns out you were just playing some kind of prank."

Stella blinked, and hot tears rolled down her cheeks. She brushed them away angrily.

"I wasn't! I'd never do that," she said, through gritted teeth.

*How can he even think that?*

"Thoughtless. That's what you are," snarled Grandpa. "No care for anyone but yourself."

"That's not true!" shouted Stella.

It was so wrong – she did care. If she didn't, why would she have tidied up his tools, or planned to make him shortbread? He didn't even realise.

"I do care about other people," she said. "And I think of nice things to do. All the time! You just don't notice. Because you're too busy being angry!"

A menacing rumble shook the air. It filled the room, making the plates on the dresser rattle.

Stella gaped at Grandpa, her heart pattering in her chest. She couldn't see the cloud, but he was here, somewhere.

This was bad. This was very bad.

"What . . . was that?" said Grandpa.

"Thunder?" said Stella, her eyes wide. She glanced at the window to give the impression that the sound had come from outside.

*Normal thunder. A normal storm. Outside the house.*

"I'm not deaf!" exclaimed Grandpa. "I meant what is thunder doing inside my house?"

Stella glanced around the room. Where was he? Behind the dresser? Under the table?

He must have followed her home; crept inside when she opened the door.

Worse than that, her cloud definitely didn't like Grandpa.

"Stop shouting," she blurted. "You've got to stop shouting. In fact, don't do anything that seems like you're being nasty."

Grandpa's mouth dropped open in shock and he stood up abruptly, making his chair screech backwards. "Nasty? You think I'm being nasty? After I've spent the day scouring the island for you?"

There was a blinding white flash and the room lit up like a camera flash.

The curtains behind Grandpa caught fire. He leapt away from them.

Stella darted forward, snatched the lid off the teapot, and threw the tea at the flames. There was a soft hiss and smoke filled the room.

When the smoke cleared, she realised she'd drenched Grandpa too. He was standing very stiffly in front of his chair. Tea dripped off his raincoat and puddled on the floor.

*At least he had his coat on,* she thought. A thrill of laughter rose dangerously inside her, but then she spotted the hardness in Grandpa's eyes.

He wasn't looking at her.

She followed his gaze. The cloud was rising from behind Gran's armchair, dark with threat and flickering with blue sparks.

*CRASH, FLASH, BOOM!!!*

Stella saw a snapshot of Grandpa's face, his eyes scrunched tight shut. The lightning shone above him. A white crack in the air. It pointed down, like an arrow, to the top of his head. Then the moment was gone.

Grandpa sat down heavily on the chair. A thin line of smoke rose out of his cap and the smell of burnt hair wafted horridly around the room.

A whirlpool of dread churned in Stella's stomach. Grandpa wasn't like Tamar. He was normal. And old, too.

The air started to crawl with electricity, like ants on her skin.

She turned around to face the cloud. It flickered like a broken bulb at the far end of the room. Another malevolent rumble trembled through the room and the air took on a metallic tang.

"Stop!" she shouted. "He's my Grandpa. He's angry all the time, but that doesn't mean you can hurt him!"

The rumbling continued, and slowly the cloud began to prowl towards Grandpa. Jagged blue sparks of electricity reached ahead of it, searing black zigzags into the ceiling with a sharp crackle.

Stella's heart contracted into a tight ball of terror.

"Please! Don't! He's the only grandpa I've got. And this isn't his fault. I broke Gran's mug. I ran away. It's my fault. It's all my fault!"

The cloud stopped in the middle of the ceiling. The sparks sputtered and dimmed. The thunder died away slowly, until there was nothing but the rapid sound of her breathing.

Stella put her hands on her hips and tried to look firm. "I mean it," she said. "No more lightning. Go outside. Up in the sky. Where you belong."

The cloud's colours shifted like a bruise and he drifted towards her. She resisted the urge to back away. As he drifted over her head, soft fingers of static electricity feathered through her hair. She stood very still.

The cloud thinned into a dark grey shadow and slipped underneath the front door.

The sudden silence was heavy in the room. She stared at the

gap under the door until she was sure he wasn't coming back, then turned to Grandpa.

He was slumped sideways against the kitchen table and his cap was scorched black on the top.

"Grandpa?" she said.

She stepped forward, but stopped, as Grandpa flinched away from her.

"Stay away from me," he said, his eyes full of fear.

She felt her heart crush like a piece of tin foil.

Grandpa thought she'd done this. Hurt him, on purpose. He was never going to forgive her.

*But I still have to keep him safe,* she thought.

"I'm so sorry, Grandpa," she said. "I'm sorry for everything."

But Grandpa wasn't listening. His eyes were distant and he was swaying in his chair.

"Can you manage to get up?" she said.

Being hit by lightning hadn't seemed to hurt Tamar, but Grandpa looked very ill. His face was waxy and pale, and his eyes weren't focused.

"Grandpa, I think maybe you should go to bed," she said.

"Bed?" he said. He blinked twice, then stood, pushing himself up on the table. Tea dripped slowly off the hem of his raincoat.

"The cloud's gone, but I'm not sure he'll stay gone," she said, glancing at the door. "If he comes back, he'll probably look for me, so it'd be safer if you're somewhere else."

"Cloud?" said Grandpa. He swayed on his feet.

Stella reached to catch him, but he found his balance.

"Please, Grandpa," she continued. "Let me help you."

"Feeling a bit . . ." he put a hand to his head. "Unsteady."

He shrugged off his wet coat and Stella stepped forward to help him. Then she took his arm and together they shuffled along the corridor to his room. Stella pushed his bedroom door open and Grandpa lurched forwards and fell onto the bed, making the springs creak.

Stella wondered for a moment if she should take his shoes off, but settled instead for tucking the blanket around him.

He looked small under the blanket – fragile – as though the lightning had sucked something vital out of him.

*Sleep is the best medicine,* came Mum's voice in her head.

Stella watched him for a while, then took a deep breath and headed back to the kitchen. She had to make sure the cloud was gone.

When she opened the front door, the cloud was right there, floating above the garden wall. A dark shadow against the twilight sky.

"Go away!" she hissed. "I don't care if it's special to have a cloud. I don't want you any more."

The cloud shuddered and sank slowly behind the wall.

Stella stepped outside. The night air was cold on her skin. It smelled of salt and damp grass. She peered cautiously over the top of the wall. The cloud huddled low to the ground on the other side.

Maybe he didn't think she meant it?

"You nearly killed Grandpa!" she said in a strained whisper. "Even if he's alright, he's never going to forgive me."

She stepped back as the cloud lifted out of the grass.

"I don't want you. You hear me? Go away!" she said.

The cloud hesitated for a moment, then began to slink away. He paused every now and again, as though hoping if he was slow enough, she might change her mind.

Each time he paused, she shook her head and pointed. *Go away!*

Stella waited until he'd floated out over the edge of the cliff, then went back inside.

The front room might have been a mess before, but now it was ruined. She picked up the teapot and put it in the sink, then mopped up the spilt tea with a dishcloth. There wasn't anything she could do about the curtains.

Grandpa had left a warm pot of stew on the stove. She ladled some into a bowl, took it to the table and sat down to eat.

She was starving hungry, but mainly, she was putting off checking on Grandpa.

What if he died?

What would she do?

There was no way to leave. Grandpa had brought her here in his boat, but she didn't know how to work it. She'd never get back to the mainland on her own.

She'd have to wait here until the end of the holidays, eating whatever was in the cupboards, until the food ran out.

*Then what?*

She thought about the limpets and mussel shells Gran used to collect down on the beach and her stomach turned over. She didn't want it to come to that.

Maybe Tamar could look after her? Feed her, at least, until Mum and Dad got here.

*Mum and Dad!*

How would she tell them? She couldn't imagine. Didn't want to. The idea of it made her insides squirm like a bucket of eels.

*No! Grandpa has to be alright. He has to.*

Stella took a deep breath to calm the churning in her stomach and crept down the corridor to Grandpa's room.

She pushed the door open slowly and listened.

The air in the room was stuffy and smelt like Grandpa, but there was no movement, no sound.

*He's dead.*

The thought sat like a rock inside her chest.

Stella tiptoed in and crouched by the side of the bed. The lump under the blanket didn't stir. He was so still.

She reached forward tentatively and poked him.

He gave a great snort and Stella toppled backwards in fright.

Grandpa rolled over and started to snore.

Nine

# BANNOCKS FOR BREAKFAST

A N unfamiliar sound slipped into her dreams. It hooked her like a fish and pulled her up to the surface of sleep.

Whistling. Someone was whistling. A jolly sea shanty. The dancing notes sang of white-capped waves and sun-bleached sails.

*Grandpa!*

Last night came rushing back.

Stella had stayed awake for ages, in case the cloud came back.

But, at some point, she must have fallen asleep.

*So much for standing guard!*

When she went into the kitchen, Grandpa was by the stove.

Not dead. Not even hurt. He was prodding the contents of a pan and looking . . . cheerful?

Grandpa gave a wide smile when he spotted her. "A very good morning to you," he said.

She stared at him. "Good morning," she said, uncertainly.

His smile changed to a look of concern. "What's up with you then? Bad dream?"

She nodded mutely. Last night did feel like a bad dream.

He broke into a grin. "Never fear! Nightmares flee in the face of my legendary breakfast skills!" He wielded the spatula in the air like a sword, struck a dramatic pose, and then paused as though waiting for applause.

Stella smiled uneasily.

"Not impressed?" he said, raising his eyebrows. "Ah, well. Sit down then." He nodded at the table. "You'll cheer up after some food, no doubt."

Stella went over to the table.

The scorched curtains hung there like an accusation.

It wasn't just a bad dream.

It was real.

Grandpa had been hit by lightning.

The only unreal thing, right now, was Grandpa. What had got

into him?

She pulled out a chair and sat down. There was a little glass vase of flowers on the table. That hadn't been there before. He must have picked them fresh this morning. She tried to imagine Grandpa out picking flowers, but she couldn't picture it. Everything was weird this morning.

"I've made bannocks," said Grandpa, flipping the contents of the pan. "A little treat for us."

"Thank you," she said, pasting on a smile. "They smell delicious."

Mum would have seen through a fake smile, but Grandpa didn't notice. He just put the pan down in the middle of the table and sat down.

As he leant forward to pull his chair in, Stella saw a red mark, like a star, in the middle of his bald patch.

It looked sore, but not as bad as she'd feared. Maybe having his cap on had helped? Or perhaps the cloud hadn't actually meant to kill him.

Her eyes slid back to the limp black tatters of the curtains.

Grandpa followed her gaze. "They're a proper mess, aren't they? I must have left a candle burning. Silly old fool."

She stared at him in astonishment.

It was as though last night hadn't happened; as though it had been wiped out of his mind. *Could lightning do that?*

He pushed the butter dish towards Stella and gave her a

sympathetic look. "Gave me a fright too, when I got up this morning," he said. "We should thank our lucky stars, I reckon."

"But, but, but what about . . ." stuttered Stella. She glanced at his head.

"Hey! Calm down. We're both alright," said Grandpa, with a reassuring smile. "That's the main thing. They're only curtains, after all. Could have been worse."

He turned towards the front door and froze. His eyes were far away, like he was daydreaming.

Perhaps the lightning had done something awful to his brain?

*But if his brain was fried, he wouldn't be able to cook, would he? Or talk normally,* she thought.

After a few moments, Grandpa blinked, shook his head, and seemed to notice Stella again. "Eat up. They're better warm," he said.

Why didn't he remember? And why was he so cheerful?

That was the weirdest thing.

Since she'd arrived, she'd seen him sad, tired, grumpy, impatient, angry, or all of those at once, but never in a good mood.

*And how do you forget being struck by lightning?* she wondered. *It doesn't make sense.*

He was spreading butter on his bannocks, and humming. *Humming!*

Grandpa nodded at her plate and raised his eyebrows, so she picked up a bannock and took a bite. It was warm and salty, dripping with melted butter.

As soon as she'd taken a bite, she smiled – a real smile this time.

"Thanks Grandpa, this is really good," she said.

"Told you, didn't I?" said Grandpa, picking up the last crumbs from his own plate with the tip of his finger. "Breakfast is my speciality. Sets you up for the day."

He scratched absent-mindedly at the red mark on his head and winced.

"Grandpa? Should you . . . maybe go to the doctor?" she said.

Grandpa raised his eyebrows.

"Up here," she said, and pointed at the top of her head. "You've got a—"

"Oh! Touch of sunburn," finished Grandpa. "Spotted that, when I was shaving. Can't think how. Must have a hole in my cap. Hardly needs a doctor though," he said, with a smile. "You done with this?" He was pointing at her plate. Stella nodded and he picked up her empty plate. "If you're all finished, why don't you head outside and play?" he said.

*Head outside and play.*

Every single day, she'd asked to go out. Every day, he'd said no. And now, all of a sudden, he was fine with it?

Stella narrowed her eyes. "You don't mind?" she said.

"Of course not!" he said. "Go and explore. Have some fun."

She jumped to her feet to get ready, but as she pulled on her coat, she paused. Would Grandpa be okay, on his own?

Stella shook her head, impatient with herself. Grandpa had actually told her to go! And it meant she could see Tamar. Tamar would know what to do.

*There. Now I've got a plan,* she thought. *How's that for grown-up and independent?*

Stella hurried to the door and shoved her feet into her shoes, squashing the backs down under her heels. *Undo them first!* Mum complained in her head, but she ignored it. Mum wasn't here. And right now, Stella was in a hurry.

She opened the front door and glanced at Grandpa. He was doing that staring into the distance thing again. "Bye then," she said.

Stella waited for a moment, but Grandpa didn't answer, so she slipped outside, and closed the door.

## Ten

# BRAIN-FOG

THE cloud was back. It was trailing along behind her like a lost puppy. As soon as they were out of sight of the house, she whirled to face him.

"Why are you still here?" she snapped. "I told you to go away!"

The cloud darkened to grey and sank down into the grass, but he didn't leave.

"Fine! Stay there then," she said, and walked away up the path. When she glanced over her shoulder, he was right behind her again. Why wouldn't he leave her alone?

She narrowed her eyes and searched around. Beside her, a tumbled dry-stone wall marked the boundary of an ancient sheep pen. She grabbed a rock off the top and hurled it as hard as she could.

It punched straight through the cloud, making a hole, and landed in the grass behind him.

"Ha!" she said. That would show him! Grandpa might have forgotten last night, but she hadn't.

The hole slowly filled with mist and disappeared.

Stella growled in frustration, then carried on walking. This time she didn't look back.

After a while, she started to wonder if she would be able to find the croft again. She didn't think it had been this far. Maybe it was hidden? Maybe she couldn't see it unless she was with Tamar?

At last, she spotted a fine thread of peat smoke, standing straight up like a signpost. Sure enough, just over the next roll of the hill, she spied the croft, nestled in amongst the folds of rock and heather. It looked just as grey and secretive as it had the day before.

Tamar was sitting outside on a rickety wooden bench by the front door, eating an apple. She gave a little wave and called, "There you are. You took your time!"

Stella walked up the slope from the cliff path and plonked herself down on the bench next to Tamar. The bench creaked in protest.

"You have to help me get rid of that cloud," she said.

"Get rid of him? What do you mean?" said Tamar, turning towards her in surprise.

"It followed me home and fired lightning at Grandpa. It's dangerous," she said.

"He fired lightning at your . . . well, he wouldn't have done that without being asked!" said Tamar. "Did you tell him to fire lightning at your Grandpa?"

"No! Of course not!" said Stella.

The cloud appeared round the bend in the path. He was floating low to the ground, snuffling along, like a dog following a scent. When he reached the bottom of the slope, he traced a small circle in the air and stopped.

*You might look all fluffy and sweet now, but I know what you're really like.*

She couldn't forget how the cloud had prowled towards Grandpa, like a predator in a wildlife programme. She hated those awful scenes where you knew something was going to die and you couldn't do anything to stop it.

"Did you think it?" asked Tamar.

"Did I think what?" said Stella.

"Did you wish something bad would happen to your Grandpa?" said Tamar.

"No!" said Stella, but then she fell silent. Had she wanted something bad to happen to Grandpa?

*Maybe,* she thought. *I definitely did when he was yelling about Gran's mug.* It wasn't like she'd broken it on purpose.

*I just wanted him to stop being angry at me.*

She shifted her bottom on the hard grey slats of the bench and looked out to sea. The clouds slid dark shadows over the waves like guilty secrets.

*And he was SO horrible when I got home,* she thought. She'd actually shouted back at him. For the first time ever! *But I didn't want him to get hurt, did I?*

Stella gave a small sigh and scowled at the cloud. "I might have done," she muttered.

"You're going to have to be very careful about that in future," said Tamar. "I can't read minds, but clouds can. That's how you tell them what to do. Your cloud was probably trying to help."

"By setting fire to the curtains and electrocuting Grandpa?" said Stella.

"Oh dear! That does sound bad," said Tamar. "Is he okay?"

"No! He's not okay," said Stella. "He's got a red mark on the top of his head and I'm worried it's done something nasty to his brain. He's not himself. He doesn't remember anything. Not a single thing! He even made me breakfast," she said. "A *nice* breakfast, and then he told me to GO OUTSIDE AND PLAY!"

"Ah, clever little cloud," murmured Tamar.

"What do you mean?" said Stella. "What's it done to him?"

"Brain-fog," said Tamar matter-of-factly.

Stella gave her a blank look.

"You haven't heard of brain-fog?" asked Tamar. "How about when people say 'my memory of that's a bit cloudy'?"

"Yes, I've heard Mum say that," said Stella. "Not brain-fog though. It sounds horrible."

"If the worst thing he said to you was 'Go outside and play', it sounds as though a brain-fog was just what he needed," said Tamar. "Like most things magical, it's really very straightforward. If you've got a cloudy memory, it's because a cloud has clouded your memory. Same thing with brain-fog. Literally a fog in your brain," said Tamar.

"What?" said Stella, in a small voice.

"Brain-fog is one of the lesser talents of clouds," explained Tamar. "Quite handy when somebody's seen some scrap of magic they really shouldn't have done. Can't go around terrifying people who have their own view of the world, can we? And when we occasionally do, it's ever so useful to be able to un-terrify them again, with a little brain-fog."

Stella blinked in confusion. Gran had never told stories about this sort of magic. Had she?

*What if she did, but I've forgotten?* she thought. *Maybe it brain-fogged me too!*

She closed her eyes and tried to work out if she was missing any important memories.

*I remember Mum, and Dad. My favourite toy is Mr Puffin.* There didn't seem to be any gaps. *My favourite book is Shetland Myths and Legends. My next-door neighbour has a cat. And the cat's name is . . .* a shiver crept up her spine . . . *What's it called?*

And then it came to her: *Inky.*

Stella let out a breath and tucked her hair behind her ear. She didn't want to lose any of her memories. *Would I still be myself? Would I even know?*

Tamar crunched on her apple and sat there chewing thoughtfully, looking out to sea. When she'd finished her mouthful, she looked at Stella. "You look perplexed, little weather weaver," she commented. "It's really not that complicated. In practical terms, your cloud must have sat on your Grandpa's head while he was sleeping, and cleverly erased all the events of last night from his memory. More, from the sounds of it. Probably rubbed out a few years' worth of worries and grumbles while he was at it, just for good measure. Hence your Grandpa's sunny disposition this morning."

"But that's awful!" said Stella. "You can't just go around wiping people's minds."

"Poppycock!" snorted Tamar. "You should be thankful! Can you imagine the trouble you'd be in right now, if he knew about you and your cloud-taming exploits?"

Tamar was right. Grandpa would be furious. Probably terrified too. Especially after the lightning.

"Stop worrying," said Tamar. "You've caught yourself a very

fine cloud, by the sounds of it." She stood, straightening up slowly, with one hand on the small of her back, then nodded at the front door. "Come on inside," she said. "Clearly our first priority today is to get that cloud of yours under control. We've got a busy day ahead."

She beckoned to the cloud and it drifted up the slope towards them.

Stella gave the cloud a dirty look as it floated passed her. Tamar might think brain-fogging people was fine, but it still felt wrong to her. Grandpa wasn't himself. He was missing bits – thoughts and feelings that made him who he was. Even if they did make him grumpy, taking his memories felt a lot like stealing.

## Eleven

# NIMBUS

"RULE number one," said Tamar, "is no firing lightning at people."

"Well, obviously!" said Stella.

"I mean you," said Tamar.

"I didn't!" said Stella. "I mean, I wouldn't! Not on purpose, anyway. I didn't even know he could do that."

"You didn't even know *you* could do that," said Tamar.

Stella gritted her teeth. *It's not my fault!* she thought. *How was I meant to know?*

A low rumble of thunder trembled around the room, rattling the glass jars. She gasped in alarm.

"Feeling angry, are we?" said Tamar, with a knowing smile.

Stella stared at her with wide eyes. "I'm not allowed to get angry? Ever?" she said. *That's impossible.*

"That's not what I'm saying at all," said Tamar. "Anyway, that would hardly be very practical, would it? From what I've seen, you get cross rather often."

Stella stiffened. That wasn't true! Not usually, anyway.

*And only when other people are WRONG,* she thought.

A sudden clap of thunder made her heart leap.

Tamar gave a patient smile. "You just need to lay down some clear ground rules," she said, "so your cloud knows how to behave. Talk to him. Tell him what you want."

Stella turned to face the cloud. "No lightning!" she said. "Never do thunder and lightning again, even if I'm angry."

"Well, I don't know about *never*," said Tamar. "How about 'Unless I tell you to'?"

Stella stared at Tamar. There was no way she was going to *tell* her cloud to do lightning. Not ever.

Tamar raised her eyebrows and waited.

Stella pinched her lips together, but it was clear that Tamar wasn't going to tell her anything else until she gave in. "Okay, fine!" Stella fixed the cloud with a firm look. "No more lightning unless I actually say so."

Tamar nodded. "Good," she said. "That should avoid any mishaps. I take it you can't hear your cloud yet?"

Stella frowned. She'd heard the thunder alright, but maybe that wasn't what Tamar meant.

"In your head," clarified Tamar. "Talking to you?"

Stella gave her a dubious look. "You can hear clouds talking?"

"All the time," said Tamar, gazing out the window with a tired expression. "Gets hard to hear myself think, sometimes," she said. "You'll hear them too, in due course. Your cloud can obviously hear you, but you're not giving him much to go on. He's just picking up your emotions and doing his best. You can start by giving him a name. Then he'll know when you're talking to him."

Stella looked at the cloud. He was gently bobbing up and down on the other side of the kitchen table, all innocent-looking. She wasn't fooled. Yesterday, she might have given him a cute fluffy name, but right now she felt like calling him Demon, or Tantrum, or Grotbag – something that told him exactly what she thought of him.

"Any ideas?" said Tamar.

Stella pouted and shook her head. "I don't know any cloud names," she said.

As she said it, she realised it wasn't true. Dad had taught her all the cloud types. High wispy *cirrus*, the huge cauliflower shape of *cumulus*, and the flat stripes of *stratus*. Thunderclouds were called *cumulonimbus*.

*I can't call him that,* she thought. *It's too long.*

"Nimbus?" she suggested.

"Perfect," said Tamar. The cloud turned a small loop-the-loop and dropped a small patter of rain. "See? He's happier already."

"Nimbus," said Stella softly, trying it out.

At the sound of his name, Nimbus bowled towards her. She squeaked and took a step back, but the cloud came to a neat stop in front of her.

Stella looked at him mistrustfully. Would he actually do what she wanted?

"Nimbus, go over there," she said, pointing to the other side of the table.

The cloud swooped low, between the table legs. When he got to the other side, he drifted up until he was floating at head height on the other side of the table. She gave a cautious smile. He *was* listening.

Then he began to sink. He drifted lower and lower until he disappeared below the edge of the table. "What are you doing?" she said. "Stay there."

"He's just playing with you, now," explained Tamar. "If you want him to do something, use his name, and give him an instruction."

"Nimbus," said Stella. "Float up, so I can see you."

The cloud popped up like a jack-in-a-box, making her jump.

"Good," said Tamar. "You see? Simple."

Stella's mouth twitched down at the corners. She hoped it was going to be that simple, but she doubted it.

"Now," said Tamar, "given that Nimbus means raincloud, why don't we start with a little raining on target? Remember to be really specific, so there's no confusion about what you want. Here, you can aim for this." She stood a large empty jug in the middle of the kitchen table. "Go ahead. Try it out."

Stella looked at the jug and then at Nimbus. She took a deep breath.

"Nimbus," she said firmly. "Rain! And aim for the jug."

Nimbus drifted down a little lower and gathered himself into a tight grey ball. Then he just floated there.

*I knew it,* thought Stella. *I knew it couldn't be that easy.*

Stella put her hands on the edge of the table and leant forwards. "Nimbus, I said rain!"

The cloud tightened in the middle, like someone had squeezed it. A jet of water blasted out of the side. It hit the jug, knocked it over, then hit Stella like a cold wet slap.

"Not at me, stupid cloud!" squawked Stella, flapping her hands.

The water kept coming, like a hose aimed at her face.

"Nimbus, stop raining!" yelled Stella.

The water jet cut off in mid-air and splattered to the ground. "I told you," she spluttered at Tamar. "He's dangerous. He's malfunctioning or something. Either that, or he just hates me. That wasn't even rain. He just fired water at me."

Tamar's eyes twinkled with amusement. She picked up a towel and held it out to her. Stella shook her head. She wasn't going to use one of Tamar's towels ever again.

"I promise you, Nimbus isn't doing it on purpose," said Tamar. "He's just being enthusiastic. You didn't ask him for gentle rain, did you?"

Stella shook her head. "No, but—"

"And you didn't specify that all the rain had to fall into the jug, did you?" said Tamar.

"I said 'aim for the jug!' How is that not clear?" said Stella.

"It strikes me that he aimed for the jug rather successfully, just not from the direction you were expecting," said Tamar.

Stella gave Nimbus a dark look. *I liked you yesterday. I thought we were going to be friends. Got that wrong, didn't I?*

The cloud sank, until it was hidden below the far side of the table.

"Why are we raining, anyway?" grumbled Stella. "You said weather weaving was about spinning; weaving magic, making rainbows! Why can't we do that?"

Tamar cocked her head and listened. "No thunder!" she said, with a smile. "So that's an improvement."

Stella puffed in annoyance and dried her face on her sleeve. She moved closer to the table until she could see the top of the cloud. She didn't want him sneaking up on her.

"Patience," said Tamar. "Training a new cloud takes time.

Besides, we can't practise spinning until he's gathered enough magic."

Stella folded her arms and hunched her shoulders, staring at Nimbus.

*Gathered enough magic . . .* she thought. *I bet you don't even know how. You can't do rain right and that's not exactly hard. You just rain down – like a normal cloud.*

Nimbus faded into a fine haze.

Stella watched him with suspicion. *What was he up to now?*

The gauze of mist drifted away to the far end of the room, becoming fainter as it went, until it was just a whisper in the air.

It was bad enough when she could see him. If he was invisible, she might accidentally breathe him in. She wasn't sure what that would do, but probably something bad.

Tamar's new reel of yarn rocked on the shelf and toppled over.

"Oh, he's not . . ." said Tamar. "He is! Stop that! Get away from there."

The yarn began to melt. It fused into a fat shiny lump.

"What did you tell him to do?" said Tamar.

"Nothing!" said Stella. "I said he should have rained down into the jug, that's all!"

"You told him something," said Tamar. "He's ruining that yarn. A whole cloud's worth of magic and it's no good for anything now!"

Silver dripped off the edge of the shelf and landed in shining spatters on the floor.

Stella wondered if Nimbus was making a mess on purpose. Maybe he was doing it to spite her?

She reached down to touch one of the tiny droplets of magic as it bounced towards her, but pulled her hand away when it fizzed and spat like hot oil.

"Oh, blast," said Tamar. "Stand back."

Stella moved behind the kitchen table with Tamar. The reel of thread had completely dissolved now, becoming a mercury pool that dripped off the edge of the shelf. The droplets made a sound like falling pins as they hit the ground. Silver beads bounced and skittered everywhere across the stone floor.

The frenzied pinging sound grew louder and harsher, like glass baubles smashing.

"Any minute now," said Tamar.

*Whump!*

A cloud of silver exploded into the air, filling the room with the smell of fireworks.

The haze gradually condensed into a small shining oval of cloud up near the ceiling.

Tamar stood with her hands on her hips, unamused. "Really?" she said. "*Really?*" She walked over and jabbed her finger into the cloud. "Not yours! Not. Yours."

Nimbus backed away from Tamar's sharp finger, but Tamar followed, poking him, as though to drive her words into the centre of the cloud.

"It's *not* on. You *gather* your *own* magic."

*He was showing me that he could gather magic,* realised Stella. A guilty feeling twisted in her stomach, becoming a little sharper each time Tamar poked the cloud.

Nimbus was peppered with little holes now. "You *don't* take another cloud's *magic*! You *know* that!" said Tamar. "*All* clouds know that."

"Stop!" said Stella. "Stop poking him."

Tamar paused and Nimbus quickly rolled away and hid behind the spinning wheel.

"I didn't want to believe it," said Tamar, shaking her head, "but perhaps you were right. This cloud is untrainable."

Stella's eyes widened. "No! He was—"

"It's a basic!" interrupted Tamar. "I have never, and I mean never, come across a cloud so LAZY that it would STEAL magic that's already been spun."

Behind her, Nimbus cowered. Guilt pressed heavy on Stella's heart.

"I told him to," she said.

"You what?" exclaimed Tamar.

"Well, not exactly," said Stella. "I didn't say 'Go and steal magic'. But you were talking about magic gathering, and I didn't think he'd even know how . . ."

Nimbus tumbled across the floor towards Stella, taking a wide path around Tamar.

When he reached her feet, she crouched down and smoothed the top of the cloud. He was looking a bit raggedy after all the poking.

*I get it,* she thought. *You were trying to make me like you again.*

She looked up at Tamar. "He didn't mean to do something bad," she said. "Probably that was just the fastest way he could think of to get magic. It's like you said – he's enthusiastic."

Tamar raised her eyebrows, but a smile tugged at her lips. "Enthusiastic, you say?"

Stella nodded.

Tamar looked down at Nimbus. "The next time you need magic," she said, "you can jolly well go and gather it elsewhere. You hear me?" She looked at Stella. "You tell him," she said. "He won't take instructions from me."

"Don't do it again," said Stella.

*But thank you for doing it now,* she thought.

Nimbus fluffed himself up and a soft sunbeam glow crept across his surface.

Stella felt a sudden surge of warmth for the little cloud. He might not get everything right, but he was trying really hard. And he was listening.

## Twelve

# SKY TUNNEL

TAMAR walked over to the shelves, her feet sending the last tiny balls of magic jingling away across the flagstones. She picked up the empty reel and held it up.

"Six month's worth of magic, that was," she said.

"I'm sorry . . ." said Stella. "I didn't realise he would—"

"Of course you didn't," said Tamar. "But do you understand now why it's important to be clear with your cloud?"

Stella nodded and glanced at Nimbus. He was cheerfully shading from peach to bright orange, to yellow, and back to peach again.

*Nimbus, can you at least try to look sorry?* thought Stella.

The moment the thought formed in her mind, Nimbus faded to a pale grey. She smiled.

Tamar shook her head. "A whole reel . . ." she muttered.

*How could they make it up to her?*

"Ooh! We could spin him?" said Stella. "Get it back for you!"

"Spinning takes patience and calm," said Tamar. "Both of which are in rather short supply right now." She turned away and went over to the spinning wheel to slot the empty reel back on the top. Tamar wasn't being angry like Grandpa would have been, but Stella still had the familiar creeping feeling that she'd failed somehow, let Tamar down.

*We have to prove we can do this,* thought Stella. She nudged Nimbus with her hip. *Help me!*

Nimbus released a light patter of rain on the floor.

Stella gave him an exasperated look, then realised what he meant.

"Shall we try rain again?" she said to Tamar. "We'll do it better this time. Honest."

"No," said Tamar, and Stella's heart sank.

"Please," she said. "Nimbus is going to try really hard. And I'll be super clear, this time. I promise."

Tamar considered the small cloud for a moment and nodded slowly. "He's fully charged right now – far more than he should be, given his size. I think for safety's sake, we'd better wear him out a bit. Maybe a sky tunnel . . ."

A wave of relief and excitement rose in Stella. "What's a sky tunnel?" she said, eagerly. "Is it like a tornado?"

"No! No! Put that out of your mind," said Tamar, looking flustered. "We definitely don't want one of those in my kitchen. No. A sky tunnel is the opposite. A still place. It protects you. It's like your own little secret passage through the weather."

"That sounds useful," said Stella.

Tamar nodded and walked over to the shelves. She began to turn jars and bottles, reading the labels and tutting to herself. She turned back to Stella.

"Go ahead and ask Nimbus," she said. "We'll see how you get on."

Stella nodded, but nerves buzzed inside her chest. She couldn't really imagine what this tunnel thing was meant to look like. She hoped Nimbus knew.

"Nimbus, sky tunnel!" she said. *Let's make it really good, okay?* she added in her head.

Nimbus floated up until he was just above her head, then he flattened into a shimmering dome.

*He's like a magic umbrella,* thought Stella, and smiled.

Pale white streamers of cloud tumbled down from the edges of the dome to the floor, until Nimbus began to look more like a jellyfish.

"Looks promising," said Tamar. "Now, let's try throwing some weather at it." She lifted a large jar off the shelf and read the label. "Blizzard. That'll do."

"What?!" exclaimed Stella, but Tamar had already opened the

jar. A plume of snow burst out of it, fountained up to the ceiling and tumbled down. As it fell, it parted, leaving an arc of clean air around Stella. It landed all over Tamar, catching in her hair and dotting her cardigan with fat white flakes.

"Perfect!" said Tamar, her face melting into a smile. "Look at that! A beautiful sky tunnel. First time."

Stella's heart danced and she broke into a wide grin. "You did it, Nimbus!" she said.

"*Both* of you did it," said Tamar. "Connection! Shared intention! A common purpose – that's what it's all about." She pointed and the snow followed the direction of her finger. It flexed in the air like a flock of white birds and swooped back into the jar. She screwed the lid on again and dusted the last few flakes off her sleeves.

"It's more like an umbrella, really, than a tunnel, isn't it?" said Stella.

"Right now, it's called cloud cover," said Tamar. "It's the seed of a sky tunnel. It should stretch and move with you. Size and shape are key for this. Too big and it'll be stretched too thin. It'll leak. Too small and you'll end up poking out the sides. It should change shape as you move. We'll try that next." She lifted a blue glass bottle off the shelf next to her. "Here's a nice little challenge," she said. "Hold on, need to get myself wrapped up, before we open this one."

Tamar opened two cupboards, one after the other. "Where's he got to?"

"What are you looking for?" said Stella.

"My house cloud," said Tamar. "Herb, where are you? Come out."

*House cloud?*

A fine mist started to pour out of a wooden blanket box. It pooled on the floor.

"There you are!" said Tamar. "Up you get, old thing. It's time for you to make yourself useful."

The mist slowly gathered itself off the floor into a small shaggy-looking grey cloud and drifted up until he was above Tamar's head.

"You have a *house* cloud?" said Stella.

"He keeps me company, don't you, Herb?" Tamar reached up and patted the little cloud affectionately. "I've never had much joy teaching him fancy tricks," she confided, "but he does a very sturdy cloud cover."

The cloud flattened into a pale saucer and the air around Tamar seemed to wobble and shimmer. "There we are, all set," she said. "I don't mind the odd snowflake, but this one may get messy. Ready?"

Stella looked up at her umbrella of cloud. "You ready, Nimbus?" The cloud above her rippled slightly, which at least told her he was listening. Stella looked at Tamar nodded.

Tamar eased the cork loose with her thumbs, then gripped the bottle tightly with both hands. Stella could see the cork moving on its own now, slowly inching its way out, until *pop!* – it flew across the room and bounced off the wall, pursued by a spume of white.

Stella flinched as the weather reached her, but she didn't get wet. Each drop burst against an invisible wall in front of her, leaving a little white splat of ice.

"It's working!" she said. "Is this hail?"

"Driving sleet!" said Tamar, with glee. "Now, I want you to walk, slowly, all the way to the spinning wheel and back."

Stella peered towards the other end of the room. She could hardly see it. It was like trying to see out of the windscreen when Mum took the car through the car wash. The air was a whirl of white, and the cloud cover around her was spotted with ice. She shivered and rubbed her arms – the cloud cover might stop the sleet, but it didn't stop the cold.

"Are you ready, Nimbus?" she checked. "I'm going to walk over there, towards the far corner. Keep me covered, okay?"

Stella took a hesitant step, and the bubble of cloud cover bulged away from her, creating a space of clear air in front of her. She walked forward with tentative steps and the bubble lengthened, becoming a shining tunnel. Sleet spattered all around Stella, but it couldn't touch her.

The side of one of the armchairs appeared inside the tunnel as she walked past. It was dotted with wet spots, where the sleet had hit the fabric. Scraps of ice crunched underfoot on the stone floor. As she stepped around the chair, she slipped. Stella threw an arm out to catch herself, and icy darts of sleet stung her skin. She yelped.

Then the cloud cover was around her again, shuddering into a new shape that encompassed her outstretched arm.

She might not be able to hear him, but somehow Stella knew Nimbus was sorry.

"It's not your fault," she said, quietly. "You didn't know I was going to slip."

"You alright in there?" called Tamar.

Stella could only just hear her over the rattle of sleet. "I'm fine," she called back. "The floor's a bit skiddy, that's all."

"Just let me . . . hold on a minute . . . there we are," said Tamar. The sound of the sleet died away to a slow patter and stopped. "Come on out, then," she said.

*We did okay, didn't we, Nimbus?* thought Stella. *It's alright. You can stop now.*

The cloud around her trembled, then furled up like a sail.

As the tunnel vanished, two lines of slush sploshed down on either side of Stella, leaving her standing on a clear path in the middle of the floor. The armchairs were dotted with damp patches, and drifts of ice were melting into puddles on the floor.

Tamar stood in the middle of all the mess with a broad grin on her face. "Outstanding sky tunnel!" she said. "Jolly good job. That is not an easy skill to master, and you breezed through it."

Stella grinned triumphantly. "I *told* you he was a good cloud really!"

"Mm-hmm . . ." Tamar raised one eyebrow, but the twinkle was back in her eyes.

*We did it!* thought Stella. She reached up and ruffled her fingers through the surface of the cloud. "That was great, Nimbus. Now we're stormproof!"

A look of concern flitted across Tamar's face.

"What?" said Stella. "I thought you said it was good?"

"Oh, it was perfect," said Tamar. "Should keep you safe in most weathers." She glanced out of the window and her face tightened. "Storms, though, deserve respect. Best course of action in a storm is usually to head indoors."

Tamar's eyes clouded with the memory of something, but as she turned back to Stella, her face softened into a warm smile.

"So, I've got a bit of cleaning up to do," she carried on. "In the meantime, why don't you two head outside and practise?"

"Do you need me to help?" asked Stella.

Tamar shook her head. "No, won't take long." She flicked the towel off its hook, onto the floor. It began to crawl across the flagstones on its own.

"I knew there was something wrong with that towel!" said Stella. She backed away as it crept towards her. "How is it doing that?"

"There's nothing wrong with it," said Tamar. "It's doing exactly what it's meant to – satisfying its thirst. It'll carry on until everything is dry. I'll teach you how to make them when we get on to weaving – thirsty towels are a nice basic project to start on."

"Thirsty towels!" said Stella. "That's what you meant! Have

you got other magic things here then? Flying carpets and stuff?" she asked, her mind racing. "Can I see them?"

Tamar looked a bit taken aback. She shook her head. "No. Just towels," she said.

"Oh," said Stella, feeling disappointed. "Why not the other stuff?"

"I weave them for other people, mostly. The towels I make for myself," said Tamar. "You'd be surprised how often a weather weaver needs a good towel."

"I wouldn't," said Stella, giving Nimbus a meaningful look.

"There's plenty of demand for the whizz-bang stuff, of course," said Tamar. "Never-empty purses, invisibility cloaks and the like. Personally, I prefer the more practical applications."

Stella's mind whirled. Just wait until she could weave! She'd start with an invisibility cloak – that would get her out of no end of trouble. And if she could get her hands on a flying carpet—

Something furry and damp wrapped around her ankle, bringing her back down to earth with a lurch. She shook her foot, dislodging the towel. It writhed on the floor for a moment, then reared into a wobbly arch, like a oversized hairy caterpillar. Stella pushed the towel away from her with the tip of her shoe. It hesitated for a moment, then began to crawl its way towards the next puddle.

Tamar opened a cupboard. A tall pile of towels tumbled out. Stella's eyes widened and she took a step sideways, towards the front door. She did *not* want to be in here with a whole swarm of creepy towels. Nimbus scudded across the room, already ahead of her.

"I'll follow you out in a minute," said Tamar. "Rain and sky tunnel. Practise, practise, practise. I want you well prepared."

*Prepared for what?* wondered Stella.

## Thirteen

# SOMETHING UNTOWARD

"WHAT do you think Tamar is preparing us for?" said Stella to Nimbus, as she walked down the slope outside. "Do you think there's going to be a test? Maybe she's planning to throw sleet at us when we're not expecting it!"

She turned to see if Nimbus was listening. He was floating at waist height behind her, whirling in a tight circle. *Like a puppy chasing its tail,* thought Stella.

"Nimbus!" she said. "We're meant to be practising. You ready?"

Nimbus stopped whirling and she smiled at him.

"Rain!" she said. "But don't get me wet . . ." she added hastily.

Nimbus bounced up higher and water began to spray out of his sides like a garden sprinkler, lighting rainbows in the air. She put out a hand and the fine spray moved away, always just out of reach. It was like trying to catch fish in your fingers.

"So, you can do it!" she said. "Why did you squirt me in the face before, then? What was that all about?"

The rain pattered to a stop and Nimbus turned a deep shade of sunset orange.

What did that mean? She gave him a long look, but he didn't give her any more clues.

"Fine. Just don't do it again. Alright?"

Nimbus faded to peach and bobbed once. *Did he nod?* Perhaps that was wishful thinking.

Stella squinted out to sea. The sky had changed while they'd been inside. Before, it was a uniform grey, but now it had cleared in patches. Pale sunlight glanced off the water with a dazzling glare. In the distance, the horizon was crowded with gargantuan clumps of cloud.

"Maybe there's a storm coming," she said. "Tamar would know that, wouldn't she? Perhaps that's what we're preparing for."

She sniffed the air – salt, grass, and the faintest tang of sheep poo. She wasn't sure what storm was meant to smell like.

Maybe Grandpa could tell her.

*Grandpa...*

The memory was like a cloud passing in front of the sun. Nimbus had brain-fogged Grandpa. Tamar might think it was okay, but was it?

Nimbus bobbed in the air.

"I know *you* think it's alright," she said.

Nimbus turned a swift loop-the-loop in the air.

"He is happier," she agreed.

Bannocks for breakfast, jokes, even whistling and humming – Grandpa was practically back to how she remembered him. Perhaps brain-fog *was* good for him?

"And it *does* mean I can be here, doing this, with you ..."

Nimbus fired a glittering fountain of rain up into the air.

"Show-off," she muttered, with a smile.

"You've got the hang of rain then," said Tamar, from behind her. "Reverse rain, too! Very fancy!"

Stella glanced at Nimbus. *Let's pretend we meant to do that...*

"Are those storm clouds coming here?" she said to Tamar. "Is that why we're practising?"

Tamar glanced at the distant clouds and shook her head. "They're not storm clouds, and no, they'll stay there for now. I've been very specific. Every cloud has its purpose, every weather its proper place."

*Every cloud?*

"Wait. Are you, like, in charge of *all* the weather here, then?" said Stella, wide-eyed.

Tamar preened slightly and smiled. "Yes, you could say that."

"Do you ever make big storms?" said Stella. "Grandpa said—"

"I don't *make* storms!" said Tamar, sounding quite offended. "For the most part, I banish them. Occasionally, I bottle them for safekeeping."

"For emergencies," remembered Stella.

"Precisely," said Tamar. "Why, what did your Grandpa say?"

"Oh, nothing about you. I haven't told him about you," said Stella, hurriedly. "No, I was thinking about the fish he caught, that's all."

Tamar gave her a look of confusion. "Fish?"

"The ugliest fish I have *ever* seen," said Stella. "Grandpa wanted me to eat it, but I couldn't . . . A *masgoom*. He said it might have been brought up by a big storm, so I thought perhaps you'd—"

"A *masgoom*?" said Tamar. "You're sure?" Her eyes were sharp with interest now. "Where did he catch it?"

"I don't know," said Stella, with a shrug. "Out on his boat?"

"And when was this, exactly?" said Tamar.

"The day I arrived," said Stella.

"But there weren't any storms. I'd cleared the skies!" said Tamar. "Wouldn't be much of a welcome otherwise, would it?"

Stella was stumped for a moment. "You knew I was coming?" she asked.

Tamar shook her head. "Not *you*, precisely. This one," she said, gesturing at Nimbus. "He'd been hanging around for a week or two. I tried catching him myself, but he wasn't having any of it. He was clearly waiting for someone else."

"Me!" said Stella, and Tamar nodded.

Stella grinned at the little cloud. "You were waiting here, just for me?"

Nimbus puffed himself up and floated a bit closer.

"A *masgoom*. Now, of all times," muttered Tamar, shaking her head in disapproval. Her mouth had puckered into a small wrinkly prune.

"What's the matter?" said Stella.

"There are one or two clouds who have some explaining to do," said Tamar. "Clear skies, clear seas . . . Honestly, I don't ask for much." She gathered up her long skirt and stomped away up the hill.

Stella had followed Tamar halfway up the hillside before she was hit by the sense of something missing. *Nimbus.* It took her a moment to spot him. He was half hidden in the long grass, nosing around a rabbit hole. "Nimbus!" she called. "Keep up."

He meandered up the slope towards her, determined to investigate every burrow he passed. By the time he'd caught up, Tamar was a long way ahead.

"Come on!" said Stella. "We're getting left behind." She waved Nimbus on ahead.

They were high up now, above the mouth of the bay. The thatched roof of the croft was a small rectangle of grey on the green hillside. Below them, a stony beach stretched back in the direction of Grandpa's house, in a series of little coves and inlets.

*So this must be the far end of the storm petrel beach,* thought Stella. She couldn't see Grandpa's house from here, but she could guess roughly where it was.

Stella turned and scrambled up the last steep bit, her breath sharp in her throat. Tamar was standing on a little plateau at the top, her fists on her hips, eyeballing the horizon.

"What . . . did you mean?" puffed Stella. "Clouds have got . . . explaining to do?"

Nimbus hung back behind Stella, perhaps worried Tamar had meant him.

"The sentinels!" said Tamar, gesturing angrily at the clouds on the horizon. "They're *meant* to keep watch!"

Stella shaded her eyes. Way out in the distance, a long row of clouds studded the horizon, evenly spaced, one after the other. She turned on the spot. The line of clouds stretched unbroken, all the way round the island. She still didn't get what they were doing there, though.

"You have clouds that watch for deep-sea fish?" she said.

"They watch for anything untoward," said Tamar. "Anything unnatural."

Stella swallowed. *Unnatural.* She was double-glad now she hadn't eaten the *masgoom.*

"They've got some explaining to do," said Tamar. "So, what do you say we put the wind up them a bit?"

Stella's attention snapped back to Tamar – the old woman's eye's danced with mischief.

"Do you spin winds too, then?" said Stella. "Like clouds?"

"Ha! No. Not unless you want a twister, and I wouldn't advise it. Unpredictable things. No. I use winds to muster my clouds," explained Tamar. "Today, though, you're going to do it."

Stella nodded nervously. "How?"

"To control each element of weather, you need to know the heart of it," said Tamar. "Joy, humour, calm, hope, sadness, fear – even fury!" Her hands danced in the air as she talked, and her eyes had taken on a slightly frenzied shine.

*Fury for lightning,* thought Stella. *But I'm never doing that again.* She didn't much like the sound of sadness or fear either.

"Today, we're after joy," said Tamar, spreading her arms wide.

Stella let out a breath. *Phew!*

"Wind needs pure joy," said Tamar, "with a thrill of excitement at its heart. So, tell me what you're feeling right now."

"Excited?"

"You don't *sound* very excited . . ."

"I will!" said Stella. "You haven't told me what I'm meant to do, yet!"

Tamar held up one finger and a breeze burst into life and lifted her hair. "Watch," she said. She pointed across the hillside and the breeze rushed away from them, flattening the grass in a long dark river. "This bit's fun," she said, in a conspiratorial voice.

She twirled her finger slowly in the air and the wind began to turn, rushing past them towards the sea and then back over the hill, round and round in circles.

Stella smiled. With the wind whipping her white hair around and a grin on her face, Tamar looked like strange mixture of witchy old lady and naughty little girl.

And she was right – the whirling air sent a thrill of lightness through Stella. It made her want to laugh, or dance, or run at top speed.

Two gulls soared in from above the cliffs and began to climb the wind, gliding in ever-wider circles. Tamar pinched her finger and thumb together and the air was suddenly still. The two birds flapped hard to stay aloft as the wind was snatched from under them. When they'd recovered, they swooped away fast, as though to cover their embarrassment.

"Go on, you have a go," said Tamar.

Stella stood with her arms at her sides, wriggling her fingers and tried to gather up feelings of excitement inside her.

*Birthdays, going to the beach, the first day of the holidays!*

She pointed her finger up in the air.

Nothing stirred. Not even a breath of air.

"You have to gather your joy and excitement first, and then point," said Tamar.

"I did that," said Stella, bringing her finger down and folding her arms. *What does that even mean?*

"Come on, what is it about wind that makes you joyful?" said Tamar. "I can tell you what I love about it, but I can't tell you the answer. It needs to be your own."

"You could at least tell me your answer," said Stella. It came out sounding whinier than she'd meant it to.

Tamar tucked in her chin, and her neck went all wrinkly like a turtle.

Stella sighed. "What I meant is, it might help me think of mine . . ." she said.

Tamar took a breath and let it out again. "For me, it's like a voice," she said. "The voice of someone I love. Whispering, singing, sometimes roaring and wild, but always full of joy." She nodded to herself and then looked at Stella.

Stella's mouth twitched. That definitely wasn't her answer. She didn't like the sound of wind. Not at all. The only time she'd heard it sound like a voice was when it moaned *Who, who?* through the letterbox at home. There was nothing joyful about that. It was plain spooky.

She glanced around for Nimbus, in case he could give her a clue. He was slinking across the grass towards Tamar, like he was stalking her. He'd gone a strange shade of apricot.

*Whatever you're planning, don't do it!* thought Stella.

"Do you play with the wind, at all?" said Tamar. "What's fun, on a windy day?"

Stella thought for a moment. "Flying a kite?" she said.

"Perfect," said Tamar. "What do you like most about flying your kite?"

"I don't have a kite," said Stella. "I was just thinking of something fun to do with wind."

Tamar groaned. "I don't want examples, I want truth. Your truth," she said, pointing a finger at Stella. "What do *you* love about the wind?"

Stella looked at the ground. She was trying. She really was.

*Joy. Wind. Playing with the wind.*

The answer whispered through her, like a breeze through an open door.

"Holding my coat out and getting blown along, like I'm flying," she said.

The feeling of it swept through her – racing down the slope in the playground with her coat held wide like a sail, light as laughter.

"There we are now," said Tamar. "That sounds exactly the right sort of sensation."

"Mrs Peck, my old teacher, used to shout at us to do our coats up. She thought we'd get cold, but we didn't," said Stella.

"Well, you wouldn't. Joy is very warming," said Tamar. "Now, I want you to gather up that feeling of flying, and point. Point like you mean it."

Stella closed her eyes, held tight to the memory of being lifted by the wind, and stabbed her finger into the air.

A light breeze lifted her hair and then died away.

Stella opened her eyes and looked around. "Is that it?" she said.

*Where's the rest of it?* She'd imagined much more wind than that.

"A good attempt," said Tamar. "A passable zephyr. I guess we'd better do it the easy way though, or we'll be here all day."

"There's an easy way?" exclaimed Stella.

"Yes – whistling," said Tamar. "You made the sky tunnel look like a piece of cake, so I thought we might skip straight to conjuring, but perhaps that was pushing our luck."

Stella let out a small growl of frustration. *Why not start with the easy way in the first place?* she thought.

Nimbus gave a small rumble of sympathy and began to drift back towards her.

*Shush!* she thought. *No thunder unless I ask you to, remember?*

"Whistling up wind is much easier," said Tamar. "Provided you can whistle, that is. Can you?"

Stella's face lit up in a wide smile. She could whistle alright. Dad had taught her how last summer. Poke a finger in each corner of your mouth, lift the corners of your tongue and blow really hard. Mum had got annoyed with her going around hissing and spitting all the time, but after two weeks of practising, Stella knew how to whistle.

She lifted her fingers to her mouth and took a deep breath.

"Wait," said Tamar, a moment too late.

The whistle pierced the air, shrill and pure and ear-splittingly loud. Stella took her fingers out of her mouth and grinned. "Yes, I can whistle," she said.

The wind knocked her to the ground.

## Fourteen

# A BIT OF A BLOW

STELLA clutched the grass and clung on tight. The wind whipped at her face, and sharp twigs of flying heather stung her cheeks. The air howled around her, making her eyes stream with tears. She opened her mouth to shout to Tamar, but the wind snatched her breath away.

"Finger and thumb," bellowed Tamar, over the wind. "Pinch together your finger and thumb."

Stella's fingers locked tight around the wiry grass. The cliff edge wasn't far away. If she let go, the wind might pick her up and throw her right over the edge. She let go with one hand and felt herself start to slide. She grabbed the grass again, tight with both fists. The stems were taut as fiddle strings in her palms. They began to snap, one stalk at a time.

"You called it!" yelled Tamar. "Now catch it! Finger and thumb."

Stella dug her fingers into the ground. She scrabbled at it, her nails bending. Against the force of the wind, the world seemed to have tilted. There was only the howling air, and the slope, and the cliff at the bottom of it.

"Do it now!" yelled Tamar.

Stella let go and pinched the air.

The wind stopped.

She let out a breath, and lay there in the sudden silence, trembling.

*I did it. I did it. I actually did it!*

Stella kept her finger and thumb tight together and raised her head. Tamar was picking herself up and dusting grass off her long skirt. Nimbus was nowhere to be seen.

"Well, I'll be . . . from zephyr to full blown gale! You're just full of surprises, aren't you?"

"Do I have to keep them pinched?" asked Stella, in a wobbly voice. Her hand was shaking.

"I would, if I were you," said Tamar. "Here, I'll bring you the bag."

Tamar slipped her bag off her shoulder, opened it and held it down in front of Stella. "Put your hand inside. All the way in.

Then, and only then, you can let go."

Stella slid her hand into the mouth of the bag. The inside felt sticky and horrid.

*Like cobwebs*, she thought and pulled a face. Even so, she pushed her hand in, until she felt the bottom of the bag.

"Now?" she said.

Tamar nodded and Stella let go. She slid her hand out of the bag again and wiped the sticky feeling off on her trousers. Tamar rolled the top of the bag over.

Stella drew in a deep breath and let it out again. Her heart was skipping in double time. She stood up on shaking legs. "Where's Nimbus?"

Tamar put a hand up to shade her eyes and looked out to sea. "Got blown a fair distance, I'd say. Silly thing. Should have hugged the ground. Never mind, he's doubtless flying back here at top speed."

"Did you know that was going to happen?" said Stella.

Tamar shook her head. "No, I was expecting something along the lines of a brisk breeze. You didn't tell me you whistle like a sheepdog trainer. I should think they heard you on the mainland!"

"Dad taught me," said Stella, smiling at the memory.

"Well, that explains it," said Tamar. "Good strong whistle *and* a hefty dose of joy. That's quite a trick. Now, I think congratulations are in order. You've caught your first wind! A gale, no less."

A blush of pride warmed Stella's cheeks and she eyed the bag. It seemed too small to hold something so large.

"Was the gale just here, round us, or was it everywhere on the island?" she said.

"Oh, all over, I should think," said Tamar. "That was a big one. I shouldn't worry though. You caught it fast. It won't have had time to do much damage."

"Don't people notice, when you do stuff like this?" said Stella.

"They'll have got a bit blown about, but that's nothing new," said Tamar. "There's plenty of weather round here. No reason for anyone to suspect magic."

Tamar walked to the edge of the cliff and pointed. "Look! You stirred them up a bit!"

The mountains of cloud were spiked with sharp tufts and wispy streaks. It looked as though they'd had a fright.

*Me,* thought Stella, in awe. *I did that!*

"Not quite the direction we were after," said Tamar. "I think we'll practise control another day, though. Yes?"

Stella nodded. Now that the gale was safely caught, her legs felt full of jelly.

Tamar's lips curled in a smile, then she turned and beckoned at the distant clouds. As she did, a light breeze began to blow. One of the narrowest wisps of cloud stretched towards them. It drew a chalky line across the sky, like an airplane trail. When it was directly overhead, the white strand of cloud scribbled down out of the sky, fading as it came.

As the tail end of it reached Tamar, it settled around her neck, like the ghost of a scarf. She pinched the air and the breeze died away, then she stood there in silence, nodding occasionally, as though listening.

Stella edged a bit closer and strained her ears, but she couldn't hear anything – nothing but birds and the hushing of the waves. Tamar's face didn't give anything away.

Stella raised her eyebrows, but Tamar held up a firm hand, like Mum did when she was on the phone. Stella sighed and turned away.

She shook her legs and stamped her feet to get rid of the last of the trembles, then cautiously moved closer to the edge, until she could see the beach below. It was a long way down.

*A long way to fall,* she thought, with a shiver.

A flock of gannets hung on the breeze above the bay. One of them folded itself up like a paper dart and plunged into the sea, with a sharp splash. Stella watched the water. A moment later it reappeared, a streak of silver in its beak.

Behind it, by the rocky outcrop on the beach, something was moving towards them along the water's edge.

Not something. Someone.

She squinted at the dark figure.

*Who was it?*

Not Grandpa. It didn't move like him. It was slinking stealthily across the stones.

*The stones! Where the storm petrels are nesting!*

"Hey!" she yelled, waving her arms. "Get off the beach!"

"What on earth are you shouting about?" huffed Tamar.

"There's someone down there!" said Stella. "They'll crush the eggs! There's eggs! Under the rocks!"

Tamar frowned and squinted in the direction Stella was pointing. Her eyes hardened as she focused on the distant figure. "Oh, no!" she said. "Not now."

Stella stared at her. All the warmth was gone from Tamar's face. She looked old, all of a sudden. Old and worried.

## Fifteen

# THE HAKEN

TAMAR stared down at the beach, a frown creasing her forehead.

"She didn't hear you," she said. "I think we're alright." Abruptly, she turned and walked away, back towards the croft.

"Wait!" said Stella. "Who is that?"

Tamar just waved her hand, as though to make the question go away, and carried on walking.

Stella looked back at the distant figure. It wasn't on the rocks any more. It was standing knee-deep in the water. The pale smudge of a face turned towards her, and a cold chill crept up Stella's spine.

In a sudden streak of movement, the distant figure dived. It twisted in the air – a fluid curve, like an eel – then disappeared beneath the inky surface without a ripple.

Stella watched, but it didn't reappear.

*One, two, three, four . . .*

She counted in her head until she got to a hundred, but nothing broke the surface.

*No one can stay under that long. Not even Dad.*

Stella gave a small shudder and turned away.

Tamar was already disappearing over the crest of the hill. Thistles snatched at Stella's ankles as she hurried to follow. When she got to the top of the slope, she saw Tamar had stopped a little way down, in a low hollow facing the sea. She stood with her arms held out wide and her chin on her chest, like she was about to conduct an orchestra. She was muttering.

"What are you doing?" said Stella. "Who was that?"

Tamar lifted her head and gave Stella an impatient frown.

"Shh," she hissed. "This needs quiet to work."

Stella closed her mouth in a thin line and tried not to think about the figure on the beach.

It had looked at her.

It had looked right at her.

And then it had disappeared under the water.

She looked out at the bay and shivered. The sea stretched out unbroken, dark and blue, all the way to the faint curve of the horizon. Far in the distance, a small white shape scudded over the waves.

*Nimbus!*

Stella took a deep breath and smiled. Whatever was going on, it would be better with Nimbus here.

Tamar dropped her chin to her chest and began to wave her arms in great wide strokes. Her cardigan flopped back and forth, like huge purple wings.

*It looks like she's trying to take off*, thought Stella, wondering if Tamar could do that.

"What are you—"

Tamar's head snapped up. "I'm summoning fog. It'll hide us."

There was a chilling urgency in Tamar's eyes.

"What are we hiding from?" said Stella.

Tamar just shook her head impatiently and flapped her arms, indicating that she should do the same.

*Just tell me!* thought Stella.

Tamar didn't get it. Not knowing was a lot scarier than knowing.

"Fog is very shy," said Tamar, in a low voice. "You can whistle winds and sing the sunshine, but for fog, you need to whisper. Now quietly, repeat after me—"

"Who *was* that?" whispered Stella, wrapping her arms around herself.

Tamar's mouth tightened like a drawstring purse, but Stella lifted her chin.

The old woman glanced out to sea. "You really don't want to know," she said.

"I do," said Stella.

Tamar narrowed her eyes, as though she'd only just realised how stubborn Stella could be. "The Haken." She spat the name, as though it tasted bad. Her jaw was set in an angry line, but her eyes darted back to the sea.

Stella felt something shrink inside her. Tamar wasn't scared of anything – not lightning, not gales, not keeping a bottled hurricane in your house . . .

"Enough!" said Tamar. "It doesn't belong here. That's all you need to know. I'll see it off, but I want you safely hidden first." She raised her arms again. "Are you going to help, or not?"

Stella studied Tamar's face for a moment, then nodded and lifted her arms.

Questions could be answered later.

Out beyond the mouth of the bay, she could see Nimbus. A lone dot of white against the dark water.

*Get back here, Nimbus,* she thought. *Quickly.*

Tamar started to chant. She flapped her arms, as though wafting her words out to sea.

Stella listened for a moment, then joined in. "*Soft as shadows, pale as death, smother sight in winter's breath. Soft as shadows, pale* as death, smother sight in winter's breath . . ."

When she looked away, to check on Nimbus, Stella saw that the clean line between sea and sky had blurred into a soft haze.

"Tamar!" she whispered. "I think it's working."

"Good," murmured Tamar. "Keep going."

Stella began to chant the words again, but her eyes were fixed on her cloud. He had passed the far headland and was skimming over the water of the bay.

If something terrible was coming, she wanted Nimbus here with her.

The gap between the creeping smear of fog and the small dot of cloud narrowed. The rocks of the headland vanished, one by one.

If he didn't get a move on, the fog would swallow him.

*Nimbus! Faster!* she thought, but as she watched, the little cloud faded into the edge of the fog.

*No! Now how am I meant to find you?*

Stella dropped her arms and watched the opaque wall moving towards them. It was growing all the time; a white waterfall of cloud endlessly falling down a hidden slope of sky.

The huge nothingness of it made her want to run, but it was coming too fast.

It rolled up over the land, erasing the green of the grass. Clumps of heather faded and disappeared, as though they'd never existed.

The fog surrounded her, wrapping everything in silence.

Tamar was nothing more than a shadowy silhouette. Stella

reached out and her fingertips found the woolly warmth of Tamar's sleeve.

"I'm right here," said Tamar. Her face drifted in and out of focus, as feathers of fog flowed between them.

Stella stared around, wide-eyed. She could see a hazy circle of grass at her feet, but beyond that, the colours faded to white.

"How are we going to get home?" she asked.

## Sixteen

# WHISPERS IN
# THE FOG

"WE'RE not going home," said Tamar. "You are."

"What?" said Stella. "No! I want to stay with you."

"I need to deal with the Haken," said Tamar. "Alone."

"But I can't find my way home in this!"

"Use your sky tunnel," said Tamar.

Stella looked at the swirling whiteness surrounding them and shook her head. "I don't even know where Nimbus is!" she said.

"I think he's lost."

"Clouds don't get lost," said Tamar. "I'm sure he's here by now. Ask him."

Stella chewed her lip. She hoped Tamar was right.

"Nimbus?" she said. "Are you here?"

Nothing.

The fog drifted around her. Rocks and thistles faded in and out of view like ghosts.

"Nimbus, if you're here, can you make me a sky tunnel?" she said.

The patch of grass at her feet grew a little larger and greener.

"You *are* here!" breathed Stella, in relief.

"There we are, then," said Tamar. "All sorted." She turned and melted away into the shifting fog. Stella heard the soft shush of her feet moving away through the long grass. "Straight home!" came Tamar's voice, from a distance away.

"Wait! Tamar . . ."

Stella stood there for a moment. The eerie silence seemed to press into her ears.

"Tamar?"

Her voice sounded small and out of place.

Even the seabirds were silent. *Even the sea . . .*

She strained her ears, but the familiar crash of waves against the rocks was gone. A heavy silence had settled over everything. It was like the fog had eaten all the sound.

"Tamar!" she called.

But there was no response.

Tamar was gone.

"She's left us," Stella whispered to Nimbus. "Can you believe that? She just went off and left us." Grown-ups weren't meant to leave you on your own.

Nimbus made the circle of green a little larger, as though to remind her she wasn't *completely* alone.

"It's still not right," said Stella. "Not if there's something dangerous nearby." She pulled her coat a little tighter around herself and squinted into the shifting fog. "Nimbus . . . do you know what the Haken is?"

The light dimmed to a murky twilight.

*Nimbus knows what it is*, she thought, then a rumble of thunder curled around her, sending shivers up her spine.

"Shh! Shh!" she hissed, in a panicked whisper. "It'll hear you! No thunder. We're meant to be hiding."

The Haken was somewhere out there. It might be coming closer even now.

*It could be standing right behind me, and I wouldn't know . . .*

Stella shivered.

She had to calm down or she'd set Nimbus off again.

*We've got to get home. Safely home.*

Stella gnawed her lip and turned in a full circle. On every side, the fog stared blindly back at her.

*Which way is it?* she thought. Then, *what would Tamar do?*

Tamar would probably tell her to be specific until Nimbus did what she wanted, but how was she meant to do that?

*He must be able to do it,* she thought. *Otherwise, Tamar wouldn't have left us here . . .*

*Would she?*

"Use your sky tunnel," she mumbled to herself.

The trouble was, a tunnel was made by walking through it. But she had no idea which way to go.

"Nimbus, can you make me a sky tunnel towards Grandpa's house?" she whispered. "Please tell me you can."

On her right, the fog parted in an arch and a narrow strip of grass unrolled ahead of her, between walls of white.

"Yes!" she said. "I could hug you right now!"

The cloud around her glimmered gold, as though the sun had caught it.

The tunnel wasn't very long. Hopefully, it would get longer when she walked into it? She just hoped Nimbus knew where they were going.

"Straight home, okay? No mucking about. We're not practising anymore."

Stella followed the green path of grass – watching her feet, avoiding the thistles. It wasn't too bad, until she glanced back and realised that the fog was swallowing the path behind her.

She moved away from it with a nervous spring in her step.

The fog followed.

"Grown-up and independent . . ." She whispered it under her breath, in time with her footsteps, trying to believe it. "Grown-up and independent, grown-up and independent . . ."

This was not what Dad had meant.

"Seriously," she said. "If Mum knew what I was doing right now, she would freak out! Walking around in fog, on my own, near the cliff . . ."

Stella slowed her pace and peered ahead. Beyond the narrow line of grass, the fog was dense and impenetrable – a thick, white shroud.

"Nimbus . . . we're not close to the cliff, are we?"

It would be so easy to walk right off the edge. She imagined the sudden lurch as her foot found nothing but air.

"Let's keep away from the cliff, okay?"

The strip of grass in front of her curved abruptly to the left. She watched it move and swallowed hard. How close had they been?

"Nimbus, don't be stupid! I can't be specific about everything. Some things are just obvious!"

The fog swept closed like a white curtain in front of her, trapping her in a narrow circle.

*No! What am I supposed to do now?*

Damp fingers of fog raised goose bumps on her arms.

"Stop it, Nimbus! I don't like it. Make the tunnel again."

But the tunnel was gone. And her cloud was silent.

*Say sorry*, whispered a corner of her mind. But she didn't want to. Why should she? Anybody would be snarky if they were lost in fog! And not going near the cliff was just common sense. *Surely Nimbus knows that?*

The fog pressed closer, cold as death. A chilling anxiety wormed its way into Stella's chest – if the fog swallowed her, she might just disappear. Never be seen again.

"Alright! I'm sorry!" she blurted. "Nimbus, I'm sorry I called you stupid! Please. Please make the tunnel again."

Like a carpet unrolling, the line of grass appeared out of the fog in front of her.

She sighed in relief. *Blooming moody cloud,* she thought.

Her eyes widened as she remembered he could hear her.

"I mean, thank you!" she said. "Don't do that again. I don't like the fog. It's creepy. And let's keep far away from the cliff."

Tamar might think it was easy to order clouds about, but maybe she'd never had a cloud like Nimbus.

The path widened into a broad strip of green and Stella lengthened her stride, but after a few metres, she slowed. There was a smell.

She couldn't tell where it was coming from, but there was a definite stink. Stella sniffed and wrinkled her nose. Rotten fish. It was so strong now, she could almost taste it in the damp air. What was it Gran used to say about fog?

*The breath of dead sailors . . .*

Stella shuddered and walked a bit faster.

*I did NOT need that thought right now.*

A high pitched keening sound cut through the silence and Stella froze. She stared over her shoulder, her breath tight in her chest.

*What . . . was that?*

She listened hard, but nothing else broke the silence.

*A bird. It was probably a bird,* she told herself, but her heart hammered a warning in her chest: *Get away. Get away. Get away.*

A dark shape bolted out of the grass, making her squeak. It bounced away and disappeared like a ghost. A rabbit. Only a rabbit. But its panic was catching. Stella's nerves twanged like elastic bands and her legs itched to run.

The sky tunnel stretched into a long narrow track. Nimbus had understood.

Stella sprang forward like a sprinter, her feet thumping the ground, arms pumping. Away from the stink, away from the scream, away from the terrified rabbit.

The tunnel snaked out ahead of her, uncovering sudden dips and sharp gorse bushes. She dodged and swerved, running until her breath was ragged in her throat.

*Home. Get home. Got to get home.*

Up ahead, something poked through the side of the tunnel. Something long and low and . . . familiar.

"The giant!"

Her feet thudded through the damp grass until she reached the rock.

The sleeping giant, Gran called it. A great curved boulder, that lay below the steepest bit of the hill. Gran said as long as it slept there, it kept them safe.

Stella jogged to a stop and crouched down in its shadow. The rock was cold against her back, but solid too – reassuringly real. She leant against it and caught her breath for a moment. The fog was fading. Tall thistles and heather bushes began to materialise out of the gloom, until she could see all the way down to Grandpa's house.

Stella huddled lower and looked back the way she'd come, scouring the hillside for any movement. The last pale shreds of fog drifted like lost spirits, but there was no dark figure following her. No monster waiting to pounce. Just a bare hillside, with a dark winding river of footsteps, that mapped her terrified run through the damp grass.

She took a deep breath and looked up, to see Nimbus rolling himself into a white ball.

"We made it!" she said. "You got me home."

## Seventeen

# FIXING GRANDPA

"**D**O you think we're safe now?" she asked Nimbus.

He bobbed once.

It *was* a nod. She was sure, this time. The fear slowly melted away, leaving exhaustion behind it. First the gale, then that creepy thing on the beach, then Tamar just going off like that . . .

Right now, Stella just wanted to crawl under a duvet and hide.

What she needed was a hug, but there was nobody to give her one. Grandpa was brain-fogged, Tamar wasn't exactly a cuddly sort of person, and Mum and Dad . . . she wouldn't see them for five whole weeks, which might as well be a million years.

Nimbus drifted towards her and wrapped around her chest.

She lifted her arms. "Is that a hug?" she said.

The cloud clung around her like a furry grey jumper, lighting a faint tingle in her skin. "Thank you," she said, with a small smile.

Nimbus glowed white in response.

She looked down the slope towards Grandpa's house and saw a movement at the back window.

"Quick, let go!" she said. "Grandpa might see!"

Nimbus gave a low grumble.

"Please!" she said. "I like hugs, but normal people don't get hugged by clouds."

Nimbus turned a militant shade of grey, but drifted away from her and floated down the slope to the chicken coop. He settled on its roof in a sulky grey heap.

"You were right, though," she said. "I needed that."

The cloud paled to light grey and she smiled. At least Nimbus never stayed grumpy for long.

"Come on," she said. "Let's go home. But stay out of sight. Find somewhere to hide, okay? And no thunder or lightning."

Nimbus faded to a whisper of mist.

Stella nodded. "Good. That's perfect."

As she made her way round to the front of the house, she slowed down. Up close, it filled her with a curious sense of disappointment. So much had happened today, but here, nothing had changed. The gate still hung wonky on its hinges and the front garden was tangled with weeds.

*I could have fallen off a cliff,* she thought, *and Grandpa wouldn't even know.* With his brain fogged, maybe he wouldn't even care.

She pushed open the front door and peeked inside. Grandpa was seated motionless in his armchair, with a cardboard box next to him. Papers and photographs were strewn over the floor all around him. The breakfast plates were still on the table.

"Grandpa?" Stella walked over to him. "What are you doing?"

Grandpa shook his head in confusion. "I'm not sure. I lost something. Something important, I think. I was looking for it," he said, gesturing to the mess on the floor, "but then I forgot what I was looking for . . ." He put a hand up to his head and rubbed at the red mark that still shone on his bald patch, then blinked and looked at her, as though she might know.

Stella gave him an uncertain smile.

*Nimbus?* thought Stella. *Brain-fog's not meant to get worse, is it?*

Grandpa gave her a quizzical look. "I know you, don't I? We've met before?"

The room seemed to lurch and Stella suddenly felt like she was going to be sick.

"It's me," she said, in a tiny voice. "Stella."

Grandpa squinted at her and shook his head. "I'm sorry, I don't . . ." His face was anxious, full of awkward embarrassment.

He didn't know who she was.

It was like falling down a deep hole. Falling and falling.

Grandpa had forgotten her. Like she'd never existed. And it was Stella's fault.

She'd done this.

*Nimbus!* she thought. *Come here right now! You've got to give his memories back! All of them. Especially the ones about me!*

She crouched next to Grandpa's chair. "You do know me, okay? You'll remember in a minute. I promise."

*Nimbus. Please hurry!*

Stella began to gather up photographs from the floor. Out of the corner of her eye, she saw a whisper of cloud appear over the back of Grandpa's armchair. It crept across the top of his head and poked misty tendrils into his ears.

"Stella?" said Grandpa, with a frown.

"You remember me!" she said, and rocked back on her heels in relief.

"Of course I remember you," said Grandpa, indignantly. "I might be old, but I'm not senile!"

Stella raised her eyebrows and slid the photos together into a neat pile. *More like himself already*, she thought.

She wasn't sure whether to feel relieved or sad. For a moment, this morning, he'd been the Grandpa she remembered. She'd miss that, when he was back to normal, back to the new Grandpa.

Stella fished a photo out from under the chair. A younger

version of her grandfather smiled up at her, his arm around the shoulders of a pretty girl.

"Is this Gran, when she was young?" she said, and looked up.

Grandpa's eyes bulged and his face twisted between surprise, and pain, and fury.

*Stop, Nimbus! You're hurting him!* thought Stella. She scrambled to her feet.

Two streamers of cloud poured out of Grandpa's ears, like smoke. He let out a long sigh and leant back in his chair. Beads of sweat shone on his forehead.

*He's old!* thought Stella. *You can't do it all at once! Not while he's awake. You'll give him a heart attack.*

Grandpa took a deep breath, wiped his face with his hankie and then sat forward in his chair.

"What have you got there?" he said. "Let me see that."

He took the photograph from Stella and held it with both hands, like something fragile. He stared at it with a faint frown on his face.

Stella bit her lip. Nimbus still hovered above his head like a fluffy hat.

*Try again, but slowly,* she thought. *Be gentle. A little bit at a time.*

A fine thread of mist slid back into Grandpa's ear.

"She was beautiful, wasn't she, your gran?" said Grandpa, and his eyes filmed over with tears.

Stella looked away. She didn't want to see him cry. It opened a little dark hole inside her, where she'd buried the sadness about Gran.

Grandpa blew his nose on his hankie and then stuffed it back into his pocket. "This was taken when we were newly engaged," he said. "We were so young, look!" He turned the photo towards her and pursed his lips. "I'll bet you can't imagine me young."

Stella looked at the young man in the photo, then at Grandpa's grizzled old face, with its stubble of white whiskers. *Not really,* she thought. She gave a nervous smile. A queue of fat little blobs of fog were appearing in the air beside his head. They were popping out of his ear holes one by one.

How much fog was in there?

"You've got that look about you," said Grandpa, "like you're up to something." He narrowed his eyes. "Have you moved my tools?"

Stella shook her head. "No, Grandpa, I haven't," she said.

*Really, Nimbus?* she thought. *The Tools Incident? Here we go again.*

She flumped down onto the armchair opposite, folded her arms, and waited. Grandpa watched her, a faint frown on his face.

"You're in a huff now? Why?" he said.

Stella tightened her lips. *How could he not remember?*

"When I put your tools away, you said a lot of very rude words and then you called me a meddling pest," she said. "I haven't touched them since then."

"I didn't, did I?" said Grandpa.

Stella nodded.

"I can't believe I'd have done that," said Grandpa.

He shook his head, dislodging one of the marshmallow puffs of fog. It floated away and drifted up towards the ceiling.

Stella scowled. He might not want to remember, but he had to. Otherwise it wasn't fair.

Nimbus darkened to grey.

*Don't you dare rain on his head!* thought Stella. *Just make him remember. Everything. Not just bits of it.*

"Did you break one of my tools?" said Grandpa.

"I didn't break anything," said Stella. "I was really careful. I just put them away. That's all."

"I'm sure you broke something," said Grandpa. "I remember . . . a crash?"

She couldn't hold his eyes. She hadn't meant to break Gran's mug, but it still pinched her heart to think about it. It was Gran's favourite, and it must have been precious to Grandpa. That's why he'd kept it.

"You've gone all shifty again," said Grandpa. "What was it?"

"I broke Gran's mug," she mumbled.

*Show him, Nimbus,* she thought. *There's no point in owning up if he can't even remember.*

Grandpa's face cleared. "Her puffin mug. I remember now. Well, that's a shame." He didn't turn purple, or shout. He just nodded.

Stella frowned. She didn't know what she'd expected, but not this.

Grandpa gave a sudden gasp, making her jump. He gripped the arms of his chair – his knuckles white – and his eyes darted around the room. "There was a cloud!" he said. "A storm! Here! In this house?"

Stella sucked in a breath. She should have told Nimbus to leave that bit out.

Grandpa put one hand to the top of his head, scattering wisps of cloud.

*Careful!* she thought. *Don't let him see you.*

"I was struck by lightning!" said Grandpa, wide-eyed.

Stella nodded and looked down at the floor. *How do you say sorry for that?* she thought.

The worst thing she'd ever done before was sneak a biscuit after Mum had told her not to. She'd never actually hurt someone.

"Argh! Get away from me!" yelled Grandpa. She looked up in fright.

Grandpa was waving his hands around, as though he was under attack.

"It's still here, Stella! Run! Hide! Get away!"

He'd seen Nimbus.

"Grandpa, stop! It's alright," she said. "You don't need to be scared."

But Grandpa leapt to his feet, swatting wildly at the blobs

of fog that encircled his head. The blobs gathered into a single storm-grey ball and floated up, out of reach.

"Get behind me!" said Grandpa, planting himself between Stella and the cloud. "It's dangerous."

This was not going according to plan. Not even slightly.

## Eighteen

# THE DREAM-SEER

GRANDPA was standing in a half crouch, clenching and unclenching his fists. He looked as though he planned to punch the cloud. He obviously hadn't thought it through.

How could Stella make him see that he didn't need to be scared any more?

As the cloud drifted closer to him, Grandpa snatched up a pile of papers and flapped at it, scattering wisps of mist across the room.

Nimbus gave a low growl of warning.

*Not again.*

"Nimbus," she said out loud. "Go outside."

The cloud faded from grey to white and floated over to the front door.

Grandpa gawped at it and turned to Stella in shock.

"It listens to you?" he said.

She nodded. "Mostly," she said.

Nimbus could have slid through the gap, if he wanted to. Instead he just hung there, pale and improbable, waiting for Stella to open the door.

*Please, for once, do what you're told,* she thought.

"Go on. Out you go," she said, in a confident voice.

She walked over and opened the door. Nimbus drifted outside in an unhurried way and settled on the garden wall.

Stella closed the door and turned back to Grandpa.

"*You* fired lightning at me?" said Grandpa, looking horrified.

"No!" said Stella. "He did that without being told to."

She felt a pang of guilt, but squashed it down. It wasn't like she'd done it on purpose.

"It was an accident! He only fired lightning at you because you were yelling at me," she said.

Grandpa glanced at the closed door and then looked back at her with an odd expression on his face.

"He was trying to protect me," she said. "He thought you might hurt me."

Grandpa frowned. "I'd never hurt you. You do know that, don't you?"

"I know," she said, and nodded. "I mean, you shout a lot, but you wouldn't actually hurt me. Nimbus didn't know that though."

"I shout a lot?" said Grandpa.

Stella frowned. *Maybe there's still a bit of fog in his head?*

"Most days, since I got here," she said. "So I know it's normal. It's just you were properly scary that night."

Grandpa closed his eyes and shook his head. "You know it's normal . . ." he murmured.

He opened his eyes and the sadness in them was hard to look at.

"I'm sorry," he said. "I'm so sorry I scared you."

Stella gave him a small smile, but a glimmer of hope glowed inside her like a candle. He'd said sorry. He'd actually said sorry.

Grandpa eased himself down into his armchair, then turned his face up to the ceiling. "You were right, as usual. And even *indoors* isn't safe from it. So now what?"

"Who are you talking to?" asked Stella.

Maybe she should get Nimbus back in? Maybe Grandpa still wasn't quite right?

"Your Gran," said Grandpa.

Stella's heart fell. All that, and it hadn't worked. He still didn't remember everything.

"Grandpa, Gran's not here, she's—"

"I know," said Grandpa. "But I can still talk to her, can't I?"

"Yes . . ."

"Fat lot of good it did, sending them away." He mumbled it, under his breath, but she was pretty sure she'd heard him right.

"What do you mean?" she said.

He paused, sucked his lips in and nodded, as though he'd come to a decision. "Your Gran saw this coming. It's why she sent you away."

"What?" said Stella.

She sank into the armchair opposite Grandpa's. Now it felt like her head was full of fog. The words grew sharp edges as they settled inside her: *'sent you away.'*

"Mum said we moved away because of Dad's work," she said, her voice brittle.

"There was that, yes. But it was your Gran who convinced them to go."

"What?! Why?" Stella stared at him. "Why would she do that?"

"She was trying to do the right thing."

"But it wasn't! Not for me!"

"It wasn't right for any of us," said Grandpa. "But try telling your Gran that!"

*Gran had sent them away. Away from here. Away from home.*

The feeling scrunched up inside her, all edges and hard corners. All the moving about, from town to town. Packing, and moving house, and unpacking again. The new schools, with their scratchy new uniforms. New faces, unfriendly and strange. All the times she'd had to smile, even though she felt like a plant with its roots torn up.

*It was all Gran's fault?*

"I never wanted you to leave," said Grandpa.

"Well, I didn't want to either! Nobody ever asked me!" said Stella. "Why? Why didn't she want us here?" she said, her voice cracking.

"Oh Stella, it wasn't like that," said Grandpa, reaching across to take her hand. "I'm not explaining this well at all. She did it to keep you safe."

"From what?" said Stella. She pulled her hand away and folded her arms.

"From the storm," said Grandpa. He looked towards the door again.

Stella's mouth dropped open.

"That's just stupid!" she exclaimed. "Gran couldn't have known about Nimbus. And anyway, that's not a reason to move house! Why would Mum and Dad listen to that?"

"She didn't tell them," said Grandpa.

"What are you even talking about?" said Stella.

Her chest hurt from all the anger inside it. Anger at Gran for sending them away, at Mum and Dad for agreeing to it, at Grandpa for not making any sense. She took a shallow breath and hunched down in the chair.

"Stella, your Gran was magic," said Grandpa. "Like you."

*Like me?*

Confusion poured through her.

"Gran knew weather magic?" she said.

"Weather magic, is it?" said Grandpa.

Stella's heart sank – he didn't know what it was. Gran wasn't like her at all.

"No . . . your gran was a dream-seer," said Grandpa. "A different kind of magic, I think. She could glimpse the future."

"Why didn't anyone tell me?"

Grandpa shrugged uncomfortably. "You were small. And there wasn't much to tell."

"Magic?" said Stella.

"Well, not exactly. That's not how I thought of it, anyhow. There wasn't any hocus pocus involved. It was just something she could do. That's all."

"But she dreamt something bad?" said Stella. "About me?" She wrapped her arms tighter around herself.

A shadow passed over Grandpa's face and he looked away.

"No! You can't do that!" yelled Stella. "Not if it's about me!"

There was a loud clap of thunder outside and both of them looked towards the door.

"Can you stop it doing that?" said Grandpa, rubbing his chest.

Stella gave a small sigh. "I can't help it. He does that when I'm angry."

She hadn't meant it as a threat, but Grandpa's face paled and she suddenly felt very guilty. "I'll get him to stop," she said. "Just tell me! What did Gran see? Why did she send me away?"

Grandpa took a deep breath. "She dreamt there was a storm coming," he said. "A storm fierce enough to drown the whole island, she said, and you . . . you were standing right in its path."

There was a moment of silence, as they both tried to picture a storm big enough to drown an island.

"And you believed her?" said Stella.

Grandpa heaved a deep sigh. "No. No, I didn't," he said, spreading his hands. "But partly I just didn't want to. The trouble is, your Gran's dreams weren't always clear, but they were always right. Every. Single. Time." He poked his finger into the arm of his chair to make his point.

"Why didn't you just tell Mum and Dad what Gran saw?" said Stella.

"What do you think they would have done, if they thought we were in danger here?" said Grandpa.

Stella thought about it. "Tried to take you and Gran away too?"

Grandpa nodded. "Exactly. So, your gran made me promise to keep it secret. Instead, she told your parents they needed to spread their wings, see the world."

"She lied, you mean," said Stella.

Grandpa sighed. "Well, it wasn't a lie, exactly."

*It was.*

"You could have stopped them," she said.

Grandpa looked helplessly at her. "I didn't want to see you get hurt."

Stella closed her mouth and looked away.

Grandpa picked up the pile of photos and began to shuffle through them. As he got about halfway through, he paused. "Here's one of us, look," he said. He held the photo out to her.

It was a picture of Grandpa with a small girl on his shoulders.

*Me,* she thought. *Me and Grandpa.*

"You were such a cheery peerie bairn," he said. "Always laughing. I've missed your laugh more than anything."

A small lump formed in Stella's throat. Grandpa in the picture was the one she remembered. Grandpa how he used to be.

Grandpa held out a hand and she took it. His palm felt like sandpaper, all rough and scratchy, but his fingers closed warmly around hers.

"You can keep that photo if you want," he said. "Might convince you not to set that cloud on me again?"

"I wouldn't do that!" said Stella. "I didn't mean to."

Her eyes were hot with tears.

"Hey, I'm joking!" he said, and gave her hand a gentle squeeze. "I won't pretend to understand what's going on here, but whatever it is, I'm on your side."

A tear escaped down Stella's cheek. She wiped it away with the back of her hand.

"Listen," he said, "I might be a grumpy auld so-and-so, but

I'm still your Grandpa. You can talk to me," he said. "I'll listen."

"You won't believe me," said Stella.

"You'd be surprised," said Grandpa. "I'm about ready to believe anything, right now."

"Also, I think it's probably meant to be secret."

"I can do secrets," said Grandpa. "Let's face it, who am I going to tell?"

Stella gave a small hiccup of laughter and wiped her nose on her sleeve.

"So, are you going to tell me how you come to have your own cloud?" said Grandpa.

Stella clamped her lips together.

She couldn't *not* tell him. He'd seen Nimbus.

But what *could* she tell him? Nothing about catching gales, or getting lost in fog, or anything scary at all – otherwise he'd never let her outside again.

Grandpa raised his eyebrows and waited.

Stella picked at a loose thread on the arm of the chair. She'd probably said too much already. And if Tamar found out Grandpa knew, she'd probably want to brain-fog him all over again . . .

*Why couldn't you just have stayed out of sight, Nimbus?*

"Well?" said Grandpa.

"I caught it," said Stella. "In a bag."

"Whatever gave you the idea you could do that?" said Grandpa.

Stella hesitated.

"Someone I met," said Stella, and bit her lips closed between her teeth, so that nothing else would escape.

"Not that Tamar, by any chance?" said Grandpa, raising one eyebrow.

Stella goggled at him. "You know her?"

"Hard not to," he said. "There aren't many people round here. I should have guessed she'd have something to do with it. Is that where you disappeared to, the other day?"

"Yes."

*How much did Grandpa know?*

Grandpa shook his head. "She's been away a long time. I didn't realise she was back on the island. Tamar's is probably the only place I didn't think to look."

"Are you friends?" said Stella.

"She was friends with your gran," said Grandpa.

It sounded like there was more to know, but Stella didn't ask. There was a quiet look of resentment on Grandpa's face. A last-person-picked-to-play kind of look, like maybe Tamar was friends with Gran, but not with him.

"Nimbus is alright, you know," she said instead. "You don't need to be scared of him. He's my friend now."

"Your friend . . ." said Grandpa.

"I *said* you wouldn't believe me!"

"No! No, I do," said Grandpa. "I'm just not sure what to make of it. That's all."

Stella narrowed her eyes. "That's why you didn't want me going out before, isn't it?" she said. "Because of Gran's dream about the storm."

Grandpa fiddled with the pile of photos on the arm of his chair and refused to look at her. It all made sense now – why Grandpa had kept her stuck in the house, why he didn't want her to go out alone: he was scared.

Except all this time, Gran had been wrong. The storm was never a threat to Stella. It was coming to meet her.

"You'd like Nimbus if you got to know him," she said.

Grandpa looked warily at the door. "He won't come inside again, will he?"

Stella shook her head. "Not if I tell him not to."

"Alright then," said Grandpa. "Good. Now, I don't know about you, but I'm famished."

"Me too," said Stella.

Grandpa stood up and ruffled her hair. "I'll get supper on," he said. "Shepherd's pie. Sound okay to you?"

Stella nodded and Grandpa walked over to the kitchen cupboard.

"Grandpa?"

He turned back to look at her. "Yes?"

"This time, Gran was wrong."

## Nineteen

# A WELL-REASONED ARGUMENT

GRANDPA pushed open the curtains and Stella sat up in bed. "What's wrong?" she said.

"Nothing's wrong. It's a beautiful day. There's not a cloud in the sky. Better still, not a cloud in the house," said Grandpa, waggling his eyebrows.

Stella rubbed her eyes and tried to smile. It was a bit early in the morning for jokes.

"I made you hot chocolate," said Grandpa, setting a mug on the bedside table.

"Hot chocolate?" she said.

"You used to like it," he said.

"I still do! I've just never had it for breakfast before, that's all."

Grandpa was still standing by the bed. He seemed to be waiting for something. Then he glanced at the bedside table. Stella reached to pick up the mug and realised – it was Gran's puffin mug! The one she'd smashed.

"You mended it!" she exclaimed.

"Nothing a bit of glue couldn't fix," he said. "Well, a lot of glue, actually. That was quite a puzzle you left me! But I didn't want to bin it. I'm fond of it."

Stella traced the fine lines that criss-crossed the curved surface of the mug. It must have taken him ages. "I'm sorry I broke it," she said.

"Not the end of the world," he said. "It's given it a bit of history. Now, when I look at it, I'll think of you as well as your Gran."

"Of how clumsy I am?" she said, with a small smile.

Grandpa shook his head gently. "You know that's not what I meant," he said. "I meant it'll remind me of spending time with you."

Stella smiled.

"Your Gran only wanted the best for you, you know," said Grandpa.

The smile dropped off her face and she rearranged the blanket, so she wouldn't have to look at him. "She was still wrong."

"We all get things wrong," said Grandpa. "And I know you're angry with her right now. But try to remember that she loved you. More than anything."

Stella didn't answer.

Grandpa prodded her knee and smiled.

"I'll try," she said.

She blew on the hot chocolate and took a sip. It was dark and bitter and made her tongue shrivel up.

"Good?" said Grandpa.

"Mm, thank you," she said.

As soon as he'd gone, she put the mug down and wiped her tongue on her sleeve. It always used to be Gran who made the hot chocolate. Grandpa might need some tips.

She knelt up on the bed and looked out of the window. The view outside was bright and clear – no hint of yesterday's fog. The sky was a wide stretch of blue. No clouds.

*No clouds at all ...*

Stella's heart clenched – she'd left Nimbus outside. All night. On his own.

The metal handle of the window was gritty with rust, but when she leant on it, it turned with a reluctant screech. The window got stuck on the warped windowsill, but the gap was just wide enough to poke her head through.

"Nimbus?" she called softly.

Tiny white flags of bog cotton danced in the breeze and every blade of grass seemed extra sharp, as though determined to stay in focus after yesterday. There was no sign of her cloud though.

She'd have to go look for him.

*Maybe he's gone back to Tamar's,* Stella told herself, trying to ignore the twist of worry in her chest.

She closed the window and climbed off the bed.

The light in the room dimmed and a grey swirl of cloud appeared against the other side of the glass.

"There you are!" she said. "Where were you?"

A curl of mist appeared under the window frame.

"Wait!" said Stella. "You can't come inside! Grandpa will . . . well, I'm not sure what he'll do, but he won't like it."

The mist faded from the window sill.

"I'll come out in a bit," said Stella. "I promise. I just need to convince Grandpa first. Now, go away, I need to get dressed."

Nimbus drifted upwards, out of view.

When she came into the kitchen, Grandpa was doing the washing up. He turned towards her with a smile.

*Now,* she thought, *while he's still in a listening mood.*

"Grandpa?" she said. "You know Gran's dream, about the storm?"

"Yes?"

"Well . . . we know what it means now, don't we?" said Stella, with a cautious smile.

Grandpa made a doubtful noise.

"Me and Nimbus – that's what Gran was talking about," insisted Stella.

She was right. She was sure of it.

She was pretty sure Grandpa knew it too, even if he didn't want to admit it.

Grandpa picked up the bowl he'd only just washed and started to rub at it, with a look of fierce concentration.

Stella waited for him to answer, but he didn't say anything – he just stood the bowl on the drainer and started washing a pot.

"Grandpa?"

He put the pot back in the water and stood there, with his hands on the edge of the sink. "I suppose it's possible," he said, at last.

"That means there's nothing to be scared about now, is there?" said Stella.

"I don't know about that . . ." said Grandpa.

"So, I was thinking, maybe I could go out for a bit today?"

Grandpa's mouth tensed and he looked up at the ceiling, as though searching for guidance.

"It would stop my cloud from bothering you," she hurried on. "I could take him somewhere else, so he doesn't try to come in the house again."

Grandpa's eyes widened. "I thought it does what you tell it?" he said, his eyes darting towards the door.

"Well, he does . . ." said Stella.

"So, tell him to stay outside," said Grandpa. He nodded, as though that settled it.

Stella gritted her teeth. Grandpa couldn't carry on being like this! Not now he knew about Nimbus. Not now he knew Gran was wrong.

"I can't stay inside the whole time I'm here!" she said.

"Your parents," said Grandpa, "entrusted me with your care—"

"*They* told me I'd be able to explore here!" she said. "At home, I'm allowed out on my own all the time."

"They don't know what your Gran saw."

"But Gran was wrong!" said Stella, spreading her hands.

"Anyway, aren't you a bit small to be out on your own?" said Grandpa, sizing her up with a slight frown.

"I'm old enough to come *here* on my own," retorted Stella. "And you used to let Dad do it when he was eleven. He told me! He even went out on the boat by himself!"

"Listen, it's my job to keep you safe," said Grandpa.

"Making me stay indoors isn't keeping me safe," she said. "It's more like keeping me *prisoner*!"

Grandpa's jaw set in a stubborn line. "I'd hardly be taking care of you if I let you go off with a cloud that'll fire lightning at you as soon as look at you!"

"He *doesn't*!" protested Stella.

Thunder rumbled outside, making Grandpa jump.

*Shush!* she thought. *That's not helping!*

Stella took a deep breath. Shouting wasn't going to work. Especially not if Nimbus joined in. She had to convince Grandpa. Make him understand. Like Mum always said: *a well-reasoned argument is louder than a shout.*

"He won't fire lightning at me, because he's *my* cloud," she explained, in a much quieter voice. "Gran's dream – that's why you were making me stay inside, wasn't it? Except Gran was wrong, wasn't she?"

Grandpa rubbed a hand over his face and gave her an exasperated look. "Eat your porridge," he said, pointing at a steaming bowl on the table.

Stella sat down and picked up her spoon. Eating had never stopped her talking before. Mum could have told Grandpa that.

"I'm big now," she said, between mouthfuls of porridge. "Mum and Dad let me go out on my own all the time. I walk to school, I go to the shops by myself and everything – that's much more dangerous. There's traffic and main roads – I mean, there aren't even any cars here!"

"Where were you thinking of going?" he said. "Back to Tamar's?"

"Mm," Stella nodded.

Grandpa dried his hands on the dishcloth. "I'll come with you, then. I'd like a word."

"What? No! You can't!"

Grandpa raised his eyebrows.

"Weather magic is secret, remember?" said Stella.

"I thought you said Tamar knows about it?" said Grandpa.

"Yes, but you're not meant to!" said Stella, her heart racing.

If Tamar found out Grandpa knew, she'd brain-fog him for sure. She couldn't let that happen. Not again.

"You *said* you could keep a secret," she reminded him.

Grandpa opened his mouth to say something, then closed it again.

"And you *know* Tamar. It's not like I'm going off with a stranger." Stella gave him a hopeful smile. "So?"

"Let me think about it," he muttered. He dried the bread knife and got the wooden board out of the cupboard.

She watched him for a moment, as he spread butter on thick hunks of bread. He hadn't said no.

She leant over to look out of the back window. Nimbus hovered alone, a little way up the hill.

*Stay there, okay?* she thought. *And please don't thunder.*

Grandpa put the bread away, then came over and thumped a baking paper parcel down on the table. "Jam sandwiches," he said, gruffly. "I wrapped them – something to keep you going while you're out and about."

Stella bounced to her feet. "Thank you, Grandpa!" she said.

"There are *rules*, though," said Grandpa, knitting his brows. "The paths are there for a reason. You stick to the path. No crossing bogs. No climbing rocks. No walking close to the cliffs."

"I won't," said Stella.

Grandpa's frown relaxed a little. "No going on the beach, either," he added.

"Because of the nests," agreed Stella.

Her chest tightened as she remembered the figure on the beach. *The Haken.* Tamar had been so frightened . . .

"Do you remember the way?" said Grandpa.

Stella nodded.

"I can't say I like it," said Grandpa. "Storm clouds and secrets and who knows what else."

*Gales, fog, creepy people on the beach,* Stella swallowed. Grandpa didn't need to know all that – he'd never let her out again. And anyway, she'd got Nimbus. He'd look after her.

"What if something were to happen to you?" said Grandpa. "What would I tell your parents?"

"Nothing will happen," said Stella. "My cloud will protect me. He wants to keep me safe, just like you do."

Grandpa raised his eyebrows.

"He's kind of like a guardian angel," she added.

It was a bit of an exaggeration, but she knew Grandpa was keen on angels.

Grandpa stood up very tall and puffed his chest out. "Well, you tell that cloud from me, if it doesn't look after you, it'll have me to answer to!"

Doubt flitted across his face as he said it. She knew how he felt.

There wasn't really any way you could threaten a cloud.

"I'll tell him that," she said with a smile, and she picked up the parcel. "Thank you!"

"You go straight there and come straight back. Understood?"

"Understood," said Stella solemnly.

*Told you I'd convince him, didn't I, Nimbus?* she thought. *I'll meet you out front.*

She grabbed her rucksack and stuffed the parcel of sandwiches into it. Then she pulled on her walking boots and laced them up to her ankles. This time she was going to be prepared, whatever weather Tamar decided to throw at her.

## Twenty

# A BOOK OF
# RAINBOWS

A S she got to the front gate, Stella turned and waved. Grandpa
stood in the doorway. Above him, Nimbus lay on the roof in
a soft heap, like a dropped pillow.

"Be back here by lunchtime," he said. "Otherwise I'm coming
over to Tamar's to find you."

"I will," she replied, nodding hard.

No way did she want Grandpa turning up out of the blue.

She might be in the middle of a gale or something.

"And you'll be careful, yes?" said Grandpa

"Yes," she said. "I'll be really careful."

Nimbus began to roll down the tiles.

"Bye then, Grandpa, see you later," she said. As he closed the door, the cloud tumbled to the ground and rolled towards her.

"You nearly landed on his head!" said Stella. "Right after I just told him you're an angel! Can't you act normal until we're away from here? Float higher!"

Nimbus launched himself off the ground and pulsed up into the air, leaving a streamer of mist behind him like a rocket trail. She shook her head. They were going to have to practise looking ordinary.

As she followed the path down the slope, her knees began to feel jittery, like they wanted to run. The coastal path was the fastest route – that was what Tamar had said – but it was also right above storm petrel beach.

What if that thing was still there, waiting for them? The Haken.

When she got to the cliff, Stella slowed her pace and flapped at Nimbus to come closer to her. Then she crouched and crept, crabwise, up to the edge. There she lay down on her stomach in the scratchy long grass and scanned every inch of the beach, wishing she'd thought to bring her binoculars.

There was no sign of the dark figure from yesterday.

Two black and white birds patrolled the water's edge, dipping their long red beaks into the crevices between stones. Further out, the bay glittered with short choppy waves, their tops ruffled white by a brisk onshore wind. Everything looked normal . . .

Stella didn't quite trust it, though.

She scrambled back until she was sure she couldn't be seen from the beach. "I think it must have gone," she said to Nimbus. "But let's be quick, just in case. Stay low."

She stood up and set off at a jog, watching all around for anything out of place. Nimbus elongated into a pointy oval and swam through the air ahead of her, his sides rippling like a cuttlefish.

Sheep looked up dozily as they passed, chewing slowly, their woolly chins stained with green. Herring gulls curved lazily on the breeze.

When she arrived at the croft, Tamar wasn't on the bench outside. Stella tapped at the door and it swung open with a low creak.

"I'm here," she called. "Tamar?"

The house was silent.

She turned and looked at Nimbus. "Do you think we can go in?" she asked. "She did leave the door open."

Nimbus gusted through the door and vanished into the house.

"Okay, I guess that's a 'yes'," said Stella, and followed him inside.

She shrugged off her rucksack and leant it against the table leg. Shadows lurked in every corner. Without Tamar here, the room felt a lot less friendly. Stella suddenly wondered whether Tamar had put the thirsty towels away. Perhaps they still here, crawling about in the gloom.

She waved at the window and half of the curtain of fog dissolved. Sunlight burst into the room. There wasn't a towel in sight, but up near the ceiling, a flurry of snow danced.

"Aren't you meant to be in a jar?" she said. "You'll be in trouble if Tamar sees you."

She pointed at one of the jars on the table, like Tamar had. The snow fell into a soft heap beside it.

"Close enough."

On the kitchen table, was a large cloth-bound book that she didn't remember from before. Stella reached towards it, but hesitated. Tamar probably wouldn't mind them being inside, but touching stuff?

She opened the cover carefully.

The pages were striped, from red at the top of the page through orange, yellow, green and blue, all the way down to purple at the bottom. The surface of the paper looked bright, like it had just been painted, but when Stella ran a finger across it, it was smooth and dry.

"Maybe this is actual rainbow," she said to Nimbus. "Like that glass, only paper."

She fanned through the pages. The whole book was striped in the same bright colours, but there were no words, no pictures. Every page was blank.

Nimbus didn't seem interested in the book. He began to nose across the cluttered table, winding misty ribbons around the wooden spinning reels and pouring himself in and out of empty jars.

"Nimbus? Look. Help me figure this out."

Nimbus drifted backwards across the heap of snow and picked up a whirl of snowflakes. He rolled towards her, like a giant snow globe.

"Stop it! Put that down," said Stella.

Nimbus blew the snow right at her, in a fine sparkling shower. Stella yelped and jumped backwards. She glared at the cloud. "Not helpful! Not helpful at all!"

Most of the snow had landed on the open book. As it melted, the colours beneath darkened into ugly wet splodges.

"Oh no," she exclaimed. "Look what you've done! You've ruined it!"

She could already hear the disappointment in Tamar's voice: *I leave you two alone for five minutes . . .*

"Get off the table, Nimbus. And don't touch anything else! You're no help at all. You're a meddling pest."

Nimbus poured off the far edge of the table and slunk away across the floor.

Stella looked down at the book and groaned. The rainbow page was now covered in a mottled patchwork of dark spots. The wet paper was starting to warp into ridges. She cast an anxious glance towards the towel by the sink, but shook her head. It might make it worse.

The book gave a sudden crackle, like a lit sparkler, and black lines began to scorch across the page. For a moment, she thought it might burst into flames, but the sound faded and the lines kept appearing, burrowing dark wiggly lines across the bright colours.

Words.

It was the same spidery handwriting as the labels on the jars – Tamar's writing. Stella leant closer and read the words etching their way in zigzags across the red stripe at the top of the page: *Fury, passion – wild lightning.*

*Wild lightning – like when I got angry at Grandpa.*

She followed the words down the page.

Orange read: *Playful, fun - sudden showers.*

The words were surrounded by tiny dots, as though they'd been caught out in the rain.

*Fun for clouds, maybe. Not if you're the one getting wet.* Still, Nimbus hadn't done that since they'd practised raining on target . . .

Was this list about her, a record of her weather-weaving lessons?

The yellow stripe now had *JOY* printed in the centre of it. A spiral of words grew in a sunburst around it: *sunshine, wind, sunshine, wind, sunshine, wind.*

*I did that too . . .* she thought.

The lines crept down into the green stripe like woodworm.

They formed two words and then wiggled to a stop.

*Secrets of*

"Secrets of what?"

Stella scooped up the last scrap of unmelted snow and rubbed it into the paper.

The last word appeared reluctantly. A faint blur of black: *stone.*

*Secrets of stone.*

It was a list. Not of things she'd done, but of things she was going to do. With Tamar.

Stella smeared her palm across the wet page, trying to coax more out of it, but no more words appeared. She rubbed harder, but the paper began to feel furry. Fine rolls of paper came loose from the surface and stuck to her skin. She wiped her hand on her jumper.

"Nimbus?" she said. "Where are you? I need more snow."

She looked up, but Nimbus was nowhere to be seen. After a moment, she spotted a trail of mist poking out from under the small table by the fire. She walked over and sat down in the armchair next to it.

Nimbus cowered under the table and Stella cringed. "You were trying to help. I didn't realise."

She knew exactly what it felt like – when Grandpa barked at her for trying to help. She'd even used his phrase, a 'meddling pest'.

"I didn't mean it," she said. "I'm sorry. You're not a pest at all."

Nimbus crept out from under the table. He still looked very deflated.

"I don't really think that," she said. "You're a brilliant cloud. You got me home yesterday, didn't you? In the fog! I would have been lost if I didn't have you. And you fixed Grandpa, too. He's almost his old self again. He might even get to like you, if you stop thundering all the time."

Nimbus turned a soft shade of yellow and fluffed up a bit.

Yellow for joy, she remembered. She hoped that meant he was feeling better.

*If I could show Grandpa what Nimbus is really like . . .*

For the first time, Stella wasn't looking forward to the end of the holidays. What would happen when Mum and Dad got here?

She didn't even know where they were moving after the summer. If it was anything like Southampton, there was no way Nimbus could come too. Not to a city. No way.

Nimbus sank to the floor and melted into a puddle of mist.

*If only we could stay here . . .*

The thought hatched like an egg.

"We *could* stay here! I bet Grandpa would agree. We can get him to ask Mum and Dad!" she said. "If they need extra convincing, I'll tell them how sad Grandpa was, all on his own. I want to live here. With you. I can't be anywhere else. When they meet you, they'll realise. We have to stay here."

The effect was startling. Nimbus mushroomed off the floor,

trailing a long skirt of mist behind him. When he reached the ceiling, he rolled, winding up the mist, until he was a perfect circle again, bobbing jauntily between the rafters.

Stella smiled up at him. "You like that idea then?" she said.

Nimbus swooped towards her, swerving away at the last moment to circle the room, in a series of wild victory laps.

*He's so happy!*

The thought gave her a twinge of worry. It was only an idea . . . she wasn't sure she could even make it happen.

Nimbus turned a loop-the-loop as though to say: *Of course you can!*

Stella swallowed. There was no taking it back now. She'd never seen Nimbus so excited about anything . . .

Her heart suddenly ached with missing Mum and Dad. What if they said *she* could stay, but *they* went away again. Could she stand being apart from them, all the time? She was used to Dad going away, but both of them?

Nimbus swooped over her head, making a mess of her hair.

Stella took Tamar's little telescope off the mantelpiece, squinted one eye closed and looked through it. Nimbus glowed like a small sun. "Alright," she said. "We'll try, at least. I'll talk to Grandpa about it tonight."

Nimbus orbited the room, faster and faster.

"Slow down!" she said.

Nimbus began to slow, but not in time. As he flew past the

window, he tangled with the remains of the fog curtain and nosedived into the sink.

Stella hastily put the telescope back on the mantelpiece and hurried over. Nimbus reappeared from amongst the pile of dirty pots and pans.

She wrinkled her nose. There was a ripe smell coming from the dishes in the sink. They must have been there a while.

A chill of worry crept into her stomach. *Maybe Tamar hasn't been home since yesterday.* It suddenly felt like a really long time since Tamar had walked away from her in the fog.

## Twenty-One

# WHERE IS TAMAR?

"SHE'S probably just popped out," Stella reasoned, "but after yesterday ..."

The pale face of the figure on the beach flickered into her mind and she shuddered.

Nimbus lifted out of the sink and drifted closer.

"Pooh, stop it. You smell of dirty dishes." She flapped her arms to stop him from trying to hug her.

Stella walked back to the fireplace and held her hand over the grate. It was cold. Not even a hint of warmth.

"Saying she'd deal with the Haken herself was all very brave and everything," she said, "but maybe not very sensible."

Nimbus rumbled his agreement.

"I think we should go and find her. Just to make sure. Do you think you can do that?" she asked him. "Find Tamar?"

Nimbus cannonballed towards the front door and bumped into it. He began to squeeze under the gap at the bottom.

"Wait!" she said. "I meant both of us!"

Nimbus popped though the gap and disappeared.

"Stop! Wait for me!" shouted Stella.

When she got outside, Nimbus was hovering at the corner of the croft.

She ran over to him. "Together," she said. "Remember? We do things together."

Nimbus brightened until he almost glowed and streaked up the hill behind the croft. Stella looked after him with a sinking feeling. It was steep, and covered in a dense maze of heather bushes.

"Hey!" she called after Nimbus. "Wait!"

*It's alright for him*, she thought. *He can just go wherever he wants, in a straight line.*

Nimbus reappeared at the top and flew back to her. He stopped a few metres away and hung there, as though to say: *What are you waiting for?*

"I'm coming too," she said. "But I have to walk, and that takes longer than flying. So you have to slow down." She stepped forward into the heather, disturbing a cloud of bees and a strong smell of honey.

Heather was hard to walk through. It hid bumps, and holes, and puddles. Even with her walking boots on, Stella had to stamp to find solid ground before taking each step. Thin branches snagged at her trousers and poked sharp spines into her ankles.

A little way up the slope, the ground had torn – a deep black rip, right down to the peat. As she tramped across it, water squelched out and the soft earth sucked at her boots.

*Stick to the paths. Promise?* Grandpa's words buzzed like flies in her head, making her twitch. She had *meant* to keep that promise, but she had to find Tamar.

Stella yanked, and, with a slurp, her foot came free. She scrambled onto higher ground and stood there with her hands on her knees, breathing hard. *I'll stick to the rocky bits,* she thought. *That'll be safer.*

Nimbus reappeared at the top of the hill and flew towards her at top speed.

"Don't panic," she said. "I got stuck, that's all."

Nimbus circled her twice. Apparently satisfied, he drifted back towards the top of the hill.

Stella shook her head and pressed on. The top half of the slope was rockier. Her boots sent little showers of scree skittering down the slope, into the bushes below.

*If I fall and hurt myself, I'm on my own,* she thought, with a shiver. *Nobody even knows I'm up here.*

The steep slope suddenly felt much colder. It wasn't interested in her. She could climb up, or fall down. It didn't care either way.

Nimbus reappeared at the summit.

"There you are! Stay with me. Stop disappearing." she said. "Also, if I break my leg or something, it's your job to go and get Grandpa."

At last, she reached the summit. The top of the hill was a smooth plateau of startlingly green grass, cropped neat and short, like it had been to the barbers.

Stella recognised the wide sweep of the bay. She was on the same hilltop where she'd called the fog with Tamar, but higher up.

"Oh!" she said. "You meant it to be a shortcut?"

Nimbus fluffed himself up. He looked very smug.

"Alright, clever clogs," said Stella. "Just try and remember that I'm not a cloud, okay? From now on, we need actual paths. Not all of us can fly!"

She turned on the spot. Tamar was nowhere to be seen.

"Is she actually here? Or did you just think this was a good place to start looking?"

Nimbus looped behind her and then drifted down the far side of the hill. He was moving slower now, following a track barely wide enough for a sheep.

*I'm going to have to explain what counts as a path.*

The trail led down to the sea. *The far end of storm petrel beach*, she realised. This end formed a little cove of its own, cut off now by the high tide. There wasn't much beach to be seen – no more than a narrow stony strip. White breakers unrolled along the rocks. "No Haken, definitely no Haken," she whispered to herself, and began to pick her way carefully down.

*We'll find Tamar, then we'll go home. And we'll eat jam sandwiches, and everything will be fine.*

The first stretch of path was an uneven patchwork of flat stones that wobbled when she stepped on them. After that, there was only treacherously smooth moss. Each time Stella's boot slipped, her breath caught in her chest.

This was *not* being careful.

As she got close to the bottom, she frowned. The black tangle of seaweed near the top of the beach was studded with piles of rock. They hadn't been there yesterday. It looked as though the high-tide line had grown teeth.

Nimbus was circling the nearest one.

Stella walked cautiously along the top of the beach, hopping between pale patches of sand and big slabs of rock, careful not to step on the loose stones. She was not meant to be here. Definitely not meant to be here. Nobody was. Grandpa would completely blow a fuse if he knew.

As she got closer to Nimbus, Stella realised it wasn't just a pile of rocks. It was a cairn.

The joints between the stones were snug, like a jigsaw. The stones were mostly grey, except for the ones at the top, which were green and speckled. It looked almost like a sculpture. It would have been beautiful, if it weren't so strange.

She was tempted to reach out and touch it, but anxiety about the Haken still hummed in her blood.

*What if the Haken had made it?* Maybe that's what she was doing down here.

Stella curled her hands closed and put them behind her back. Maybe it was safe, but maybe it wasn't.

Nimbus circled the cairn, swinging round and round, in ever tighter circles.

"Can you stop doing that? You're making me dizzy," she said. "And I don't think we should touch it, so don't go any closer."

Nimbus stopped on the far side and Stella walked round to join him.

Tamar lay in a crumpled heap on the ground.

## Twenty-Two

# SEA WITCH

"TAMAR!" shouted Stella. She darted forward to crouch at her side. "Tamar!" she said again. *Is she dead?* Her mind whirled with the impossibility of it. *Tamar can't die. Tamar is magic. She's got to be okay.*

Stella touched Tamar's wrist, then snatched her hand back. Tamar's skin was damp and cold. The idea of touching a dead body made her stomach clench, even if it was someone she knew.

She put her hand close to Tamar's mouth.

There . . .

A breath.

A whisper of warmth on her hand.

Stella shook Tamar's shoulder. The old woman's head rocked from side to side, but her eyes didn't open.

"What's wrong with her?"

Nimbus floated closer, but didn't offer any answers.

"I think we should get her onto her side," instructed Stella. "I read about it in my walking guide – recovery position."

She pushed at Tamar's shoulder and her hip, but it was tricky.

There was something special you were meant to do with the person's arms to stop them getting in the way, but Stella couldn't work out what.

She stopped and looked along the beach. There was nobody here. Nobody who could help.

"She's too heavy," she said to Nimbus. "I can't even roll her over. What do we do?"

*Get Grandpa?* she wondered, then shook her head. He'd probably call the coastguard, or something. Tamar definitely wouldn't want that.

*No.*

"Wait, maybe you can help?" she said to Nimbus. "Can't you do some magic thing? If you can wake her up, I can help her home."

Nimbus contracted into a dense grey ball and edged away from them – he looked very unsure of himself.

"Please. Think!" said Stella. "Come on, you can do brain-fog

191

and hear thoughts. I know you can do this! Just imagine you're her alarm clock."

Nimbus hesitated, then drifted down until he was floating above Tamar's limp hand. Stella frowned. What was he planning?

*BZZZZT!*

A small blue spark shot out of the cloud and hit Tamar's arm.

"No!" shouted Stella.

"Ouch!" yelped Tamar and sat bolt upright.

There was seaweed in her hair and a pink imprint of pebbles on the side of her face.

"You're awake!" said Stella, in relief.

"Did you just zap me with your cloud?" asked Tamar, with a frown.

Stella eyed her, trying to work out if she was angry or just surprised.

"It was only a little spark," she said. "I couldn't wake you, so I got Nimbus to help. Are you alright?"

"Of course I'm alright. I was having a little nap," said Tamar. She clambered to her feet with a groan and stood there blinking.

Stella narrowed her eyes at Tamar. "You weren't napping," she said. "I'm not stupid, you know."

Tamar dusted herself down. "You'd need a nap, if you'd spent the night shifting rocks."

But Tamar couldn't have moved all those rocks. Not on her own. Why couldn't she just tell Stella the truth, for once?

"Stop lying!" she blurted out.

Tamar looked at her in surprise. "About what?"

"I don't know, do I?" snapped Stella. "That's the point! How am I meant to help, if I don't know what's going on?"

"You use your cloud, just like you did," said Tamar. "A little jolt was exactly what I needed. Now, let's get back, shall we? I could do with some food. Then maybe I'll start feeling human again."

She hobbled over to the boulders at the top of the beach, searched about for a moment, then turned round, holding her green bag. She looked up and down the empty beach. "Herb? Herbert! You can come out now."

A ragged grey tuft of cloud appeared from under one of the boulders.

"Good. All set then," said Tamar. "Off we go."

Stella folded her arms.

"No," she said. "You have to tell me what happened. I thought you were dead!"

"Oh, pish and twaddle. Dead indeed," said Tamar. She looked out at the sea. "I'm a tough old bird. It'll take more than one lousy sea witch to kill me."

Stella stared at her and Tamar stared right back.

"You asked," she said. She turned and walked away up the path with Herbert trailing behind her.

Stella looked out at the bay. Was it her imagination, or did the sea look darker than before?

The sea witch from *Shetland Myths and Magic* curled cold fingers around her heart. So many times, she'd woken up paddling backwards in bed, trying to escape those clutching white hands.

"Wait, a sea witch!" said Stella. "They're real?"

Tamar ignored her and kept walking. The trail up from the beach was too narrow for anything but single file, so Stella had to wait until they got to the top before she could ask anything else. At the top, they both paused to catch their breath.

"The Haken? The Haken is a sea witch?" she said. "There was a sea witch here? An actual sea witch—"

"There *is* a sea witch here," corrected Tamar, looking down at the beach. "She's not gone, more's the pity. Still, at least I stopped her from getting her hooks ashore."

"What happened?" said Stella. "Did you fight her?"

"Oh, nothing that impressive," said Tamar. "I built a few cairns to keep her off the beach. Seems to be working, for now."

"That was her? On the beach yesterday?" asked Stella.

The dark figure. The figure who had turned and looked right at her.

"I thought sea witches have to stay in water, that's what the stories say," she said.

*Shetland Myths and Magic* was pretty specific about that. It was how the selkies had won. They took the sea witch out of the sea. No sea; no magic.

A wary expression passed over Tamar's face and she glanced

away. For a moment she looked distinctly shifty. "That's why it was at the water's edge," she said.

"So why bother building cairns?" said Stella.

Tamar sighed. "Let's just say, the Haken is not your standard sea witch," she said. She rubbed her shoulder and grimaced.

"Are you hurt?" said Stella.

"No, no. I'm fine," said Tamar. "A bit worn out, that's all. There's nothing glamorous about moving rocks. Think I've pulled a muscle. But hey ho, we're weather weavers. That's part of our job."

"What do you mean, 'our job'?" said Stella.

"Well, my job," said Tamar, "Not yours. Not yet, anyway. As this island's weather weaver, one of my roles is to protect it – from sea witches, amongst other things."

Stella looked down at the sea below. The inky water seemed to stare back at her, willing her to come closer.

The waves whispered and hissed.

She tore her eyes away from it and found Tamar watching her.

"It's a lot to take in," said Tamar, with a sympathetic smile. "You were going to find out sooner or later though. Might as well be now. Do you need to sit down? You've gone a bit pale."

Stella shook her head. "No, I think I'd like to get further away first," she said.

Tamar nodded. "Probably wise."

## Twenty-Three

# SECRETS OF STONE

"WHAT did you mean by 'not your standard sea witch'?" asked Stella, as they approached the croft. "Is that worse, or better?"

Tamar glanced uneasily at the sea. "Different," she said. "Just different."

"Different how?" insisted Stella.

"Most true sea witches have little interest in land," said Tamar. "But the Haken's not 'most sea witches.' She's fixated on this island. It's an obsession for her."

"The cairns will keep her away though, right?"

"For now," said Tamar, with a sigh.

Stella felt a tickle of electricity in her hair. She glanced up. Nimbus was just above her head.

*Well done for waking Tamar up,* she thought. *You were great. I'm glad I've got you.*

Nimbus bobbed in response.

Was it odd to find that reassuring? How much had Stella changed in a few short days?

She followed Tamar and the two clouds into the croft. Tamar closed the door and bolted it, top and bottom.

*Not that a door is much use against a sea witch,* thought Stella.

Herb headed straight for the wooden blanket box and disappeared inside. Whatever he'd seen on the beach, he wasn't happy about it.

"Poor old thing," said Tamar. "He does an excellent cloud cover, but he's not much use against a sea witch – not a shred of gumption in him."

Stella flopped into a chair at the kitchen table.

*A sea witch.*

There was a real sea witch.

Here.

She felt a sudden wish to be very far away from the sea.

*Trouble is,* she thought, *on an island, nowhere is far from the sea.*

Nimbus circled the room twice and settled up in the far corner of the ceiling. *Like a puppy going to bed,* she thought, smiling. *At least one of us is relaxed . . .*

Her rucksack was still leaning against the table leg, where she'd left it. Stella got out the parcel of jam sandwiches Grandpa had made and unwrapped it.

Tamar's eyes lit up. "You brought food!" she said. "Good thinking." She took a sandwich.

Stella's mouth twitched. She'd been intending to eat it herself, but it was too late to say anything. Anyway, Tamar probably needed it. She picked up the other one, before Tamar could decide they were both for her.

"You didn't tell me you knew my gran," she said.

"Oh, is that what all the fuss was about?" said Tamar.

"No! It's because there's a sea witch and you weren't going to tell me."

"Of course I would have told you," said Tamar. "Just maybe not down on the beach!"

"Oh," said Stella and sank a bit lower in her chair.

Right now, she wished she didn't know.

"Did Gran know about the sea witch?" she said.

"Lizzie knew most things that went on round here," said Tamar.

"What about Grandpa?" said Stella

Tamar snorted. "Hardly."

*No wonder he felt left out,* thought Stella.

"You found my book, I see," said Tamar, running a finger down the rainbow page and pursing her lips.

*Uh-oh.*

The words were fading as the damp patches dried, but the pages were still crinkled, like it had been dropped in the bath.

"It got a bit of snow on it . . ." said Stella.

Tamar sighed. "For future reference, any magic-charged weather will unlock it," she said. "I usually opt for sunshine . . ."

"Sorry," said Stella, "We didn't know where you were. We thought it might give us a clue. It got stuck though, on green."

"That's next then," said Tamar. She snapped the book closed and strode over to the mantelpiece, munching her sandwich as she went. She picked up a small basket, brought it back to the table, and tipped out a pile of pebbles. They rattled across the table and one of them rolled off onto the floor. Tamar stooped to pick it up. "Given our unwelcome visitor," she said, "we need to get you prepared. So, secrets of stone . . ."

"Prepared for what?" said Stella. She bit her bottom lip.

"Prepared to defend yourself," said Tamar.

Stella stared at her. She'd guessed Tamar was going to say something like that, but hearing it out loud still made her stomach shrink.

"You do know I'm only eleven?" she said.

"The Haken won't care how old you are," said Tamar.

"Why would she even care about me at all?"

"You're a weather weaver," said Tamar. "She has a particular hatred for weather weavers. Besides which, you're not experienced yet, so she'll look to steal your cloud."

"What?!" yelped Stella.

Over in the corner, Nimbus jumped as though he'd been stung. He bounced off the ceiling and two of the walls before tumbling towards Stella. He hit the table, sprawled across the stones, and slid to a stop as he reached her.

*Sorry,* she thought. *I didn't mean to scare you.* She ran her hand through the cloud and soft curls of mist wrapped around her fingers.

Tamar began to rapidly arrange the stones in a circle on the table, setting each one down with a clunk. She sorted them by colour until there was almost a complete rainbow. "Right, are you ready? You've a natural talent for this, so I'm hoping you'll pick it up quickly."

*A natural talent.* The unexpected compliment glittered in Stella's chest. *You hear that, Nimbus?*

Nimbus rolled himself up into a ball and moved closer to her.

Tamar looked at the cloud, huddled against Stella's chest, and shook her head. "He might be a clumsy little thing," she said, "but he's remarkably powerful for such a young cloud, so I'm particularly keen that the Haken doesn't get him."

"Never mind that," said Stella. "Nimbus is mine! The Haken can't just take him."

"That's the spirit," said Tamar. "And that's why you need to be ready to fight."

*Me and my big mouth,* thought Stella and glanced down.

Nimbus looked very small inside the circle of her arms.

"Don't worry," she whispered. "I'm not going to let some evil old sea witch have you."

She set her jaw, looked at Tamar, and nodded. "So, what's the secret?" she said.

Tamar ran her finger around the circle until she came to a sparkling black stone. She picked it up between finger and thumb. "Stones are absorbent," she said.

*No, they're not,* thought Stella. But she kept her mouth shut and waited for Tamar to explain.

"Stones absorb all sorts of things," continued Tamar. She brandished the black pebble in the air, as if to underline each word. "Memories, emotions, sounds, magic; whatever they come into contact with. They're a hidden library of life."

Stella picked up a purple rectangle of slate and tried to picture it as a tiny book. "People used to write on slate," she said. "We learnt about it in school. In the olden days, they used slates instead of exercise books."

"Very true," said Tamar. "Humans share a long history with stone. They used it to build homes to keep them safe, roads to mark their journeys, and castles to proclaim their power. The stones have been listening all that time – saving up stories – so it's no wonder they get a bit leaky sometimes."

Stella put the slate down and picked up a white egg-shaped

stone. It was smooth and dry. It didn't feel leaky at all. She fitted it into the hollow of her palm.

"What do they leak?" she asked.

"Usually, it's what people call ghosts," said Tamar.

The hair on the nape of Stella's neck stood up, as though someone had run a cold finger along her spine.

"Ghosts?" she said, with a quiver in her voice.

"Yes. People call them ghosts, but it's actually stones leaking stories. Stones soak everything up, you see? Joy, hope, fear, fury, all of it. When they get too full, the stories start to leak out. It's frightening for people who don't understand, of course."

*First sea witches, now ghosts!* thought Stella. She'd never actually seen a ghost, but she could believe they existed.

She set the white stone carefully down on the table.

"You're alright with that one," noted Tamar. "That's a touchstone – highly absorbent. I'd keep it if I were you. Give it to your Grandpa. It'll help keep that temper of his in check, if the brain-fog doesn't hold."

Stella closed her mouth in a tight line. Tamar didn't know she'd de-fogged Grandpa.

Nimbus slid out of her arms and off the side of the table.

*Come back,* she thought. *Stop acting guilty.*

Nimbus crept up onto the far end of the table, as far away as he could get.

*Not telling her isn't the same as lying,* she thought. *And it's not like she doesn't keep secrets . . .*

Tamar hadn't noticed – she was too busy talking. "I don't want to give you the impression that leaky stones are always bad," she said. "Sometimes it's a beautiful thing. You can feel it in sacred spaces."

"What? Ghosts?" said Stella.

"No, prayers," said Tamar. "You can feel the silence; it's like a living thing. That's prayers, leaking out of the old stones. Hundreds of years of people coming to hope, or think, or pray. The stones absorb it all, until they're full to bursting. Then they start to leak a sense of peace. It's called sanctity . . . just don't go telling people that, alright? You'll get some funny looks if you do!"

Stella shook her head. She had no intention of telling anyone. It was bonkers. And yet, despite that, she could kind of believe it.

"But here's the key thing you need to know," said Tamar. "Apart from stories, stones leak magic. Did you spot those green stones in the cairns I built?"

Stella nodded.

"They're serpentine," said Tamar. "A superb sea-witch deterrent. Layered with magic and chock full of stories of the seas drying up, ocean beds rising to meet the sky. To a sea witch, they sound like a horror story." She pulled a ghoulish face and waved her fingers in the air.

Stella smiled uncertainly. She didn't much like the sound of stones full of horror stories.

"Anyway, that's enough of me prattling on," said Tamar. "Time for you to practise." She slung her green bag over her shoulder and unbolted the front door.

"Wait! What about the sea witch?" said Stella.

## Twenty-Four

# THE BROCH

THE sea witch loomed large in Stella's mind. It was bad enough when it was only a nightmare: the gut-lurching terror of waking, the sea witch's cold hands trying to pull her back beneath the surface of sleep. Now it was real.

And it was outside, waiting for her.

"We'll be safer where we're going, than staying here," said Tamar. "But we do need to get a move on."

Stella looked around for Nimbus. He was edging away along the wall. He looked about as keen to go outside as she did.

"Just to be on the safe side," said Tamar, "Nimbus can ride in here, until we get there." She opened her bag and held it out towards the cloud.

Nimbus scooted under the kitchen table.

"Oh, for goodness' sake," said Tamar. "There's not many clouds I'd let ride in my bag, you know! And it's only a precaution."

Stella leant down to look under the table. Nimbus sparkled with frost. He was pressed right up underneath the table top, where he'd be hardest to reach.

"Come out," she whispered. "We need to do this, to keep you safe."

She held out her hand, but Nimbus shrank away.

"What about if I carry the bag?" she said, quietly. "Would that make you feel better?"

Nimbus hesitated, then moved slowly towards her, extending a misty point to touch her hand.

"I'll keep you hidden," said Stella, "and we'll go to this safe place to practise. It'll be alright. You'll see. I promise – I'll look after you."

She stood up and held out her hand for the bag.

Tamar raised her eyebrows. "Talked some sense into him, have you?"

A little knot of defensiveness tightened in Stella's chest. Nimbus wasn't being difficult, he was just scared.

"I'm going to carry the bag," she said.

"Fine," said Tamar, handing it over. "Just get a move on." She peered out of the window. "It's all clear now, but there's no time to waste."

Stella held the bag open under the table. Nimbus hesitated for a moment, then poured into it like smoke. She waited until the last wispy tendrils had disappeared inside and then rolled the top closed and stood up.

"We're ready," she said.

"Good," said Tamar. "Off we go then."

Stella followed her outside.

It was very bright and clear. The sky was a smooth fish-belly grey.

*It should be easy to see the Haken coming,* she thought, but a doubt tiptoed into her mind. *Easy for the Haken to see us, too.* The bright clifftop suddenly felt very exposed. A cool breeze made Stella shiver. She put a protective arm around the bag.

"Where are we going?" she asked.

"The broch," said Tamar.

"What's that?"

"The safest place there is," said Tamar, the sparkle back in her eyes. "A fortress! Amazing place. Ancient stone. You're going to love it."

Stella gave Tamar a sideways look. "Are there ghosts there?" she said.

"Not ghosts," said Tamar. "Stone stories, remember? Yes, there are plenty of those. But you'll like them," she added. "They're *our* stories."

She turned away from the sea and headed along the grassy path towards the other side of the headland.

Stella began to notice every rock and pebble they passed. The boulders on the hillside didn't look ordinary any more. Each one seemed to be silently waiting, watching. Their stillness made even walking seem fast.

*I wonder how many people they've seen hurrying by,* she thought. *Probably hundreds. No, thousands.*

She couldn't imagine what it was like to be around for centuries. It made her brain ache to think about it.

Tamar finally stopped by a tall dry-stone wall. A series of larger rocks had been set into it and poked out like rough steps. "Up you go," she said, gesturing for Stella to go ahead.

Stella climbed over the wall. Its coarse beard of lichen was rough under her hands. Every stone was different; a patchwork of colours. They spoke of purple heather, green grass, brown rabbits and the grey sky above. She climbed down the other side and waited for Tamar.

"They've soaked up the island, haven't they?" she said, as Tamar's head appeared over the top.

Tamar gave a satisfied smile. "You noticed," she said.

Stella grinned briefly, but the sea witch swam back into her mind, making her shiver. "Are we nearly there yet?"

"Yes, not far now," said Tamar, pointing up the hill.

As they came over the ridge a few minutes later, Stella's mouth dropped open.

The broch stood on a curl of land that protruded a little way out into the sea; a gigantic stone tower, like a fat chimney stack. The walls were a tight mosaic of dark-grey stone. It was absolutely massive.

"It's huge!" said Stella.

"That it is," said Tamar. She sounded as proud as if she'd built it herself. "Three storeys high, if you care to measure things in houses. Been here since the iron age. Nobody knows who built it. Early Picts is what's generally agreed, but I prefer to think that it was built by the first weather weavers."

The great curve of stone radiated calm and safety.

A path of broken slate led down the hill. Stella followed Tamar towards the vast, still presence of the broch.

On the far side, nearest the sea, there was a small rectangular opening. A door.

"Can I go in?" she said.

"Of course you can," said Tamar. "That's why we're here."

Stella ducked under the great slab of the lintel stone. It wasn't just a doorway. It was a short tunnel, with iron rings set into the walls on either side.

She shuffled along it, wary of hitting her head. At the far end, she stood up and gazed around, opened-mouthed.

The heart of the broch.

It was a large circular room, its earth floor studded with slabs of stone. Stella had expected it to be dark, cave-like, but it wasn't.

It was bright. She looked up to see a circle of open sky high above.

"It's got no roof!" she said.

"Easier to call clouds in, with no roof," said Tamar, straightening up as she came inside.

"But I thought sea witches use weather, too?" said Stella.

Tamar nodded.

"So, she could send a storm in from the top?" said Stella.

Tamar gave her a patient smile. "This is a sanctuary," she reassured her. "A safe space. It sings the stories of every defeat the sea witches have ever suffered. The Haken won't bother us here."

Stella looked up at the sky. Sanctuary or not, she would have liked it better with a roof.

"Go on, have a look around," said Tamar. She pointed to a narrow opening in the far wall.

Stella hopped across the slabs on the floor, peered into the dark doorway, and smiled in delight.

A secret tunnel!

She hadn't realised the broch had two walls. In the narrow gap between them, steep stone steps curved up out of sight. The centre of each stone dipped in a smooth bowl.

*Stone stories,* she thought. *Thousands of footsteps. Enough to shape stone.*

She began to climb.

Gaps in the inner wall threw a dim light down the stairs. Stella peered through them as she passed, and each time she was higher than before. She began to feel quite dizzy from going round in circles, so when she got to the next gap, she sat on the narrow step and looked down at Tamar far below.

The bag at her side rumbled.

"Oops! Come on out," she said.

She pulled the bag onto her lap and unrolled the top. Nimbus burst out in an angry purple ball. Stella pulled a guilty face.

"I'm sorry! I forgot you were in there . . ." she said.

Nimbus crackled with sparks and shot sideways through the gap, into the centre of the broch.

"Sorry," she called after him.

Nimbus reappeared at the gap and gave a low grumble.

"I know," she said, "but you're out now." She grinned. "Let's explore!"

Nimbus disappeared straight up and Stella scrambled to her feet. "Hey! Not fair." She ran up the stairs, in awkward little steps.

Whoever built this place must have had tiny feet. Or really short legs. Maybe both. She giggled as she pictured grown-ups smaller than her. She'd be like a giant to them.

As she reached the top of the stairs, Stella gasped. "Oh!"

The whole coastline spread out before her. Soft rolling curves of purple and green and ahead, the wide sparkling blue of the sea.

"Take a look down here," echoed Tamar's voice, from the bottom of the broch. "You should be able to see it better from the top."

Stella peered over the inside wall and her stomach lurched. It was a long way down.

The floor of the broch was a distant circle below her, studded with stones.

"Can you see it?" said Tamar.

"There's a pattern," said Stella. "A spiral."

"A power spiral," said Tamar. "It directs the flow of magic from this." Tamar patted the stone at the centre of the spiral. "The sanctuary stone. It's super-saturated, constantly singing our victory stories. Sea witches can't stand it. Can you hear it?"

Stella listened. She couldn't hear it, exactly, but she could feel a warm hum deep inside her chest, like the harmony to a forgotten song.

Twenty-Five

# LIGHTNING AND
# DISASTER

"CHECK the sea while you're up there," called Tamar. "Tell me what you see."

Stella gazed out across the bay. It was strange to look down on it from so high up, even higher than the cliffs. It looked almost like a map. Patches of wind trembled across the surface. *Cat's paws*, she remembered, and smiled.

Dad would love it up here. In fact, he must have been here!

You couldn't grow up on the island and not know about this place.

*He probably stood right on this spot, like I am now.* The thought was as solid as sun-warmed stone.

Stella tried to look at the sea like Dad had taught her, with a sailor's eye. A dark smear of smooth water streaked the surface around the point on the far side of the bay. Currents, probably. Maybe the tide coming in. But a flash of movement there made her heart clench.

She squinted at the distant rocks. It was hard to tell, at this distance. It might be a seal? The stone song changed to a high-pitched whine that found its way inside her teeth and made her nerves feel tangled.

"Tamar . . ." she called.

"Anything to see?"

"Yes!"

Nimbus shot up out of the centre of the broch and stopped a few metres above her.

"Get down!" hissed Stella.

Nimbus dropped like a stone. He reappeared a moment later, slinking around the stone walkway, a coiled rope of mist.

"What do you see?" Tamar called up.

Stella leant over the inner wall to look down at her. The sheer drop made her insides clench, but at least she was expecting it this time.

"I think the Haken's back!" she said. Her voice curved around the broch and the ancient stones picked up the echo. *The Haken's back, Haken's back, Haken's back...*

There was a sudden rattle as Tamar dropped something down below. "Down here," she said. "Both of you! Right now. And stay out of sight."

Stella dropped into a crouch and shuffled to the dark mouth of the stairs. Nimbus poured over the edge and disappeared into the gloom.

Stella risked one more peek over the wall. All across the bay the water sparkled and moved, ragged with whitecaps, but around the far headland a smooth patch of darkness was spreading across the water like an oil stain.

She ducked down and began to clamber down the steep stairs, her heart racing in her chest.

When she got back to the ground, Tamar seemed to be having a silent argument with herself. She was pacing back and forth, making angry cutting motions with her hand.

"Tamar?" said Stella.

"There you are," said Tamar, giving her a smile that was a little too wide. "Right, let's get started."

"What were you doing, just then?" said Stella.

"I was having a little discussion with my clouds," said Tamar. Her face twitched in a sudden frown, as though she'd heard something she disagreed with. "It's all settled now, though. I've told them you're absolutely ready. Aren't you?"

Stella nodded nervously. *Ready for what?*

Tamar looked up. "You'll need to get that cloud under control though."

Stella looked up the curved stone wall. High above them, Nimbus was spinning around the top edge of the broch in dizzying circles, like some sort of demented pinball.

*Nimbus! Please,* thought Stella. *This is serious now.* She took a deep breath and mentally beckoned her cloud.

Nimbus darkened slightly, then spiralled slowly down the centre of the broch, coming to rest in a soft heap on the central stone. He looked distinctly grumpy.

"Get off that! You don't sit on sanctuary stones," said Tamar, sounding scandalised.

Nimbus drifted off the stone, but instead of coming to Stella, he floated over to the far side of the broch.

Stella's heart fluttered with nerves. Nimbus didn't look in the mood to take instructions. Maybe he was unsettled by the sea witch? Either that or he was still cross about being left in the bag. It wasn't a promising start.

"Shall we?" said Tamar, raising her eyebrows.

Stella threw a doubtful look at Nimbus, but nodded anyway.

"Righteous anger," said Tamar. "We're going to tap into your rage."

Stella shook her head and kept shaking it. She knew exactly what rage was for.

"No way," she said. "I'm not doing that again."

"Lightning isn't something to be afraid of," said Tamar. "I know it didn't go so well the first time, but that's only because you weren't expecting it."

*Didn't go so well!* thought Stella. *Grandpa might put that another way.* She bit her lip and gave Nimbus an anxious look.

"Where was the Haken, when you saw her?" said Tamar.

"On the rocks off the headland," mumbled Stella. "I think it was her, anyway. I mean, it could have been a seal."

"What did the stones tell you?" said Tamar.

Stella sucked her teeth. They were still aching from the sound.

"There we are then," said Tamar.

"But you'll protect us," said Stella. "It's your job – that's what you said. And you've got loads of clouds."

Tamar winced slightly and looked away.

Nausea crept into the back of Stella's throat.

Tamar bent and peered out of the entrance of the broch. "I was planning to whisk them all in when we got here, but they're having trouble getting back. Wrong side of a storm front, or some such nonsense. We're going to have words later!" She shook her head in annoyance. "They'll make their way here as soon as they can, but until they arrive . . ."

Stella swallowed and stared at Tamar. "But the Haken is already . . ." She pointed at the door. "And I can't, I *definitely* can't—"

"Shush, shush, just listen," said Tamar, holding up her hands to calm Stella's outburst. "You'd need to learn it sooner or later, and most likely you won't need it. But I need you to try. I'm *certain* you can do it. It's just a question of controlling your fury."

Stella could still picture the moment when the lightning hit Grandpa. It was sickening. Violent. She didn't want to do it again. Not on purpose. Not even to a sea witch.

"I'm not really feeling cross at the moment," she said.

Tamar narrowed her eyes. "We'll soon fix that . . ." She nodded towards Nimbus, nosing around the shadowy nooks on the far side of the broch. "The Haken has got her eyes on your little cloud."

Indignation sparked inside Stella's chest. "She can't have him," she said.

Tamar gave a sly smile and a slight shrug. "What's to stop her taking Nimbus right now?"

"I won't let her," said Stella, squaring her shoulders.

Nimbus swerved towards her, as though she'd called him.

"Perfect. That's a good place to start," said Tamar. "Now I want you to channel that feeling into your cloud. He mustn't let it out, just hold on to it."

*Nimbus, can you do that?* thought Stella. *Please don't fire any lightning, just feel what I'm feeling.*

She thought of the sea witch trying to steal her cloud, and anger began to glow inside her like a hot coal. Beside her, Nimbus darkened like a bruise, swirling navy blue and purple.

"Perhaps send him a bit further away," said Tamar. "We don't want to be in the firing line if he accidentally lets a few sparks fly."

Stella's eyes widened. "Should we be doing this indoors?" she asked.

"We don't have a choice," said Tamar. "With any luck, the Haken doesn't know we're here. I'd like to keep it that way."

Stella took a deep breath and wiped her hands on her trousers. She stamped her feet to try and get the tremble out of her knees, then nodded at her cloud.

Nimbus drifted up the great stone tube of the broch until he was floating halfway up. He hung there like the shadow of a cannonball, heavy with threat.

"Next, we need to amp things up a bit," said Tamar. "You need to stay really focused while we do this, Stella. Concentrate on the feeling with your cloud. No flying off the handle, just a slow boil. A calm fury."

Stella nodded, keeping her eyes fixed on the dark seething surface of the cloud.

*No sea witch is going to steal you,* she thought. *I won't let her.*

Nimbus rumbled in agreement.

*You're MY cloud! And I'm your weather weaver,* she thought, with a sudden, fierce burst of love.

Nimbus paled until he shone like a golden harvest moon.

"No, no, no, no, no," said Tamar. "You're meant to be thinking angry thoughts, not happy ones. This is no time for joy! Even with the sanctuary song, the Haken has made it ashore. The cairns won't hold her off for ever."

The image of the sea witch swam into Stella's mind, sucking her courage away. Empty eyes, grasping hands, and the endless depths of the sea beneath her.

They couldn't fight that.

A flurry of snow puffed out of Nimbus and drifted down to the ground.

Tamar gave a small sigh and shook her head. "Shall I tell you what sea witches do to clouds?" she said. "That should stoke a little fury."

Stella's mouth twitched down at the corners. She didn't want to know. It was bound to be horrible.

Tamar began to pace slowly around the inner wall of the broch, her hands clasped behind her back. "Weather weavers," she said, "are chosen by their clouds. Not so, for sea witches. No cloud would choose a sea witch, but sea witches crave their power." She stopped pacing and looked up at Nimbus. "So, they trap them," she said. "Imprison them. In small sea caves so deep underwater that the clouds never see the sun. They keep them there until they are half mad."

Stella gaped at Tamar in horror. Nimbus had gone a bit mad after half an hour in a cosy bag. She couldn't imagine what he would feel like trapped in a cave, down in the cold blue darkness. At the thought of it, she shivered and Nimbus shuddered in the air.

"When they're finally let out," continued Tamar, "the clouds are broken. So desperate for the sky, they'll do anything the sea witch demands. Anything to avoid being dragged back down to the darkness."

Stella's eyes filled with hot tears and she blinked hard.

"Do you want that to happen to Nimbus?" said Tamar.

Stella shook her head. "No," she said, through gritted teeth.

"Are you going to let that sea witch steal your cloud?" said Tamar.

"NEVER!" yelled Stella.

Nimbus ignited with a flash that lit the stone walls white and made Stella jump. She squinted at the cloud, blinking at the brightness. He shone like a star, bright with arcs of blue and purple sparks.

"Good," said Tamar. "That's perfect. Hold that thought."

Stella stared up at Nimbus, her heart burning with fury for the poor trapped clouds.

*The Haken is evil!* she thought. *Torturing clouds. Making them into slaves.*

A fierce hum echoed her thought. It swarmed through the air like wasps.

"Steady," said Tamar. "Cold fury."

*We'll stop her,* thought Stella, clenching her fists. *There's no way she's taking you! If she tries, we'll blast her back into the sea.*

Bright sparks began to shower down from the shining cloud.

"Rats," said Tamar. "It's too much."

"Oh no," breathed Stella. "No, Nimbus! Stop!"

Tamar grabbed Stella's arm and yanked her backwards.

A jagged streak of lightning stabbed down and struck stone. A crash tore through the air and thundered around the stone walls, shatteringly loud. The sound was battering at her, grinding and rumbling until her skull felt too tight for her brain.

When the noise died away, it left a needle-thin whistle, a mosquito whine.

Stella stuck her fingers in her ears, but it didn't stop.

It was inside her head.

Tamar rushed over to the stone in the middle of the broch. When she looked up, her eyes were full of shock. Her mouth stretched wide around urgent words, but Stella couldn't hear them.

*I've gone deaf,* she thought.

She saw something move on the far side of the broch, a faint tremble of mist, falling down the stone wall.

*Nimbus.*

The light in the broch dimmed and Stella looked up.

A bird. It was just a bird, riding the wind in the open circle of sky.

Not a sea witch. Not yet.

*But I bet she knows where we are, now,* Stella thought, with a chill.

She walked over to Tamar and stared in shock.

The sanctuary stone had shattered.

Fine cracks radiated out like a dark star from its blackened centre.

She began to hear Tamar's voice, but it was like listening underwater. The words boomed and whooshed, soft-edged in her ringing ears. Stella pointed at her ears and shook her head at Tamar.

"I can't hear you . . ." she mouthed – or maybe she shouted, she wasn't sure.

Tamar frowned and nodded. She gestured at the skulking mist that now surrounded the sanctuary stone, then turned and marched towards the entrance of the broch.

*Come on, Nimbus,* thought Stella.

The pool of mist rippled then subsided. She knew how he felt, but now was not the right moment to sink into a puddle.

*Please,* she thought. *We've got to go.*

"Are you two coming or what?" shouted Tamar from the doorway. The words were still blurred around the edges, but loud.

"My hearing's coming back!" said Stella.

"Thanks be for small mercies," said Tamar. "Now, move!"

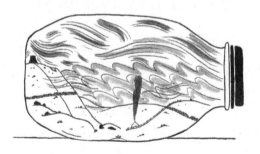

## Twenty-Six

# A GATHERING STORM

OUTSIDE, a sharp wind blew and the sea was flecked with foam.

"Tamar?" called Stella. "Where are we going?"

"To fetch my weather. We'll bring it back here."

"But the Haken's coming here!"

"If we hurry, we'll make it back first. It pains her to be out of the water, so that's on our side. Even without the stone, this is the easiest place to defend."

"Without the stone?" said Stella. "It's not working any more?"

Tamar shook her head. "Didn't you see?" she said. "It broke. Honestly, of all the things you could have hit in there . . ."

Stella suddenly felt too heavy to stand. She swallowed hard.

*I broke it.*

"It's not keeping us safe any more?" she said, in a wobbly voice.

Tamar hooked her arm through Stella's and hustled her along. "Why do you think we're in such a hurry?" she said. "The stone song was keeping the Haken away. No stone, no sanctuary. She'll raise the storm to end all storms, if I don't stop her."

A cold line of fear trickled down Stella's neck. "You can stop her though, right?" she said.

Tamar's jaw clenched. "I hope so."

*The storm to end all storms.*

Stella looked out towards the point of the bay. She couldn't see the Haken any more, but the weather had changed. The wind carried the grey smell of rain and, behind the green of the headland, the sky was the colour of iron.

She picked up her feet and crunched along next to Tamar, up the slate path, away from the sea. As she scrambled over the steps set into the old wall, Stella shook her head. "All stones have stories in them. That's what you said. Even pebbles. So why's it not working?"

Tamar let out a short puff. "The stone needs to be whole to sing," she said, as though explaining something very obvious. "Otherwise it's nothing more than whisper and rumour. No use at all." She turned away and beckoned for Stella to follow. "I'll explain later."

*There might not be a later!* thought Stella.

She jumped off the bottom step and glanced back to make sure Nimbus was close behind.

*We have to do something,* she thought. *We need to mend it somehow.*

Nimbus drifted closer and wrapped himself around her shoulders.

"We'll think of something," she murmured to him. "Don't worry. Whatever happens, I'm not letting the sea witch take you."

She glanced out to sea and her heart fizzed with fear. Far out, the horizon had vanished into shadow – the water and the sky bled together in a long dark stain.

"Tamar, look," said Stella.

Tamar's face turned a strange colour. "She'll drown the land to come ashore," she muttered.

"What?!"

"You heard me," said Tamar. "Now, hurry! We need that weather."

*Drown the island. Drown all of us!*

"I've got to warn Grandpa!" said Stella.

Tamar gritted her teeth, as though battling not to say something, then she took a deep breath and let it out.

"You're right," she said, finally. "This isn't your fight. Has your grandpa got a cellar? A storm shelter? Anything like that?"

Stella shook her head. "I don't know. I don't think so."

"Ask him," said Tamar. "He's weathered winters here. He'll know what to do. If nothing else, tell him to put his storm shutters up and you can wait it out. If it gets really bad, head for high ground."

Tamar touched Stella's arm. It felt like goodbye.

"What about you?" said Stella. "What if you don't . . . What if you can't . . ."

Tamar's mouth was set in a hard line.

"I didn't mean . . ." said Stella. "But without the sanctuary stone?"

"I've never lost yet," said Tamar.

The words were the same as always, but her voice was as tight as piano wire.

Stella looked out at the distant storm clouds. The dark underbelly of the storm flickered and glowed with lightning.

"Look after your cloud," said Tamar, "and your grandpa. That's your job now." She pushed Stella's shoulder to get her moving.

Stella hesitated, but a boom of distant thunder made her mind up. First, she needed to tell Grandpa. Then, she could worry about everything else. She gave Tamar a swift nod and set off down the hill.

The wind was stronger now, surging in from the sea like a turning tide. There were no birds in the sky.

*They're all hiding*, thought Stella. *They know what's coming.*

Nimbus scudded along ahead of her. Every few metres, he bounced sideways, buffeted by gusts of wind.

She picked up the pace until she was running, her breath sharp in her throat. Did Grandpa even have a cellar? Stella didn't think so.

At last, she saw the house. Grandpa was out the back, hammer in hand, fixing the roof on the chicken coop.

"Grandpa!" she called. He straightened up and waved.

"I was starting to worry," said Grandpa, as she ran up to him. He sniffed the breeze. "The weather's on the turn."

Stella doubled over to catch her breath.

"What is it? What's wrong? Are you hurt?" said Grandpa.

"No. No," she said, shaking her head and straightening up. "Out of puff. Inside. Let's go inside. Have you got a, you know, like, shutter things—"

"Slow down," said Grandpa. "Tell me what's going on. What's got you in such a fluster?"

But Stella wasn't listening. She was looking at the toolbox by his feet. She took a deep breath and swallowed.

"Grandpa?" she said. "You know about fixing things, don't you?"

He gave a curious frown and nodded.

"Do you know how to fix stone?" said Stella.

Twenty-Seven

# GRANDPA HELPS

"I KNOW a fair amount," said Grandpa. "Why?"

Stella hesitated. If she told him, it would mean admitting she hadn't been careful at all. But he might be the only one who could fix it.

"Come on, spit it out lass," said Grandpa.

"There's this stone, down in the broch. It's really important for weather magic. It keeps the island safe, from storms. And it's broken . . ." she said.

"From storms?" he said, and his eyes widened. "From storms?"

He stabbed a finger towards the dark smear of clouds on the horizon. "Tell me the truth, Stella! What did you do?"

"I didn't make that storm!" she said. "It's not me, I promise! There's other people who do weather magic too, you know. I've just got one little cloud. That's all."

Nimbus sank down beside her and made himself pale and fluffy. He was starting to get the hang of looking, if not ordinary, at least unthreatening.

Grandpa looked down at the cloud floating like a lamb at her side and shook his head. "You can understand why I might have thought—"

"Please, Grandpa. We have to go and mend the stone!"

"Can't Tamar sort it out?" said Grandpa. "Why is it your problem?"

Stella looked back in the direction of the broch and winced.

"The thing is," she said, "I broke it."

Grandpa's eyebrows shot up, and he gave her and Nimbus a long look.

"You're getting a bit of a track record with breaking things," he said, finally.

Stella ran a hand through the top of her cloud and looked at her feet.

"I'm not sure I'll ever get used to that," said Grandpa, with a smile in his voice.

Stella looked up.

His eyes were twinkling. He looked so much like the old Grandpa that she almost wanted to hug him.

"Grandpa, can you help? Please?" she said. "It's really important."

Grandpa gave a rueful smile. "I can hardly say no to that, can I?" he said.

Stella's eyes lit up and Nimbus turned a small somersault next to her.

"Just tell me this isn't your gran's storm we're talking about," said Grandpa.

Stella swallowed hard and looked out at the dark horizon.

"Oh, good lord!" said Grandpa, and his face paled. "If there's even a chance of that, we should stay indoors. Hunker down. Wait for it to blow over."

"But it won't," said Stella. "Not until we fix the stone."

The wind was getting stronger by the minute and there was no hint of joy in it. It felt full of spite – hissing through the grass, whipping Stella's hair into her eyes, rattling the newly fixed roof of the chicken coop.

Grandpa looked out to sea. There was worry written deep in every line of his face. "You're sure about this?" he said.

Stella nodded. "It's the only way."

"If you knew how much you sound like your gran," said Grandpa, and shook his head.

"Please?" said Stella.

Grandpa tucked his shirt into his trousers, picked up his

toolbox and glared at the horizon. He looked like he was readying himself for battle.

When he turned back to Stella, there was a bright determination in his eyes. "Okay. Let's figure out what we need."

Stella took a deep breath. It was going to be alright! Grandpa could fix it.

* * *

Grandpa didn't immediately object when Nimbus followed them inside, though he watched the cloud warily until it had settled on top of the dresser.

"So," said Grandpa. "What kind of stone are we dealing with?"

"Er, a grey one?" replied Stella.

Grandpa's eyebrows pinched together. "I'll need more than that," he said. "Otherwise I won't know what to bring."

*Uh-oh.* Maybe this wasn't going to be simple after all.

Grandpa blinked at her and put his tool box down on the kitchen table. "How big is it, then?" he said, gesturing with his hands. "What shape?"

"About this big," said Stella, holding her arms out in a circle. "It's flat. It's on the ground."

Grandpa nodded. "Well, that's good. If it were round, like a boulder, we'd struggle. Flat on the ground is promising. How is it broken? Chipped? Crumbled? Split?"

"I don't know!" said Stella. "Into lots of pieces."

"Into pieces," said Grandpa. He twisted his lips. "We'll have to hope the rain holds off then. Mortar and water don't make a good mix." He fished about in one of the kitchen drawers and pulled out a pair of work gloves. "I'll grab some things from the shed. I dare say we should bring water, too. I doubt we'll find a tap at the broch. They weren't much for plumbing in those days." He smiled at his own joke. "In the meantime, you can get yourself some lunch."

"There's not time!" said Stella.

Grandpa's expression grew stern. "There's *always* time for food," he said. "Can't work on an empty stomach." He opened the front door, letting in a gust of cold air. "Bring it with you, if you like," he conceded, then went outside, closing the door firmly.

Stella hurriedly grabbed a random selection of things from the cupboard and stuffed them into Grandpa's satchel.

When she and Nimbus went outside, the weather's mood had darkened even more. The sky was steel grey, heavy with threat. The wind rushed inland in hurried gusts.

The shed door banged open on its hinges and Grandpa appeared. He was carrying a tarpaulin and two large bags.

"Sharp sand and black rock," he said, putting them into the wheelbarrow. "Wait there." He disappeared back into the shed and reappeared with a sack. "Lime," he said. "Don't touch this. It's nasty."

Stella took a step away from the wheelbarrow.

"Oh, *now* you're cautious," said Grandpa. "Why did you think I didn't want you in my shed, before?"

"Because you didn't want me messing with your tools?" said Stella.

"Well, that too," said Grandpa. "But no, it's because that's where I keep all the nasties – lime, weed killer, rat poison . . ."

"Oh."

*He wasn't angry, before,* she realised. *He was worried. Worried about keeping me safe.*

It was like a little chink of brightness, which painted all Grandpa's bad moods in a different light.

Grandpa bolted the shed door against the wind, then lifted a jerry can into the wheelbarrow with a clang. "Right. All set," he said.

Stella felt a cold dot of water on her cheek. As she looked up, the rain began to fall.

*Cloud cover, Nimbus,* she thought.

The little cloud shivered into an umbrella above them and Grandpa looked up in surprise.

"That's a neat trick!" he said. "Could do with one of these clouds myself!"

"We need to hurry," said Stella. "It's going to get worse."

Grandpa lifted the handles of the wheelbarrow. "Lead the way!" he said.

By the time they got to the broch, the rain was hard and steady, drumming against the cloud cover and puddling on the earth floor.

"Not ideal, this rain," said Grandpa. "Still, at least it's not cold. You'll never get lime to set in the cold."

Stella looked up at the circle of sky above them. She hoped the Haken couldn't hear him – she could probably make it cold in a heartbeat.

Grandpa crouched to look at the sanctuary stone. He raised his eyebrows at Stella when he saw how it was broken, but he didn't ask. He just pulled on a heavy pair of work gloves and set about mixing a mortar.

Stella watched, with a warm swell of gratitude.

"Stand well back," he said. "I don't want you anywhere near this. Lime is caustic. You don't want it on your skin and don't even get me started on what it'll do to your eyes."

Stella backed away until she could hear the rain thrumming against the dome of cloud cover. She pictured the Haken moving closer and her stomach clenched.

*This has got to work,* she thought.

"You can eat while you're waiting," he said. "This'll take a little while."

Stella made a pretence of looking in the satchel, but she wasn't hungry at all – her stomach was in knots.

Grandpa began to wedge the mixture into the cracks, finishing each line with a long scrape of his trowel. He worked with a smooth, sure motion.

At last, he sat back on his heels. "That's the best I can do," he said. "You're lucky it's more of a slab than a boulder. I've used a nice black rock for the mix, should hold together fine, as long as you don't plan on moving it?"

Stella shook her head and looked up at the cloud cover. The rain still hammered down against it. If anything, it seemed to be raining harder than before.

She closed her eyes, but she couldn't feel the warm hum of the stone's song. Maybe the mortar needed to set first?

Stella opened her eyes again and gave a small smile. "Thanks Grandpa," she said.

Grandpa washed his tools with the last of the water and then stood up. "Come on then," he said. "Let's get home."

Stella shook her head. "I need to stay here, with Nimbus," she said, "to keep it dry."

Grandpa frowned and shook his head. "I'll cover it up," he said. "Lime mortar takes ages to go off. Hours. Sometimes days. You can't stay here and wait for it!"

"It'll stop raining soon," she said, looking up at the smear of sky. "We've fixed the stone now, so it should do."

Grandpa pushed a hand through the cloud cover and drew it back in again, dripping wet. "It's not showing signs of stopping," he said.

"Stella? Is that you in there?" Tamar's voice was indistinct through the drumming of the rain.

"Yes, it's me," called Stella.

Tamar appeared through the edge of the cloud. Her hair hung in dripping hanks and her clothes stuck to her. She glared at Grandpa.

"What's *he* doing here?" she said.

"I came to help my granddaughter mend this stone here," said Grandpa, drawing himself up to his full height.

Tamar rolled her eyes. "With what, exactly? Cement? This isn't just any old stone, you know," she said.

Grandpa pulled his chin in. "Cement? You won't catch me using cement. I used a good lime mortar," he said, obviously offended.

Stella went over and stood next to Grandpa. He didn't deserve Tamar being rude to him. He'd come out here to help, just because she'd asked him to.

"I asked him to mend it," she said to Tamar. "Grandpa knows lots about stone. Anyway, why are you all wet?"

"I'm conserving my cloud's energy," said Tamar. "You should do the same. Call off that cloud cover."

"Wait!" said Grandpa. "The mortar hasn't had a chance to go off yet. Let me get the tarp over it first."

"Why have you dragged him along?" said Tamar to Stella. "He knows nothing about this. Nothing!"

"I know you've created a whole mess of trouble and it somehow involves my grand-daughter," growled Grandpa. "So, unless you're a stonemason by trade—"

"Mortar might hold it in one piece, but it won't restore the magic!" said Tamar. "Besides, she'll need her cloud at full power for the battle."

"Battle?!" said Grandpa. "If there's going to be some sort of battle, I don't want Stella anywhere near it!"

Tamar's face was full of impatience, but with her wet clothes stuck to her, she looked bedraggled and frail.

*She can't do this on her own,* thought Stella.

Grandpa put his arm around Stella's shoulders. "Come on, Stella," he said. "We're leaving."

Stella stiffened, resisting the gentle push of his arm. Tamar could have said it in a nicer way, but she was right. Grandpa didn't belong here. He didn't understand what was going on. And even if he wanted to, he couldn't protect her. Not against a sea witch.

She put her hand over Grandpa's gnarled fingers. "Grandpa, I've got to stay," she said. She turned to look him full in the face. "Gran was right. She was always right. I have to help Tamar stop this storm."

Grandpa looked down at her, and frowned. He scowled at Tamar in silence for a moment, then let out a breath. "Then I'm staying too," he said.

"Grandpa, you can't," said Stella. "There's so much you don't . . . I can't even explain."

Tamar shook her head. "Ugh!" she said. "It's simple. Broken sanctuary stone," she said, stabbing a finger at the stone. "Evil sea witch," she said, gesturing to the door. "Imminent storm battle! There we are, all caught up!"

*Typical Tamar* . . . thought Stella. That wasn't how she would have explained it.

Grandpa looked from Tamar to Stella, and back again. She saw him realise that Tamar was serious. The weight of it settled on his shoulders. There wasn't anything she could say to make it better. At last, he frowned, and gave a short nod.

"I might not know much about magic, but I'll do what I can to help," he said, and gave Stella a small, determined smile.

The real Grandpa was back, she realised with a burst of joy.

On an impulse, she wrapped her arms around him. His jumper smelt exactly like she remembered – wood smoke and wet wool. He wrapped a big arm around her back and Stella leant into him. It felt like being home.

"Right, well, I'm glad you two are getting along now," said Tamar, "but we've got work to do."

Stella gave Grandpa a last squeeze and let go.

"What do we need to do?" she said.

"First of all, get that cloud down," said Tamar. "I'd like him tucked safely away in some cosy corner, out of harm's way."

*Corner?* Stella looked around the circular room and raised her eyebrows at Tamar.

"Oh, you know what I mean. Tell him to hide," said Tamar. "And you!" she said to Grandpa. "Was that your wheelbarrow I saw outside?"

## Twenty-Eight

# LIQUID MAGIC

STELLA looked up at Nimbus. "You've done a brilliant cloud cover," she said, "but Tamar says you need to rest now and stay out of sight."

Nimbus, stubborn as ever, stayed where he was.

The percussive beat of the rain was loud against the thin membrane of magic. Nimbus was almost transparent, stretched taut as a drum skin.

"I know you want to keep trying," she said, "but you heard what Tamar said."

She ran her hand down the cloud cover. It tingled under her fingertips.

"Sticking the stone together hasn't fixed it," she said. "The song has gone."

The rain beat faster against the cloud, as though it sensed weakness.

Nimbus still didn't move and Stella gave him a small sad smile. "We'll keep trying. I'll think of something, I promise," she said. "But you need to be strong, for when the Haken comes."

The edges of the cloud cover began to lift. Bouncing raindrops splattered her ankles, then the rain poured in, soaking cold through her clothes and plastering her hair to her head. Stella blinked water out of her eyes and looked at the little cloud floating above the sanctuary stone.

"Go and hide," she said. "Go on."

Nimbus hesitated for a moment, then poured himself into a hole in the wall and disappeared with a flourish of mist.

Stella stood and watched, shoulders hunched, as the heavy rain began to throw spurts of mucky water from the soft mortar.

*We tried,* she thought.

"Chin up," said Tamar, from the doorway. "We're not beaten yet."

Stella looked up. "Where's Grandpa?" she asked.

"I sent him back to mine, for more weather jars," said Tamar. "He might turn out to be useful, after all. Could have done with a wheelbarrow, for this lot." She set a large wooden box on the floor. The contents jangled as she put it down.

"You sent him outside!" said Stella. "What about the sea witch? And the storm!"

"Stop worrying," said Tamar. "Herbert has gone along to keep an eye out. The Haken's not interested in your grandpa anyway. Besides, you were the one who brought him."

Stella's heart pinched with guilt. If Grandpa got hurt, it would be her fault. Again.

Tamar began to lift jars out of the crate. "I've got the basics here," she said, "but without the sanctuary stone to help, we'll probably need more than usual."

Stella looked at the sanctuary stone. "I was so sure he could fix it," she said.

"You had the right idea," said Tamar. "Trouble is, mortar's got no stories in it. It's the same as a break in the stone. The magic only works when it's all one piece, all singing the same story."

"What about the sand?" said Stella. "Grandpa said he used black rock. Doesn't that have stories in it?"

Tamar gave her a sympathetic look. "Too many stories," she said. "All of them different. The stone was like a choir before, all singing in harmony. Sand is more like standing in a crowded room, with everyone talking at once."

*I was right then,* thought Stella. *I could hear it singing, before.*

"I've only ever known one sanctuary stone that was mended,"

said Tamar, her eyes suddenly distant. "Beautiful thing it was. You could still see the cracks, but somehow it still sang."

A tiny spark of hope rekindled in Stella's heart. "How?" she said.

"Nobody knows," said Tamar, shaking her head. "It was too long ago. Mended with magic, they say, but the truth is, no one remembers."

Frustration twisted in Stella's chest. She looked up the broch to make sure Nimbus wasn't sparking, but the curved wall was dark and silent. Wherever he was, the little cloud was well hidden.

"Here, help me get this lot unpacked and in the right order," said Tamar.

Stella came over to the crate and picked out two jars. "'Hard Frost' and 'Sudden Thaw'," she said. "Where do these go?"

"Next to each other," said Tamar. "You use one and then the other, creates a wonderful confusion. We'll make a cold collection over there. Blizzard goes last in the line," she said, tapping the lid of a large blue one. "It's a weather of last resort."

Stella carried the two jars over to the far wall and set them down in the gap between *Freezing Fog* and *Blizzard*.

An idea was lurking at the back of her mind, but she couldn't get it to talk to her.

*Mended with magic,* thought Stella. *Nimbus! Come here a minute.*

A white mist squeezed itself out of the wall in thin worms, like toothpaste. The worms gathered together into a soft bulge of cloud that strained away from the wall. Stella thought for a moment

Nimbus was stuck, but then he popped free and flew across the floor.

"What are you doing out here?" said Tamar. "I thought she told you to hide?"

"Wait!" said Stella, "I've had an idea."

She scrunched her eyes shut and pictured exactly what she wanted, then opened them to see if Nimbus had understood.

He had.

Nimbus scooted over to the sanctuary stone. He compressed until he was a dense shining globe. Then, he began to drip. Silver spattered onto the broken stone. Stella nodded in excitement and ran over to watch.

The drips came faster and faster, until they became a thin stream, dribbling out of the cloud and onto the stone. The magic poured into the cracks like mercury.

With a start of recognition, Stella felt the low hum of the stone thrum to life. It was working!

Tamar came over, her arms full of jars, crouched down next to the stone and set the jars on the ground.

Nimbus faded as the magic ran out of him, until he was little more than a ghostly shadow in the air. The shining ball of magic shrank to the size of a marble and then dropped from the air, falling into place with a single high note, like the peal of a bell.

The cracks in the stone shone like the silver spokes of a wheel.

"Look," said Stella.

Tamar poked a finger down into one of the cracks and prodded at the line of magic in the bottom. "Solid. Who'd have thought it? Ingenious."

Stella shared a triumphant grin with Nimbus.

*I told you I'd think of something, didn't I?* she thought.

Tamar gave the stone a little pat and gathered up her jars again. "Right, suck it all up again, then come and give me a hand with the rest of these jars."

Stella's mouth dropped open. "What! But—"

"There's not enough!" said Tamar. "Can't you tell? I can barely hear it and I'm standing right here. It's certainly not going to drive a Haken away, so get your cloud charged up again, and come and help."

Stella closed her eyes. When she concentrated, she could definitely hear a soft hum, but Tamar was right. It was barely louder than a distant bumblebee. She scrunched her face up and willed it to get louder, but it didn't. She opened her eyes and gave Tamar a furious look.

"But don't you see? We've got to get more!" she said. "This is how we mend it! What if your cloud did it too?"

Tamar shook her head. "Herbert won't be able to do that."

"Why not?"

Tamar grimaced. "He's useless at learning new tricks. If you knew the number of times I'd tried to teach him raining on target . . ."

"I can tell him what to do!"

"No!" barked Tamar. "You can't!"

Stella took a step back.

Tamar shook her head in apology. "I don't mean I won't let you," she said, in a quieter voice. "I mean it's not possible. He's *my* cloud. We're linked, so he only listens to me. Same way Nimbus only listens to you. If I don't know how, if I don't have that feeling in my bones, he can't fix it!"

Stella could do something Tamar couldn't? Another time, that might have made her feel clever, but right now it just made her feel alone.

"If we get through this, the stone will need to be mended," said Tamar. "You can give me a lesson for a change! But we'll need a whole host of clouds to have enough magic, and right now, we don't."

Stella ran a finger down the line of silver in the bottom of one of the cracks. She could feel the song trapped inside it, bursting to get out.

"Come on, get that cloud of yours powered up again," said Tamar. "Keeping the pair of you safe, that should be your priority right now."

Stella took a deep breath. If the Haken was coming for them, she wanted Nimbus strong. Strong enough to fight.

*Nimbus?* she thought. *You know what to do.*

Beside her, the stone began to fizz and hiss as the magic boiled up out of it. Nimbus solidified in the air, slate grey, tight as a clenched fist.

"Ready?" she said, and Nimbus crackled in answer.

"We've got company," said Tamar, looking up at the sky.

Twenty-Nine

# TO CATCH A SPY

STELLA looked up. A small pale-grey cloud was nosing its way around the top edge of the broch. It looked a lot like Nimbus.

*Hello, little cloud,* she thought, but it didn't give any sign of having heard her.

She turned back to Tamar.

Tamar pulled a shimmering net out of her bag.

"Here, grab a hold of this," she said, flapping the edge of it towards Stella. "I need a hand to spread it out."

Stella took one side of the net. It clung to her hands like

cobwebs. She began to walk backwards, pulling it out of the bag. The net kept coming and coming, like some sort of conjuring trick.

"Lift it up, don't drag it," said Tamar. "It's a moonbeam blend, so it's easily snagged."

Stella reached the far wall and laid the net carefully on the floor, then walked round the edge of it to Tamar, wiping her hands on her top as she went.

"What's it for?" she said.

Tamar nodded meaningfully at the cloud that was beginning to meander its way down the inside wall. "That little pest there, that's the advance party – a spy. We need to stop it from reporting back," she said.

Stella looked up. The cloud poured itself through a gap in the wall and then popped out again further along. If it was a spy, it wasn't very good at it. It didn't seem to have noticed them at all. It looked more like it was exploring.

"The net won't hurt it, will it?" she said.

Tamar stopped straightening the net and fixed Stella with a firm look. "Listen," she said, "Haken-slaves are nothing like your cloud. They're not your friends. They're dangerous. You'd do well to remember that."

Stella pressed her lips together and looked up at the cloud. It was snuffling around in a spiral, just like Nimbus had this morning. It didn't look very dangerous. It didn't even look very interested in them. It had almost reached head height, but it was still just nosing around the wall.

Tamar edged towards the cloud with a determined look in her eye, holding the edge of the net in both hands.

The cloud was stitching its way through the wall, pouring itself into the gaps between the stones and reappearing a metre or so further on, each time a little closer to them.

Nimbus still floated above the sanctuary stone. He'd calmed to a light grey. Had he seen the other cloud? If so, he didn't seem worried.

As the Haken-cloud bulged out of the wall just in front of them, Tamar spun the net through the air. "Got you!" she grunted, pulling the edges of the net together.

The cloud flew desperately from side to side. It bulged in narrow quilted diamonds, as the net tightened against it.

Stella couldn't understand why the cloud didn't just flow through the gaps and float away, but it didn't. The net seemed to stick to it, trapping the cloud in a messy bundle and pulling it to the ground.

Tamar heaved a rock onto the edge of the net, pinning it down.

"Well, that's one safely out of the way," she said. "That was easy. Must be new. Maybe its first time out. I expect the worst ones are being held in reserve."

Stella took a step towards the agitated cloud. It crackled with white sparks.

"Watch out!" said Tamar. "Don't get too close. That'll hold it in place, but it'll still give you a nasty shock if you touch it. Help me move these weather jars further away. Don't want it getting any ideas." She gathered an armful of jars and carried them over to the sanctuary stone.

Stella waited until Tamar had moved away, then crouched down by the edge of the net.

"It's alright," she whispered. "We don't hurt clouds."

The sparks died down. The trapped cloud was listening to her.

"We'll let you go later," she said. "We just need to beat the Haken first."

She hoped that was true. Stella wasn't actually sure what Tamar had planned.

*I'll make it true,* she promised herself.

"Look alive," said Tamar. "Here come the rest of them."

Stella looked up. The top edge of the broch had disappeared under a black furry mould of cloud. It began to creep down the walls like the edge of night. The trapped cloud next to her shivered a sparkle of frost over the net and flattened itself on the floor.

She grabbed the nearest two jars and backed towards the centre of the broch, where Tamar and Nimbus waited.

"Here, this is for you," said Tamar. She was holding out a leather strap strung with glass bottles and vials. Tamar was wearing one already, like a belt. "Compressed winds. No need to whistle, just pop the top and out they fly."

Stella put down the jars and took the leather strap. She tried putting it round her waist, but it was far too big, so she slung it over one shoulder.

"I was hoping Herb would be back by now," said Tamar.

*And Grandpa!* thought Stella, with a sudden stab of worry.

"Let's hope Nimbus can cover both of us," said Tamar.

Stella nodded and took a deep breath to calm her nerves. It was time to fight. She hoped she'd remember everything. She understood now why Tamar had been so worried. These clouds looked evil. Poisonous.

*Cloud cover,* thought Stella. Nimbus spread smoothly into a shimmering dome above them in the nick of time. She jumped as hailstones hammered into the cloud cover above. It sounded like a washing machine full of pebbles.

Stella wanted to flinch away from the noise, but she didn't. Nimbus needed to know she trusted him. She moved closer to Tamar, though. At least he wouldn't have to stretch as far to cover them.

Tamar pulled the *gaa* glass out of her belt, squinted one eye closed and peered up the broch. "There you are. I see you. Vicious little beasties."

"What can you see?" said Stella.

"Take a look," said Tamar, handing Stella the little telescope. "I think we'll give Nimbus a swift dose of rainbows. Then we'll both be able to see what we're doing."

*How are rainbows going to help?* thought Stella.

She put the *gaa* glass up to her eye and looked up through the cloud cover. Six red suns glowed like monstrous eyes in the sky above them. Stella stared at them in horror. "What are *those*?"

"Clouds," said Tamar. "Haken-slaves. Very nasty ones, by the looks."

Stella took the *gaa* glass away from her eye.

Tamar was fumbling the lid off a jar of rainbows. She dropped the lid on the floor and began flinging handfuls of rainbow rings up towards the protective ceiling of cloud. They stuck, leaving little popped bubble circles on the surface. The cloud cover began to glow red.

"Stop! What are you doing to Nimbus?" exclaimed Stella.

"Just lending him a little rainbow," said Tamar. "It won't hurt him. Just turns the whole cloud cover into a giant *gaa* glass – so we can spot them coming, but keep our hands free."

Stella could see the Haken-slaves overhead now. The hail hammered against the cloud cover, a constant sharp rattle, making the air tremble and her ears ache.

"Keep your eye on just one of them," said Tamar. "They'll run out of hail soon. The moment there's a pause, we'll drop the cover and blast a couple out of the top."

One by one, Stella lifted the glass bottles hanging at her chest, trying to make out the labels in the dim red light: *Storm Gust, Arctic Blast, North-Sea Hoolie*.

"Any of them will do," said Tamar. "Just be sure Nimbus makes a hole in the cloud cover before you pop the cork."

Stella tucked the little telescope through a spare loop on the leather belt and pulled out the bottle labelled *Storm Gust*. She clutched it in trembling fingers.

*You ready, Nimbus?*

The hail was slowing. The constant clatter dropped to a rattle, then an erratic tapping.

"Now!" said Tamar.

Stella fixed her eyes on one of the glowing red clouds and pictured what she wanted. Nimbus split the cloud cover open like a burst balloon and she yanked out the stopper. A gust of wind screamed up out of the bottle.

"Cover up," said Tamar. Stella blinked and Nimbus swept a smooth sheet of cloud cover over their heads again. Now there were only four red suns shining above them. She slid another glass bottle out of the strap and looked at Tamar with wide eyes.

"Good shot," said Tamar, giving a sharp nod of approval.

The air filled with a fierce hiss. *Rain,* thought Stella.

It fell in a steady spray, bursting against the cloud cover above them and running down the sides. Rivulets of water began to snake under the edges of the cloud cover and pool in dark vermillion puddles on the ground. Soon, the ground had become a shallow lake, that lapped at the spiral of stones.

*They're trying to flood the broch,* she thought and then remembered the small cloud, still pinned to the floor under the net. Could clouds drown? She took a shaky breath and squinted through the cloud cover.

"Tamar, the other cloud! It's gone!" she said.

Tamar peered through the wall of cloud. "No, it's still there."

Stella stared at the little pile of shadow at the foot of the wall. "Why isn't it glowing then? Is it dead?"

Tamar shook her head. "No, it's fine. Just not as toxic as these ones up here. The rainbow shows truths and intentions, remember? It's not about to attack us, so it's not glowing."

Stella frowned. *Maybe it's not evil at all?*

"We're going to get a bit wet this time, but it can't be helped," said Tamar briskly. "Are you ready to go again?"

Stella threw a last worried glance at the captured cloud, then nodded and looked up. The red-glowing clouds were moving now, circling in a sinister dance.

"Now!" said Tamar.

Stella nodded and the cloud cover split. Water poured onto her face, blinding her, making it hard to breathe. She tried to pull the cork, but the wet glass was slick. The bottle slipped from her fingers and fell, bouncing off the stone with a sharp clink. It disappeared into the dark water with a splosh.

A wind screamed out of Tamar's bottle somewhere nearby. "Cover! Cover!" spluttered Tamar.

At a thought from Stella, the cloud cover slid back into place. She crouched and ran her hands through the muddy puddle at her feet, but she couldn't find the bottle. Stella straightened up, wiping her hands on her thighs. "Sorry," she said. "I dropped mine. It was slippery." She hung her head.

"Don't worry," said Tamar. "Easy mistake to make. You'll get the hang of it."

Stella gave Tamar a half smile.

"A proper deluge, that was," said Tamar. "They're really putting on a show for us. How are you holding up?"

Stella wiped her face on her sleeve and gave Tamar a determined smile. "I'm alright," she said. "Wet, but alright."

"How about your cloud? Not tired yet?" said Tamar.

Stella looked up and her face tightened in worry. Above their heads, the cloud cover was smooth and firm, but at the edges, she could see dappled patches of mist. They looked thinner than the rest.

Above her, the Haken's clouds burned a violent scarlet, as bright as branding irons. She didn't want to face them without the cloud cover.

But how long could Nimbus keep this up?

## Thirty

# A BREAK IN THE WEATHER

"AHOY in there!" Grandpa's shout was hard to hear against the constant hissing of the rain.

"Grandpa!" called Stella. "Quick! Come inside!"

A lumpen blue form appeared through the side of the cloud cover. Grandpa's smile beamed, under the broad brim of his oilskin hat.

"You took your time," said Tamar. "Did you get the weather?"

"Caught a fair amount of weather on the way back, yes," said Grandpa. "But you'll be talking about these, I imagine?" He reached back through the cloud cover and dragged the wheelbarrow through the curtain of cloud.

Tamar hurried over and began to check the labels. "Dawn Mist? Useless. Light Dew. Oh, grief!" she moaned. "I should have gone myself."

"Why are you all wet?" said Stella. "I thought Tamar's cloud went with you?"

"It obviously decided I could look after myself. It's fine. I've got a perfectly good oilskin," he said, tugging at his raincoat.

"Stop lazing about and get yourself up now," said Tamar. "Can't you see this poor cloud is struggling?" Grandpa turned and looked at her in surprise, but she wasn't talking to him. "Cloud cover. Now!" she said. The misty dome around them thickened and paled, as Herb joined Nimbus.

"You're not dressed for this weather at all," said Grandpa, casting a disapproving glance at Stella's sodden clothes.

"It's not ordinary weather!" said Stella.

"Well, lucky for you, I grabbed some spare rain gear and towels too. Here, get yourself dry. You'll catch your death otherwise."

He threw a towel to Stella. She put it cautiously to her face, but it was just an ordinary, scratchy old towel. One of Grandpa's. He must have stopped off at home. She set the bottled winds gently on a stone and peeled off her sodden cardigan. Grandpa handed her a crew-neck sweater and a bright yellow raincoat. They were big on her, but once she rolled up the sleeves, they were okay.

"Now you look the part," said Grandpa. "That was your Gran's sailing gear. You can hang on to it. She'd have liked that."

Stella pulled up the hood. It felt for a moment like Gran was here too, wrapping her up warm. Protecting her from the storm. She picked up the belt of bottled winds and slung them in a jingling diagonal line across her chest.

*Now we're ready,* she thought, looking up at the dim circle of sky above.

"Enough chin-wagging," said Tamar. "We've got work to do."

She hurled another handful of rainbows up into the pale-grey cloud cover and it simmered down to dark red again. Three scalding spots of red ignited in the centre of broch above them.

"What the devil are those?" said Grandpa, knitting his eyebrows together.

"Evil clouds," said Stella, with a smirk. "They've been trying to get us, but we're winning."

Grandpa looked very unsettled by the explanation. He scowled at the glowing clouds and then turned a worried look on Stella.

"It's alright," said Stella quickly. "We blasted some of them out of the top, so now there are only three."

"Only three?" muttered Tamar. "If only . . ."

"How many, then?" blurted out Grandpa, before Stella could ask.

"Lots," said Tamar. "There are three here inside, but they're only the advance party. I would estimate she's brought two, maybe three hundred more."

Stella's mouth dropped open. "Two? Two, or three . . ."

"Hundred," said Tamar.

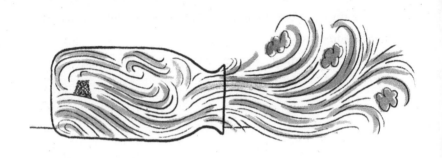

## Thirty-One

# DANCE OF FREEDOM

"NO need to panic," said Tamar. "We defend the broch. It's a solid stronghold."

Stella could hear the gnash of the waves outside. Between each hissing crash, there was a low sucking gurgle, as the water drained down through the black rocks.

"But what if the Haken comes ashore?" asked Stella.

The sea witch's pale fingers flexed in her mind, waiting to drag her down.

*If she comes ashore, she'll come right through that door.*

"She won't," said Tamar. "Your stories were right. Sea witches rarely come ashore. The sea is the source of their power, so they're not keen to leave it."

*Drown the land to come ashore* . . . remembered Stella. But she didn't say it out loud. Grandpa looked worried enough already.

"Let's start by dispensing with these three, shall we?" said Tamar. She held up a large jar. "Stella, would you like to do the honours?"

Stella took the jar from her. It vibrated under her fingertips, with a tingle that sent a shiver up the nape of neck.

"Stella's Unseasonal Gale," she read, and looked up at Tamar. "It's my gale," she said. "The one I caught!"

She glanced at Grandpa and gave him a small, proud smile. Grandpa stopped unloading the wheelbarrow and stared at her in bafflement.

"Potted it for you," said Tamar, with a twinkle in her eye. "Seems only fair that you're the one to use it."

*Are you ready, Nimbus?* thought Stella. *Hold on tight and open up when I say. I don't want to blow you away.*

"On three," she said. "One, two, THREE!"

The cloud cover burst open and a wintery cold smacked Stella's face. Icy snow whirled around her. She held up the jar and unscrewed the lid.

Nothing.

No screaming wind.

Not even a whisper.

The storm clouds churned down in a boiling rush, and the blizzard swallowed her whole. Freezing cold gripped Stella with icy claws, biting her skin and aching through her bones like an illness.

"Whistle!" came Tamar's voice, urgent in the darkness.

Stella stuffed two frost-stiffened fingers in her mouth and winced as her teeth chattered closed on them.

*Too cold!*

Her lips were numb. Freezing air burnt in her throat as she breathed in.

She blew.

The shrill note knifed through the air, kindling a thrill of joy inside her.

The gaps in the walls answered with a graveyard moan. Soft at first, a long low groan of wind stirred the shadowy darkness and pushed it higher. It flipped Grandpa's hat off and whirled it up into the rising black clouds. The wind grew to a howl, gaining in confidence and power until it was one great roar that whipped Stella's hair into knots and brought tears to her eyes.

"Cloud cover!" she shouted, as the wind began to fall. She hoped Nimbus had been holding on tight.

The shimmering bubble of cloud popped back into place. Grandpa stood there with his mouth hanging open.

Stella took a deep breath and blinked in relief. She turned to Tamar. "Was that okay?"

Tamar looked straight up. The snowflakes tangled in her hair sparkled like diamonds in the sudden brightness. "I should say so," she said. "Blasted a hole clear through."

Stella looked up. Sunlight glimmered gold through the dome of cloud cover and, far above, a circle of blue sky shone.

A constellation of small suns darted out of the stone walls near the top of the broch and began to dance.

"What are those?" she said.

"I'm not sure," said Tamar.

"How about we don't find out?" said Grandpa.

*Down cloud cover,* thought Stella.

Six small white puffs of cloud circled in a maypole frenzy near the mouth of the broch. One of them detached itself from the group, and began to spiral down towards them.

"Careful," said Tamar, pulling a bottle out of her belt.

"Wait!" said Stella. "It glowed yellow. It's not going to hurt us."

"We don't know that. We can't trust it – it's been tortured by the Haken," said Tamar, her eyes fixed on the approaching cloud.

"But now it's free," said Stella. "You saw! They're full of joy."

Tamar pursed her lips, but she tucked the bottle back into her belt.

Stella smiled up at the little group of clouds spinning helter skelter around the top of the broch.

*Free! You're free now!* she thought.

The single cloud circled down and bowled towards her. Tamar's eyes widened in alarm and she fumbled with her bottle of wind.

The cloud burst against Stella's chest, soft as a sigh, and wrapped itself around her, a soft circle of white around her chest.

"Get away from her! Leave her alone!" exclaimed Grandpa. He stepped forward and started to flap at it, stirring curling tendrils of mist from its surface. "It's not dangerous, is it?" he asked Tamar, anxiously.

Tamar shook her head. "No. Not right now," she said.

"It's a hug," said Stella. "My cloud does this. It's just saying thank you. That's all. We freed it."

A look of sadness slipped over Tamar's face. "It's too early for a thank you," she said. "When the Haken gets close, she'll take control of them again."

Stella looked up at the white clouds dancing high in the mouth of the broch and then down at the soft fur of cloud that encircled her. Her eyes filled with tears.

"We've got to save them," she said.

"Be practical," said Tamar. "We're only just managing to save ourselves. The best thing would be to send them as far away as possible. If they fly fast—"

But it was too late.

The light in the broch dimmed. Stella looked up. The blue sky was disappearing in a murky haze.

"Get down here!" Stella shouted. The little white clouds at the top of the broch slowed their dance. "Come here!" she shouted again.

The clouds stopped moving. They hung like a circle of uncertain moons in the gathering shadow.

Stella felt a sudden chill around her chest and looked down. Frost sparkled in the cloud around her.

Grandpa tried to scoop it away from her in handfuls. "Shoo! Go on. Away with you," he said. "Tamar? Help me. It's trying to freeze her."

Stella shook her head and put a hand on Grandpa's arm. "It's just frightened. That's all," she said.

Grandpa gave the sparkling cloud a doubtful look and turned to Tamar, looking for support.

Stella looked anxiously down at the glittering cloud.

It had glowed gold, so it couldn't be evil. *Could it?* But a cold ache had started to spread through her chest, as though the ice was trying to find its way inside.

"Let go," she whispered. "You're hurting me."

The glittering cloud streamed away from her.

*You didn't mean to, did you?* thought Stella.

The cloud began to zigzag around the broch, zipping from one side to the other in frenzied triangles, like a trapped fly.

"I told you," said Stella to Grandpa. "It was just being friendly and then it got scared. These little clouds don't want to hurt us."

Grandpa closed his mouth in a grim line. He took a deep breath and let it out again, but he didn't argue.

She glanced up at the little clouds hovering near the mouth of the broch, then looked around for the lone cloud. It had found a nook in the wall and pressed itself inside. It wasn't good at hiding. There was a pale glitter of frost on the wall all around it that made it easy to spot.

"Get your friends down here," she said. "Hide under the cloud cover with us. We'll protect you."

The cloud stayed where it was for a moment, then slipped out of the nook and began to circle up the wall of the broch. It left a line of frost on the stone, like a snail trail. It got about halfway round and then stopped.

"What are you waiting for?" said Stella. "Hurry!"

She walked towards the cloud and realised why it had stopped. It floated above the net. The net that was pinned to the floor with a rock. The net they'd used to trap a cloud.

The cloud beneath it was barely visible now.

*Trapped,* thought Stella. *Like the Haken traps clouds.* She hurried across.

"We're not like the Haken," she said. "We were just defending ourselves. We don't trap clouds. Look, I'll prove it."

She crouched down and heaved at the rock. The edges of it were sharp against her fingers and her shoulders strained. It was too heavy to move.

"What are you doing?" said Tamar, indignantly. "If you let it out, it'll just be one more we need to fight."

Stella shot her an angry look and turned back to the trapped cloud. The net lay almost flat over the unmoving pool of grey mist.

"You're alright," she said, hoping it was true.

She turned to Grandpa. Surely he'd be on her side?

"Please Grandpa?" she said. "We've got to let it go. Otherwise we're just as bad as the Haken. That's what its friend is thinking."

She looked up at the white puff of cloud, which hovered in uncertainty about a metre above her head, then back at Grandpa. He turned to Tamar, looking for her approval.

Tamar threw up her hands. "Fine, fine," she said. "I don't think it's wise, but if you're going to do it, be quick about it."

Grandpa smiled at Stella and wrapped his large hands around the edge of the stone. He hefted it off the side of the net and dropped it to one side with a thud.

Stella lifted the edge of the net and dragged it off the cloud. "I'm sorry we trapped you," she said. "You're free now."

The pool of mist didn't move.

"Come on, wakey wakey," said Grandpa, batting a hand through the middle of it.

"Grandpa!" said Stella, but then saw it was working. The mist shrank away from his hand and rolled itself into a dark grey ball; a small furious globe of thunder cloud.

"Uh-oh," said Stella, standing up and backing away.

"Uh-oh?" said Grandpa with a worried look. "What do you mean—"

The cloud fizzed and crackled.

"Look out!" said Stella, but as she spoke, a white blur swooped down from above. It smothered the storm cloud and mingled with it. Streamers of white twined through it, in swirls and curlicues, until there was just one cloud hanging in front of them, pale and still.

Stella let out a breath in relief. That was close. Grandpa almost got fried again. And this time, it would have been completely her fault. No question about it.

"Are we quite finished?" said Tamar. "Perhaps there's an electric socket you'd like to poke next? Don't say I didn't warn you!"

Stella nodded.

"Good," said Tamar, "because that was just the first wave. There'll be more, any moment now."

The broch flashed white and shards of stone exploded off the ground.

Stella screamed.

"Cloud cover!" yelled Tamar.

"Cloud cover!" echoed Stella.

The cloud cover pinged back into place.

*But if those little clouds want to come in, you let them*, she added.

She couldn't tell whether it was the weird light, or the lightning strike, but Grandpa's face looked grey.

"We'll be okay," she said, reaching out and touching his arm. "Tamar's done this before. She's an expert. And she's got a plan." Stella looked at Tamar, who was gathering a new collection of weather jars around the sanctuary stone.

Tamar looked up. "What?"

Lightning flickered white and blue overhead, sending shivering shadows skittering across the ground.

"I was saying, you've got a plan. Haven't you?" said Stella.

"A plan? Oh. Yes, of course . . ." said Tamar, but for the first time, she didn't sound sure.

## Thirty-Two

# HAKEN-SLAVES

STELLA walked over to stand by Tamar. "So? What's the plan?" she said quietly.

"Wind, ideally," said Tamar. "We use wind to hold the broch. When the Haken makes her move, that's the moment to strike—"

"Stella?" said Grandpa.

"Wait a minute, Grandpa," she said.

Couldn't he see they were in the middle of a conversation?

"That gale of yours worked wonders, the trouble is that was the best one I brought with me," said Tamar, with a sigh. She lifted the bottles at her waist and shook her head at the labels. "Most of these are good defensive winds," she said. "They'll see off a driving rain, even a light hail . . ."

"You two! Listen!" said Grandpa.

"What?" said Stella and Tamar.

"I think your cloud bubble thingummy has a puncture," said Grandpa. He pointed at the ground. A soup of mist was snaking in across the floor.

It was already up to their ankles and getting deeper. A lake of cloud.

"Oh, for goodness sake!" said Tamar, giving the cloud cover a cross look. "What's the point in putting a roof over our heads if you're going to leave a leaky bottom? We're paddling in Haken-cloud down here!"

She pulled a bottle from her belt and turned to Stella. "This is where a strong breeze comes in handy," she said. "We'll blow them out of the side. Ready?"

"Wait!" said Stella.

She looked at the pale mist creeping across the floor. It glittered with frost. Frightened cloud.

*These are the good ones, aren't they?* she asked Nimbus. *You gave them a way in.*

She was sure. Nimbus wouldn't have let them in if they were dangerous.

A smile stole across her face. *I trust you,* she thought.

She looked at Tamar and Grandpa and stood up tall. "These ones can stay," she said.

Tamar opened her mouth, but for once nothing came out.

"Are you sure about this?" said Grandpa, lifting his feet, as though they might disappear if he couldn't see them.

"Yes, I'm sure," insisted Stella. "They're on our side. They're not trying to hurt us."

"Not yet . . ." said Tamar, doubtfully.

"They were golden!" said Stella. "You saw it. All they want is to escape the Haken." She put her hand over the bottle in Tamar's hand. "We have to help them," she said. "That's what we'd do if they were our clouds."

Tamar shook her head. "The Haken won't like that," she said, but then she smiled. "The Haken won't like that at all!" She slid the bottle back into the loop at her belt. "Alright," she said. "They stay, for now. But I warn you, at the first sign of trouble, they're out."

Lightning crackled overhead. It lit up a mottled patchwork of white and grey. The cloud cover rippled. It looked thinner than before.

"Did you see that?" said Stella.

The tight expression on Tamar's face said 'yes', she had.

Stella glanced at Grandpa. It was probably better that he hadn't noticed. It wasn't like he could help.

Tamar began to rummage urgently through the remaining jars in the wheelbarrow, tutting in exasperation as she read the labels.

"Summer Breeze? Fat lot of use. Strawberry jam! Did you even look at the labels before you loaded up the wheelbarrow?" she said.

Grandpa grunted and sat down on the sanctuary stone, with his back to her.

"You don't *sit* on a sacred sanctuary stone!" said Tamar. "Why does everybody think it's some sort of sofa?"

Grandpa ignored her.

Stella looked down at the little clouds swirling round her ankles. Lightning cracked again in a searing flash and they glittered with fear.

She'd promised to keep them safe, but she wasn't sure if she could.

She crouched down, gasping as the cold reached her stomach.

"Have any of you got any magic in you?" she whispered.

The clouds drifted away from her and heaped up against the far side of the dome like windblown snow.

"Nimbus, can you explain?" she said. "Tell them how it works. If they help too, we might have enough magic . . ."

Tamar looked at the slumped heap of cloud and shook her head dismissively. "You're not going to find help there."

Stella ignored Tamar. *Surely it was worth a try?*

She moved closer to the little bank of cloud. It melted away from her as she came towards it. "We're on your side," she explained. "You have to be brave now though. Help us fight back. Help us protect you!"

"Look at them!" said Tamar. "They're too terrified to be useful. Now come and help me sort this lot."

"Please!" said Stella to the clouds. "If you help us, we can drive her away. Then you'll be properly free."

One small cloud separated itself from the others and nosed across the ground towards the centre of the broch. It slid up the side of the sanctuary stone, towards Grandpa's bottom, making him stand up in a hurry. The cloud spread across the stone in a milky pool.

"Well, will you look at that?" said Tamar. "Proper little cloud whisperer, aren't you?"

The cloud shuddered and a fine powder of snow sparkled in the air and landed around the stone like a halo.

*Had it understood?*

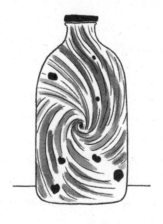

## Thirty-Three

# THE EYE OF
# THE STORM

STELLA knelt down by the stone. In the very bottom of the cracks, a fine line of silver shone like the wire spokes of a bicycle wheel.

"Yes!" she exclaimed. "Thank you!" She turned to Tamar and Grandpa. "It did it!"

She turned to the other clouds in excitement.

"Please!" she said. "Share your magic. If you all help, we might have enough. If we fight the Haken together—"

At the name of the sea witch, a flurry of snow puffed out of the clouds.

"—we can beat her. I know we can!" she pleaded.

They backed away from her in a slow meandering dance, each one trying to slide behind the others.

*Tamar's right,* she thought. *They're too scared.*

"The lightning's stopped," said Tamar.

Stella looked up at the cloud cover. Tamar was right. Perhaps the worst of the storm was over?

"We should make the most of it and get organised," said Tamar. "Bring that wheelbarrow over, would you?" she said to Grandpa. "Let's see if you brought anything more useful than strawberry jam."

Grandpa snorted at her but hefted the wheelbarrow and wheeled it over to the sanctuary stone. "You're welcome," he said pointedly.

Tamar ignored him and began to turn the jars and read the labels.

Stella sighed. "Thank you, Grandpa," she said.

Tamar straightened up. She had a yellow earthenware jar in her hand. She nodded. "This might come in handy. Stick it in the bag, would you?" she said, handing it to Stella.

Stella looked around for Tamar's bag and raised an eyebrow. Nobody was allowed to sit on sanctuary stones, but apparently, it was okay to put bags on them. To be fair, the ground was a mess of puddles. The stone was the only dry spot.

She slid the jar into the bag and slipped its strap over her head.

"Sounds like the storm's blown itself out?" said Grandpa, with a hopeful smile.

Stella gave him a small smile. She wanted to believe it, but the little clouds still sparkled with fear.

"Not likely," snorted Tamar. "Now, what else have we got in here?" She rummaged through the remaining jars until she almost got to the bottom. Her face lit up in a wolfish grin.

"What?" said Stella.

"This," said Tamar. She held up the *Heart of Hurricane* bottle.

Stella's palms itched with the memory of touching it. "I thought you said it was only for emergencies?" she said.

"This qualifies," said Tamar. She handed it over.

As Stella slid it gingerly into the bag, she realised there was a new sound building outside the broch. A long, low howl. It gradually built into a grinding roar. A rattle of pebbles echoed around the broch.

Tamar looked up and went very still. "Tornado," she said. "That's not good."

"What?! But, but, we don't get . . ." stammered Grandpa.

"Can we catch it?" said Stella, pinching her finger and thumb together.

Tamar shook her head. "You'd be a mile up in the air before you knew it," she said. "That's a long way to fall, when it stops blowing."

There was a thud and a splash. Tamar looked down at a large chunk of rock that had landed right next to her.

"Oh no . . ."

Another block landed with a splash, spattering Stella with muddy water. She sprang away from it.

"Run!" bellowed Grandpa.

The cloud cover burst, unleashing a torrent of stinging rain, and Stella ran to the entrance.

She reached it, ducked under the shelter of the heavy stone lintel, and looked back.

The stones from the top of the broch wall were toppling down, thudding to the ground like missiles and throwing up gouts of muddy water. On the far side of the broch, Grandpa was hauling Tamar into a nook in the wall.

"Tamar!" she screamed.

"I've got her," called Grandpa. "Stay where you are!"

Stella flinched back as another rock landed at her feet, embedding itself in the soft mud. A rock like that could split your skull – crack it like an egg. Her scalp tightened at the thought.

"Tamar!" she called, again.

"She can't hear you," said Grandpa. "She took a bit of a knock. We're safe here though. You stay where you are."

*But we need Tamar to stop the Haken.*

Her heart clenched at the thought of the sea witch and she looked behind her.

She couldn't see out. Beyond the narrow tunnel that led outside, the air was solid grey, streaked with flying water. A skeletal branch whipped past.

*We're trapped,* she thought.

"Nimbus?" she called. Her voice sounded thin against the roar of the wind. "Nimbus!"

"The clouds are still in here," called Grandpa.

*The Haken-clouds, yes, but where's Nimbus?*

Where had he gone after the cloud cover burst?

She risked a glance up the inside of the broch. It was like looking down a deep well. Above it, the sky turned, a whirlpool of cloud. It made her head spin, as though she might fall straight up, into the sky.

*The eye!* she thought. *We're under the eye of the tornado.*

A small cloud-shaped hole gaped in her heart.

Nimbus must have been pulled outside, sucked up into the tornado!

*Taken by the Haken...*

Stella ducked back under the lintel and her face crumpled. She'd promised him. She had promised she'd keep him safe.

Now Nimbus was gone and Tamar was hurt and the sea witch was coming. All she wanted to do right now was press herself into the wall and disappear inside it like a cloud. Hide until it was all over.

Why did Tamar have to get hurt? Tamar was the one who knew

what to do! She was meant to protect the island. It was Tamar's fight, not Stella's.

Stella peered across the broch. Even the shadows seemed to tremble at the violence of the wind. A shred of cloud cover clung to the far wall. *Herbert*, she realised. Still trying to protect Tamar . . .

Grandpa had Tamar cradled in his arms. He was crouched in one of the little cave-like nooks on the far side. Another rock thudded down and she flinched back. There was no way to get to him.

In the centre of the broch, a cluster of clouds spiralled over the sanctuary stone.

Her stomach twisted.

They were still here. But Nimbus wasn't. It was so wrong.

"You have to help!" she shouted. "Now! I can't do this by myself."

One of the clouds settled like a white cloth over the stone, then lifted off again.

Had it given its magic? She closed her eyes and listened.

*Yes . . .*

She could feel it. A faint hum of defiant joy.

Another cloud settled on the stone and the feeling grew louder. Hope began to resonate in her bones. She slapped her palm against the wall of the broch. *Yes!*

"You can do it," she shouted against the wind. "Be brave. Fight back!"

*If all of them helped, there would be enough magic. Enough to drive the sea witch away.* Stella just knew it.

A tiny seed of courage settled in her chest. She put her hand over it and her fingers met the strap of Tamar's bag.

*Heart of Hurricane.*

She took a deep breath. Did she dare?

She slipped the brown bottle cautiously out of the bag. *DO NOT OPEN*, said the label, in Tamar's curly capitals. The top was sealed with a small cage of wire.

*Except in emergencies,* thought Stella.

She edged along the wall towards the entrance. Her coat flapped wildly, like a broken sail.

"Stella? Where are you going?" shouted Grandpa. "Get back here! Stella!"

She hesitated. "Remember Gran's dream?" she called. "This is what she meant! Not Nimbus. This."

"Stop!" exclaimed Grandpa. He laid Tamar gently on the ground and stood up.

She shuffled back towards him. "I know what I'm doing," she called. "Trust me."

"I do trust you," said Grandpa.

"Gran knew," said Stella. "I have to stop the storm."

"You can't go outside," said Grandpa. "That's madness."

"I'll come back. I promise! Look after Tamar. And say kind things to those clouds. They're trying to help."

Stella turned away and edged along the tunnel, before she could lose her nerve.

As she looked outside, her heart beat like a trapped bird. There wasn't one tornado, she realised. There were many.

Twisted tentacles of wind reached down out of a mountain of cloud. They ripped across the headland, throwing up clods of mud and broken bushes of heather. It sounded like the island was being torn apart.

There might not be an island for much longer, if she didn't do something.

She fixed her eyes on the nearest twisting grey column, in the centre of the bay, hooked her arm through the iron ring in the wall and untwisted the wire, to loosen it from the top of the bottle.

As the wire came free, the bottle blasted from her hand and smashed behind her. A solid wall of wind exploded out of the broch. She held on tight, the metal ring biting hard into her elbow as the wind dragged at her.

The hurricane tore a strip of white across the surface of the bay.

It sliced through the tornado. For a moment, the twister writhed like a beheaded snake, then it disintegrated in a splattering shower.

The white wake of the hurricane sliced straight out of the bay, towards open sea.

"No! Come back!" shouted Stella.

She brought her fingers to her mouth and whistled, the note clean as a blade, and her heart thrilled as the hurricane turned.

She was doing it! Calling a hurricane!

It carved back, raising a white wave in the mouth of the bay and scythed towards the ravaged headland. The twisters fell, one by one, in a heavy shower of mud.

An enormous curve of blue opened in the dark sky, and sunshine broke through. A fierce joy rose through Stella at the sheer wild power of it.

A hurricane! Her hurricane. Slicing through the Haken's storm like a knife.

The sky curdled into clots of darkness. Hundreds of smaller storm clouds were breaking ranks and moving off in different directions.

*The Haken's army are running away!* Stella realised, with a sudden surge of hope. *She's lost control. Her clouds are escaping!*

She slid her arm out of the metal ring, leant against the stone wall and laughed in relief. The whisper of the sanctuary stone laughed with her, twining her story into its song. Warning sea witches to stay away.

She'd done it!

Tamed the storm!

Beaten the Haken . . .

Stella took a deep breath. Now that the wind had died away, a putrid stink of dead fish and rotting seaweed drifted in from the sea. She wrinkled her nose and swallowed hard. It was so strong, she could almost taste it.

*Yuck!*

Maybe it was churned up by the tornadoes? All the sludge and muck from the bottom of the bay?

As a wave rolled in along the length of the rocky beach, with a slurping gurgle, fear trickled into Stella's heart.

*There's something wrong with the water . . .*

## Thirty-Four

# THE DEEP

THE water looked oily, dark – as smooth and muscular as an octopus. Above it, the sky crawled with clouds – the ragged remnants of the Haken's army, moving slowly away. Nimbus was nowhere to be seen.

*He probably got blown really far,* she told herself. *He's probably flying back here right now. As fast as he can.*

But she didn't believe it.

An ache of loss tightened around her chest. *Nimbus, where are you?*

Stella stepped outside and followed the path down to the water's edge.

The crunch of the crushed slate underfoot was loud in the sudden stillness. The water rippled and surged forward between the rocks, setting up a chorus of greedy sucking noises. Like it had heard her . . .

"Go away!" she shouted. "You lost! Leave us alone."

A lone wave swelled in the mouth of the bay, with a long hump on the surface, like a whale surfacing. It moved silently towards the rocks.

When it reached the shore, it didn't break. It just heaved forward and then slithered back into the sea, in one smooth, wet motion.

When it retreated, Stella's heart clenched.

A dark figure stood in the shallows.

*The Haken!*

She stared wide-eyed at the sea witch.

*Still in the water,* she thought. *She has to stay in the water.*

The Haken's hair hung down in a dark knotted mat. It tangled with the frayed lace of stinking black seaweed that covered her body.

But it was her face that was the worst.

Slippery smooth as a squid. No nose, no lips. Even up close, it was nothing more than a pale blank, with a thin slit where her mouth should be. Only the eyes were human. They stared at Stella. Cold and black. Filled with that same gaping hunger that had haunted her nightmares.

"Apprentice." The word came out of the Haken as a venomous hiss and the waves seemed to whisper it amongst themselves, along the shore.

*Apprentisss, apprentisss, apprentisss.*

Stella took a step backwards, closer to the broch. "Where's my cloud?" she blurted.

The Haken opened her slit of a mouth in a cold-blooded smile, revealing rows of needle-sharp teeth. She raised her arm slowly and it caught the light. The skin was pallid green, etched with fish scales.

Behind her, a thick umbilical twist of water rose slowly out of the bay. Trapped inside it was a small powder-puff of cloud.

"Nimbus?" said Stella. "Nimbus!" She ran forward a few steps, but as she did a dark wave licked towards her over the rocks and she skipped backwards.

The sea witch laughed; a wet sound, like slime gurgling in a blocked drain. "Nimbusss, Nimbusss," she echoed, mockingly, and lowered her hand. The column of water sank back into the bay, taking Nimbus with it.

Nimbus wouldn't last ten minutes in a sea cave, never mind years. Stella's heart felt brittle just thinking of it. Nimbus, all alone, in the dark.

The Haken stepped up out of the water. A slick of black water slid up onto the rocks, under her feet.

"You can't do that!" said Stella. "That's cheating."

She realised how stupid it sounded. Why would a sea witch follow rules?

The Haken narrowed her black eyes and a river of water poured uphill ahead of her, making a glinting, sinuous path over the grey stones towards Stella. She looked down and took another deliberate step. Her foot squelched as it touched the rock. Maybe it had suckers underneath?

Stella turned and ran.

*Drown the land to come ashore,* Tamar had said. This was what she meant.

Where the sea witch went, the water came too.

When Stella reached the grass by the broch, she turned and looked back.

The Haken was still coming, but slowly. She seemed to consider each step before she took it. Dark water streamed uphill, over the rocks ahead of her, onto the slate path. It was heading for the open door of the broch.

*No!* thought Stella. *Not in there!*

Grandpa and Tamar – they'd be trapped.

The Haken spread her arms wide. Behind her, the surface of the bay stopped moving, as though the water had thickened to slime. A rotten low-tide smell belched out of the shallows. A low wave folded itself over the rocks and a fat finger of water began to ooze up the short slope, like a slug.

*I've got to stop her!* thought Stella.

She looked around for anything she could use as a weapon. She should have grabbed a rock from the beach. There was nothing on the grass that looked like it would hurt the Haken.

*Weather!* she thought. *You're a weather weaver, aren't you?*

The black storm clouds were scattered all the way to the horizon. The hurricane must have flown far away by now, but maybe she could call it back?

She poked salty fingers into the corners of her mouth, took a deep breath and blew as hard as she could. A long shrill whistle. Loud enough to be heard on the mainland.

But the wind didn't answer.

*Joy,* she thought, in horror. *It needs joy.*

The air remained still, heavy with the foul reek of decay.

The Haken swept her arms forward and the horrible black tongue of water grew longer, pushing stones aside with sharp cracking sounds, like breaking bones. It surged up over the rocks, onto the slate path and in through the mouth of the broch, as though to choke it.

"Grandpa!" shouted Stella.

He'd drown.

He'd drown, unless . . .

She stuffed her hand into Tamar's bag.

She had one more jar. The yellow one. *Sahara Sunshine.*

The Haken was getting closer, taking one careful step after another through the dark water that flowed up the slope.

Stella pulled the stopper out and thrust the jar forwards.

The wave of heat burnt her cheeks and dried her eyeballs. Centuries-dry air. It smelled of spice and sun-baked sand.

The Haken turned towards her and hissed.

The sound made Stella's stomach lurch, but she gritted her teeth and held the jar out in front of her like an offering.

The water in the mouth of the broch writhed like a trapped worm and began to shrink. It shrivelled in the searing heat, until it was no more than a smear of sludge on the ground.

Stella let out a shuddering sigh of relief.

*Dry!* she thought. *Try walking on that, sea witch.*

The rocks on the beach paled from black to grey.

The Haken took a step closer. As her foot touched dry rock, there was a disgusting sizzle. She looked down at the dry rocks, curled her long fingers into claws, and took another determined step.

Stella stared at her and waved the jar in desperation, but she could feel the air beginning to cool already.

The jar was empty.

She glanced at the entrance to the broch, but there was no sign of Tamar. Or Grandpa. And if she went inside too, they'd all be trapped.

*I did everything right,* she thought. *Why?! Why is she still coming?*

"What do you want?!" she said, in desperation.

The Haken raised her head. "I want . . . what isss mine," she hissed.

"Nimbus isn't yours," said Stella, her voice cracking. "You stole him!"

She had nothing left. No wind. No jars. No cloud. Nothing that would stop the Haken.

Stella backed away, until her heels met the solid wall of the broch.

The sanctuary stone was singing now. Loudly. Was it loud enough to stop a sea witch? The low hum of it thrummed in her blood, and courage surged through her heart.

"There's nothing here that belongs to you," she said.

The song echoed her words. A riotous chorus of defiance.

Stella clenched her fists and squared her shoulders. "This place isn't yours," she said. "This island isn't yours. Nothing here is yours." She put a hand on the rough stone behind and fury swarmed through her.

"Most of all," she said, her voice rising, "Nimbus isn't yours!"

A pale patch of lightning bloomed under the water of the bay like a white flower, and Stella gasped.

*Nimbus!*

Right there. Just under the surface. And he could hear her!

"Nimbus is my cloud," she shouted. "Mine! Not yours!"

The lightning flashed again, like a beacon, sending jagged white lines skittering across the inky swell.

The Haken bared her teeth and Stella's blood sang with rage.

"LET MY CLOUD GO!"

A white star of pure fury exploded under the water and a dark geyser of water exploded up into the air.

The water spattered down in heavy drops. High above it, a cloud shone like a second sun in the sky.

"Nimbus!" she yelled. "Get away from the water. Now!"

As Nimbus arced towards them, the Haken raised her arms. A wave surged over the rocks and onto the grass. Stella yelped as it wrapped round her ankles, cold as death.

The Haken tilted her head to one side and pointed at Stella.

There was a sudden sharp, burning pain. She looked down at her shoulder. With a jolt of panic, Stella saw a fine black spine poking through the fabric of her yellow raincoat. *Nimbus, help!*

Nimbus plummeted, like a shooting star.

He hit the Haken and ignited, a furious ball of white lightning, crawling with sparks.

The Haken screamed.

Her arms crinkled and peeled like snakeskin. Scales flaked down and fizzed as they touched the dark water. The seaweed around her body started to crackle and spit, like a deep fat fryer.

Stella stumbled back against the solid curve of the broch, but she couldn't hear the stone any more. Its song was drowned out by the terrible screams of the Haken.

Steam began to pour out of the Haken's body, hissing into the air, until all Stella could see was the lightning, pulsing purple and blue in searing flashes.

"Stop!" she shouted. "Nimbus, stop!"

The lightning flashed once, twice, and then stopped.

A tremor started in Stella's hands and then in her knees. Dread – it clutched at her scalp and sent shivers down her spine. What had she done?

She swallowed hard, as the mist began to drift apart.

*I have to look,* she thought. *I did this.*

A dark shadow materialised out of the haze, and Stella's mouth dropped open in shock.

The Haken wasn't gone.

She still stood there on the rocks, between the broch and the sea. A pale silhouette against the dark thunder cloud that crackled just behind her.

The Haken was a girl.

A thin scraggy-looking girl standing barefoot in a tattered blue dress.

No more water, no more power.

The sea witch glared at Stella. Her eyes hadn't changed. They were still dark and hungry, as though everything human had been hollowed out of her.

Her lips peeled back in a snarl and Stella flinched. The needle teeth were still the same too.

"Tell Tamar I will have what is mine," she hissed. Then she turned and ran across the rocks.

When the Haken reached the water's edge, she dived.

The sea swallowed her without a ripple.

Nimbus fired a fork of lightning into the shallows, throwing up a plume of spray.

"Stop! Let her go," said Stella. "We won."

Her shoulder was throbbing now. She touched a finger to the thin spine that poked out of her jacket and yelped.

Nimbus dropped out of the air and wrapped himself around her.

"Thank you," she said.

"Stella!" Grandpa's voice was hoarse with worry.

"I'm here. I'm alright," she called. "You can come out."

Grandpa and Tamar appeared in the doorway of the broch.

Tamar wasn't in good shape. She had Grandpa's hankie pressed to her head as a makeshift bandage and she was leaning heavily on his arm.

"I got rid of the Haken," said Stella, her voice wobbling. She took a deep breath and swallowed hard. "I did it. I got rid of the Haken." It sounded more convincing the second time she said it, though she couldn't keep the note of accusation out of her voice.

*Where were you, Tamar?*

Tamar gave a weak smile. "I heard the fireworks," she said. "I'm sorry I missed it."

Grandpa stared out at the fractured sky. There was a look of fierce readiness on his face, as though he expected the Haken to reappear at any moment.

"She's gone, Grandpa," said Stella. "I beat her. I stopped the storm."

He turned back to her, his face full of awe. His lips moved, but no sound came out. It looked like there were too many different questions fighting to get out.

"How?" he said finally.

"Hurricane, Sahara sunshine, and then Nimbus did a horrible lightning thing," said Stella.

Tamar nodded in approval. "Righteous fury. A powerful weapon if you use it right."

"And you're okay?" said Grandpa.

"Mostly," said Stella. Nimbus settled closer, his touch soothing and cool against her sore shoulder.

Grandpa let out a breath. "I told you, didn't I?" he said. "Your gran was right, about the storm."

Stella shook her head. "Not about me, though."

"No, not about you," said Grandpa. "But she'd be delighted to be wrong on that count. Delighted and proud." He smiled.

A mess of clouds billowed out of the doorway of the broch behind him.

"Oh," he said. "They did it, by the way. Those little clouds of yours. I kept them at it, and they mended the stone! Not all of them mind, but it was enough, wasn't it?"

"Yes. It was enough," said Stella, and gave them a grateful smile.

They'd done it. They'd found their courage and mended the sanctuary stone.

Without the stone song, she didn't think she'd have beaten the Haken.

The clouds tumbled towards Stella and whirled around her in a dizzying circle, until she laughed.

"Free!" she said. "You're free!"

"They've got you to thank for that," murmured Tamar. "I would have blasted them out of the broch without a second thought, if you hadn't stopped me."

Stella smiled at her. *Tamar admitting she was wrong?*

She turned back to watch the joyful little clouds. Nimbus wrapped himself closer around her. Maybe he was a tiny bit jealous . . .

*You're the best cloud of all, Nimbus,* thought Stella. *You're my cloud.*

The horizon wobbled and she sat down. Now all the excitement was over, her shoulder was starting to throb. A hot, heavy ache, that spread down her arm and made her want to lie down in the cool grass and sleep.

## Thirty-Five

# CULLEN SKINK

TAMAR and Grandpa had argued a lot about the best way to treat sea-witch venom.

"Sun soaked moss," Tamar had said. "That'll sort you out in no time."

Grandpa had maintained that Tamar was talking nonsense – he advocated tweezers and antiseptic. Eventually, Stella had agreed to both, just to shut them up.

She rubbed at her shoulder. It was itchy now, rather than sore. The moss under the bandage had felt uncomfy at first, but it had helped. Or maybe it was the antiseptic. Who knew?

She pulled on her Fair Isle jumper, being careful of her shoulder. It felt so good to have dry clothes again. Maybe Tamar was right about the towels? She wrinkled her nose.

*No. I still don't like them.*

When she opened her bedroom door, she was greeted by the rich smell of food.

Tamar was laying out cutlery on the kitchen table and Grandpa was standing at the stove, stirring a pot of cullen skink. It felt back to front. When Gran was here, it would have been the other way round – Grandpa laying the table, Gran at the stove.

Still, it felt nice – more like it used to. The house was a lot cosier with four people in it. Well, three people and a cloud . . .

Nimbus was curled up small, on top of the dresser. Maybe he was tired? Maybe just giving Grandpa some space? Stella looked at the shelves below him. Gran's puffin mug was back in its place. Everything looked a lot neater generally.

"Have you tidied, Grandpa?" said Stella.

Grandpa made an exasperated face, as though she'd given away a secret.

"We've got guests," he said.

*Guests,* she thought, and smiled to herself. *He's including Nimbus.*

Nimbus fluffed up a bit and slipped off the top of the dresser.

Stella walked over, to make sure he didn't get too close to

Grandpa. As she did, she realised what was different about the room.

"Gran's seal painting!" she said. "You put it back!"

Grandpa turned towards it. "Put it up this morning. Looks right there, doesn't it?"

"Yes, it does," agreed Stella.

"I put all your Gran's stuff away, a while back. I just couldn't . . ." Grandpa tailed off, then gave his head a sharp shake. "But I think it's time we get it out again. Going through that box the other day, I realised there were a lot of happy memories hidden away in there, too."

The cardboard box was still on the floor, next to Grandpa's armchair.

"Can I?" said Stella. Grandpa nodded.

Stella went over and opened the lid. Nimbus followed her and tried to pour himself into the box.

"Out! Out, Nimbus," she said. "I can't see if you do that."

Nimbus lifted out of the box and floated off towards the table, with a slight air of huff.

Tamar patted the top of the little cloud. "I've got him," she said. "You carry on."

The first thing Stella spotted was the knitted chicken.

*It's still here!*

She lifted out the chicken and gave it a squeeze. It smelled fusty from being in a box. She sat it on Gran's chair by the fire. It looked happy to be back in the right place.

Stella glanced at Grandpa, to check it was okay. He was watching with a fond smile on his face, so she grinned and delved deeper into the box.

She unwrapped a small parcel of newspaper, and smiled. The driftwood seal! She ran a finger along the smooth curve of its back, then carried it to its spot on the window sill.

The room looked better already.

"Come here," said Grandpa, pulling out a chair at the table. "I discovered something else you'll like."

As Stella sat down next to Tamar, her heart did a little dance of excitement. It almost felt like her birthday.

Grandpa put a soft bundle on the table in front of Stella. *Gran's blue scarf.*

It rattled when she picked it up and out spilled hundreds of purple periwinkles, a shower of jewels.

"My beach treasures! You kept them!"

Grandpa smiled.

Tamar took a corner of the scarf and rubbed it between finger and thumb. "I made this for your Gran," she said quietly. "Years ago. A gift."

"I didn't know that," said Grandpa.

Tamar nodded.

"Do you want to keep it, then?" he said. "A memento?"

Stella looked up at him in surprise. It felt like a big thing to offer. Especially since he and Tamar didn't really get on.

Tamar shook her head. "I think Stella should have it."

Grandpa smiled. "Good idea. Lizzie would have liked that."

Tamar carefully tipped the rest of the shells onto the table and then gave the scarf a gentle shake to get the sand out of it. She flapped Nimbus out of the way, then swept it around Stella's shoulders.

The fabric was warm, as though it had been lying in the sun rather than tucked away in a drawer.

Stella mouthed the question at Tamar, so Grandpa wouldn't overhear. "Magic?"

Tamar's eyes crinkled at the corners.

"Cloud magic?" mouthed Stella.

Tamar gave an almost imperceptible nod.

Stella ran her fingers over the soft fabric and took a breath.

"Thank you," she said. "Both of you."

"Don't be silly," said Grandpa. "It's me who should be thanking you. Having you here – it's made this place a home again."

Stella's heart glowed. She glanced at Nimbus and clasped her hands together nervously. If ever there was a right moment . . .

"Grandpa," she said. "Nimbus and I have something important to ask you."

"Yes?"

"Can we stay here? For good, I mean. Even after the holidays . . ."

Grandpa raised his eyebrows. "Your parents didn't tell you where you're moving next?"

Stella frowned and shook her head. "They never do. It's Dad's work that decides. But it can't be better than here."

Grandpa smiled and his eyes shone. "Stella, you *are* moving here. That's the plan, anyway."

Stella's mouth dropped open, then she jumped to her feet and wrapped him in a tight hug.

*Home. I'm home!*

Grandpa rubbed her back. "What with you starting secondary school, they didn't want to be constantly moving you about anymore," he explained.

"That's brilliant!" said Stella, her words muffled by his jumper.

"I've got a slight confession, though," said Grandpa, smoothing her hair as he let go. He pulled out a chair and sat down.

A cool thread of worry wound slowly through Stella's excitement. She sat down next to him and tried to catch his eye.

Grandpa studied his hands for a moment, then looked at her sheepishly. "When they asked me," he said, "I told them it was a terrible idea."

"What?!" squawked Stella.

Nimbus jolted in the air and rushed to her side.

"I was still worried about the storm!" said Grandpa. "I thought you might all be safer elsewhere . . ."

"Grandpa!"

Nimbus turned gunmetal grey.

*No lightning!* instructed Stella swiftly.

Grandpa patted the air with his hands to calm the pair of them. "I'll tell you what we'll do," he said. "We'll take the boat over to Lerwick tomorrow. Call them. Tell them that it's all settled. They're coming here."

"But what if they—"

"They'll say yes," said Grandpa. "To be honest, I don't think I changed their minds. They still brought *you* here, didn't they?"

"You're sure?" said Stella.

"Certain," said Grandpa, putting his hand over hers.

"I'll have a little word, if you like?" said Tamar. "I'm sure I can convince them."

Stella shot her a worried look. She wasn't sure what Tamar had in mind, but she suspected it might involve brain-fog.

"It's alright," she said. "Grandpa and I will talk to them."

The thought of it sent a little thrill of excitement through her. *I'll actually get to talk to Mum and Dad tomorrow! Hear their voices.*

She took a deep breath. Everything was going to be perfect. All of them together – her and Nimbus, Grandpa, and Mum and Dad too! At last, they'd all be together.

Nimbus took that as a cue to try and hug Grandpa.

Grandpa stood up abruptly and backed away flapping his hands.

Tamar chortled rudely.

"Nimbus! I don't think Grandpa wants a hug from you," said Stella, laughing. *Come on, leave Grandpa alone.*

Nimbus drifted back to her, looking distinctly peachy.

Grandpa dusted himself down, as though to get rid of any remaining cloud, then stepped over to the stove and clattered the ladle in the saucepan, obviously keen to reassert a bit of normality. "Supper," he said briskly. "Let's get this table clear, please."

As he turned back to the stove, Tamar rolled her eyes rudely. "I still can't believe he tried to *mortar* a sanctuary stone," she said.

"I didn't see you fixing it," said Grandpa, over his shoulder.

"No, that was *all* Stella," said Tamar, turning to look at her. "You're going to have to explain to me how you did that."

"It wasn't all me, actually," said Stella. "Turns out Grandpa's a bit of a cloud whisperer, too!"

Tamar scoffed. "You're telling me that someone with no cloud knowledge whatsoever, convinced those Haken-clouds to mend the sanctuary stone?"

*Urgh!* thought Stella. *Really, Tamar?*

Grandpa glanced at Stella. He looked embarrassed. "To be fair, Stella did most of the convincing," he said.

"I suspected as much," grunted Tamar, and Grandpa deflated.

"Grandpa did help!" protested Stella.

"He did?" said Tamar.

Grandpa stood up a bit straighter. "Yes," he said. "I did! I kept them at it. You know, after Stella went outside."

"And how did you do that, then?" said Tamar.

Grandpa gave Tamar a haughty look. "Wasn't that hard really," he said. "They're much like chickens."

"Chickens?" snorted Tamar. "They're nothing like chickens."

"They are so!" said Grandpa. "They just need a bit of reassurance. Someone to talk kindly to them, let them know they're safe."

"And it was *Grandpa* that gave me an idea of what would fix it," said Stella.

"Don't tell me you just thought of mortar!" exclaimed Tamar, rolling her eyes.

"No," said Stella. "Love." She looked up at the puffin mug on its shelf. "Gluing everything together."

Grandpa glanced at the dresser and smiled. He knew what she meant. He ladled the soup into three bowls and gave Nimbus an uncertain look. "Clouds don't need . . . feeding, do they?" he said.

Stella laughed. "No, Grandpa!"

He pulled out a chair and sat down, then gave a sly smile. "I seem to remember, Tamar, that while Stella and I were mending the sanctuary stone, you were taking a nap? That's probably why you don't remember."

"Touché," said Tamar.

Stella looked down at her bowl, to hide her smirk. All this time, she'd been worried what would happen if Grandpa and Tamar were to talk, but it turned out he had a real knack for answering her back. That could be fun.

She scooped up a spoon of soup, blew on it and put it in her mouth. It was rich and creamy, and had flakes of smoked fish in it. It was better than anything else Grandpa had cooked since she'd been here.

"This is so good!" she said.

"It's your Gran's recipe," said Grandpa. "Spotted her cookbook tucked away up there – thought I'd give it a go."

"And you promise there's no *masgoom* in it?"

Grandpa shook his head. "Not a scrap," he said. "Only smoked haddock."

Tamar slurped her soup noisily off her spoon. "You can certainly cook," she said.

Grandpa nodded stiffly, unused to Tamar giving him compliments.

"By the way," said Tamar to Grandpa, "if you ever find *masgoom* on your line again, you'll let me know?"

"Sure," said Grandpa. "If I catch another, I'll bring you some too. Doesn't happen often though."

Tamar shrugged. "You never know your luck."

Stella looked at Tamar with a sudden chill.

The *masgoom*! That's how Tamar known the sea witch was coming – monsters rising out of the deep, just like in the book!

Stella shivered. Hopefully that was the last *masgoom* Grandpa would ever catch. And the sea witch wouldn't be coming back anytime soon. Still, it might be worth re-reading *Shetland Myths and Magic* tonight – see if there was anything else she should be watching out for . . .

"You're home for good then," said Tamar, pulling Stella out of her thoughts.

Stella grinned widely and nodded. She still couldn't quite believe it!

"So you'll be able to carry on training?"

"Training?" said Grandpa, lowering his eyebrows. "I'm not having Stella involved in any more storms. One was quite enough, thank you very much."

Stella put her spoon down. "Grandpa, you can't stop me doing weather magic."

Grandpa gave her a hurt look, and wiped his mouth with his napkin. "Just because you're suddenly all grown-up and can take care of yourself doesn't mean I'm going to stop worrying about you!"

"I know," said Stella.

She smiled inside. *Grown-up.* At least he realised now. Probably it would just take a while to sink in.

"I *can't* stop," she said. "I've got my own cloud now! And once you've found your cloud, they're yours forever." Nimbus settled in a white puff around her shoulders, as though to prove the point.

Grandpa huffed and gave Tamar a dark look, but Tamar just nodded – Stella was telling the truth.

"I need to keep learning!" said Stella. "We don't want more accidents. Remember the curtains."

"Not forgetting my head!" said Grandpa.

"No. Not forgetting your head," she said, with a guilty smile. He was never going to let her forget that.

Grandpa took another spoonful of soup and they ate in silence for a moment. Stella gave Tamar a wide-eyed look, that meant: *Don't say a word! Let him think about it!*

At last, Grandpa fixed a firm gaze on Tamar. "You're keen to teach her all this, are you?" he said.

"If she'd like that," said Tamar.

Stella nodded eagerly.

"Can you guarantee that it's safe?" said Grandpa. "No more storms or sea witches, nothing dangerous?"

"Absolutely," replied Tamar, smoothly.

Stella shot Tamar a glance, but didn't say anything.

"And is there much more for her to know?" asked Grandpa. "I mean, you've already got her whistling winds out of the sky and firing lightning to order. What else is there?"

"Oh, lots!" said Tamar. "We've barely started. We haven't even done any weaving yet."

"Weaving?" said Grandpa.

"Weather weaving," said Stella.

# ACKNOWLEDGEMENTS

Lauren Gardner, my brilliant agent, who accidentally conjured a storm when first reading this book – you are more marvellous and magical than you know.

To my amazing editor, Hazel Holmes, and all the team at UCLan – it has been an adventure and a delight working with you. Tilda Johnson, line editor extraordinaire – thank you for bringing it all into focus.

David Dean for the marvellous cover – you have captured the spirit of weather weaving. There was dancing in the kitchen when I saw it! Thanks too, to Hannah Blackman-Kurz for the wonderful weather jars – Tamar would approve. Becky Chilcott, master designer, for conjuring it all into a book!

Huge thanks to the brilliant tutors and writers on the MAWYP at Bath Spa University, especially Anna Wilson, Janine Amos, Lucy Christopher and CJ Skuse. Stella crept timidly onto the page – with your help she grew in confidence, until she was ready to face any adventure.

Thanks to the MAWYP gang, for befriending the new girl. Also, to the alumni workshop group, for cups of tea, edits in purple ink, and utterly decadent cheesecake.

Heartfelt thanks to Callen – for endless support, late night phone calls, sessions with scissors, and brilliant insights. Your eagle-eyed reading skills are second to none. You have calmed my panics, cheered my successes, and lifted me higher at every step.

To Elizabeth and David, for welcoming me home with warm company, food, and cribbage, when I'd spent the days wandering the Shetland coastline, notebook in hand. Linda, thank you for the wonderful family tree.

Alison Powell, for scribbling lunches, Sherbet Club, The Artist's Way, WriteClub, and regular writing escapes. I'm always grateful for your playful and lightning bright spirit.

Cat, for giving me a quiet bolt-hole and encouraging me to read everything aloud. Your poetry, humour and grit are an inspiration.

My earliest readers, the Solsbury Siblings – Leonardo, Isabella, Lily, Georgina, Freya and George. Thank you for sharing this wild journey – I owe you all massive mugs of hot chocolate with shortbread.

Cath and Catherine – for laughter, lasagne, and late-night harmonies. You are my sanctuary stone – you fill my heart with songs and courage.

My parents, for boundless support and encouragement, and teaching me to delight in working hard at what matters.

My husband, Bernardo – you are my sense of belonging, my home, my love. Thank you for the bottomless coffee pot and for keeping all the plates spinning while I was busy dreaming.

And above all, thank YOU! Yes, I'm talking to you. Thank you for letting this story sweep you up and carry you along. Now, look up, look outside – what weather have *you* conjured while you were reading?

# HAVE YOU EVER WONDERED HOW BOOKS ARE MADE?

UCLan Publishing are based in the North of England and involve BA Publishing and MA Publishing students from the University of Central Lancashire at every stage of the publishing process.

BA Publishing and MA Publishing students work closely with our company and work on producing books as part of their course – some of which are selected to be published and printed by UCLan Publishing. Students also gain first-hand experience of negotiating with buyers, conceiving and running innovative high-level events to leverage sales, as well as running content creation business enterprises.

Our approach to business and teaching has been recognised academically and within the publishing industry. We have been awarded Best Newcomer at the Independent Publishing Guild Awards (2019) and a *Times* Higher Education Award for Excellence and Innovation in the Arts (2018).

As our business continues to grow, so too does the experience our students have upon entering UCLan Publishing. To find out more, please visit: www.uclanpublishing.com/courses/